Margarita Meklina

The little Gaucho who loved Don Quixote

ISBN : 978-1-911424-87-1
SKU/ID: 9781911424871

ORIGINAL COVER:
Title: THE LITTLE GAUCHO
Artist: Fabio Perla
Technique: monochrome pencils on card board mounted on wood
Year: 2016

Editor: Monica Turoni
Book design by: Wolf

Publishing Company:
Black Wolf Edition & Publishing Ltd.
2 Glebe Place, Burntisland KY3 0ES, Scotland
www.blackwolfedition.com

For adorable anchors of my life,
Marianna, Irene and Federica

— II —

NOTE OF THE EDITOR

— *III* —

The writer's usage of dashes to indicate direct speech has been maintained in this book edition.
In Russian тире [-] "dashes" are used in literary texts, like short stories, novels, and plays to indicate "direct speech".
In this novel English-like quotation marks to punctuate dialogues have been used as well to indicate reported direct speeches in the narrated stories.

1

Little Naftali was born in Russia.

In those times, the pictures of Russia that decorated children's books were always full of snow. There were rounded mounds of snow, untamed drifts of snow that formed wherever they wanted... Nothing but white snow, with no beginning and no end – just like Russia herself, that huge, faraway land.

And when it snowed, it was very cold.

Even now, adventurers who've traveled to Russia boast about surviving the Russian winters at temperatures that were so far below zero, little creatures without warm dens were nipped by the frost, birds would freeze in mid-flight, and people's noses turned into icicles.

But Naftali remembered a different kind of cold from his childhood. It wasn't the kind of cold where you had to put on high felt boots with galoshes and you shivered whenever an icicle fell down your fur collar, or the kind of cold that made your fingers numb and nipped at your ears, nose and chin, and anything else sticking out of the large scarf your grandmother wrapped around your face, and turned them red. It wasn't the kind of cold that would keep the meat and sausages you hung outside the windows fresh, either.

Naftali felt a different kind of cold – like when he passed by some neighbors on the street, for instance, who wouldn't even look at him and only muttered things under their breath.

Once, when he was walking along the street, Naftali was almost run over by a large horse-drawn carriage with a drunken coachman, who laughed, as Naftali scrambled to escape the horse's hooves. Another time, when his kitten disappeared, a neighbor grinned at seeing Naftali cry and search for his 'Murzik.' And still another time, a stranger at the marketplace grabbed the yarmulke off of Naftali's head and threw it so high, it got stuck on the highest branch of a birch tree.

Naftali's father loved to say that the frost froze not only those people's noses and ears, but even their hearts.

– But is everybody like that? – Naftali asked.

– No, – replied his father, who was known in the town of Tulchin, where they lived, as a wise man. – Frost tries to reach into people's hearts with its icy fingers, but even though it's very strong, there's a way to resist it, and thaw your heart.

– And how do you thaw your heart? – asked Naftali

– By doing something warm, every day, – his father replied. – Remember how everybody gathers at our house and tells stories and sings and prays? It feels like we don't need to put more wood into the stove, and that suddenly our usually cold room has become warm.

– Yes, it's true, – Naftali seemed surprised. – And what else can you do to thaw your heart?

– You can warm a samovar and invite your friends, – said his father, – so they can warm up, too, by drinking tea.

– Now I understand why there are always so many people in our house during Shabbat, – Naftali said.

Naftali's father was a learned man. During the day, he was a station master, supplying travelers from far away with horses, and serving them borscht and hot tea, and in the evening he studied the Torah. Many Jews who lived in the city of Tulchin came to him when they had questions about something in the Torah or Talmud, the two major Jewish religious books. When they were discussing something, it was very loud in their house. Everybody was shouting and seemed very angry, but then, after the discussion ended, people left with smiles on their faces, as though studying had made them much happier.

But they discussed more than just religious matters. Sometimes the conversation shifted to a certain school boy, who joined a traveling circus he'd encountered on his way to yeshiva one day, and abandoned his studies. Suddenly somebody would sigh and say:

– I wonder how Yankel is doing in America now..., – and then everybody imagined what their former neighbor from Tulchin had achieved there.

– I heard that in America people have forgotten how to walk, – one guest would say, – because they have such good railroads... They don't need horses to carry water or logs, like we do; they only use their horses for racing, because everybody in America is so rich, they don't know how to spend their savings...

– I heard that in New York you can be blinded by electric lights on the street – not like here, in Tulchin, where you can break your leg coming home in the pitch darkness...

– I heard that with special machines Americans can sew a woman's shoe in thirty minutes, and people there have so many pairs of shoes, they can't fit on one shelf. Meanwhile, our children sometimes have to wait their turn to go to school, because they have to wear their brother's pair of shoes!

– This is all rubbish, – Naftali's father would say,

and everybody would quiet down. – Money and horse races are not what dutiful pupils of the Torah should occupy themselves with! There are other, more important things in life!

– What do you mean, Lazar Evseevich? – the guests would ask, and Naftali's father would speak very slowly, so that everybody would understand the importance of his words.

– I heard that in the United States people are free, – he would say, and all the guests would look at him with hopeful eyes. – There, in America, Jews can go and live anywhere they want!

– Do you mean we could pick the best city in the U.S. – the one with paved roads and city lights, and many jobs and shops and universities – and live there?

– Yes, you surely could!

– That would be incredible, – the guests would say, – because here we can't live in Moscow or Saint Petersburg or other large cities, unless we are doctors or bankers, but we are neither – we are blacksmiths and shoemakers and tailors and yeshiva teachers, and even milkmen...

– And also, – Naftali's father would say, – in America our kids could go to school with non-Jewish kids, and nobody would be surprised!

– Do you mean that our kids could apply to American universities, and if they studied hard and did well, they would be admitted? – asked the guests, eyes still glimmering with hope.

– Yes, that's true! – Naftali's father would nod.

– That would be incredible, – the guests would repeat, – because here, out of a hundred openings in a university, only three are allotted for Jews, so you need to be smarter than ninety-seven kids to get in!

– And our sacred books would be safe in America! Nobody would dare burn them! – Naftali would exclaim suddenly, and everybody would grow silent, and assume very serious expressions. It wasn't because boys weren't allowed to speak up when adults were talking – on the contrary, Naftali's father always encouraged his son to participate in conversations as an equal to grown men. It was because everybody still remembered how, one night, drunken Cossacks broke into the synagogue, took the Torah and other books from there, and set them on fire.

The Jews had looked out their windows and seen the huge flames, but they couldn't do anything. It wasn't the first time such a thing had happened: the year before, when a young man ran out of his home to try and save the books, he was beaten by a mob and had to spend several months in bed, recovering from his injuries. One of the neighbors ran for the police, but they never came.

The guests became very upset after what Naftali had said. They knew he was right, and that somewhere, far away from Russia, there was another country – perhaps America, perhaps some other nice foreign land – where a better life awaited them.

2

Naftali was five years old when he learned to read: his mother, who wore a scarf on her head even on the hottest summer days, was too busy with household chores, and his father was too preoccupied with earning a living, so Naftali, who was always left to his own devices, spent his time 'reading' the books that lay within his reach.

At first, he held them upside down while looking for pictures. But before long his parents noticed that when Naftali took a book, he held it correctly, and if the book was in Yiddish, he flipped through it from right to left, and if the book was in Russian or Spanish, he thumbed through it from left to right. Naftali's parents were very proud that Naftali had taught himself to read – in three languages, no less – and they attributed his remarkable achievements to their own resourcefulness. He could barely walk, when they started hanging the letters of the Yiddish and Russian alphabets from the ceiling, on colorful pieces of yarn, over Naftali's bed.

But when they boasted to others about Naftali's gift for languages, people didn't believe them and laughed.

– Are you going to become the next Spinoza? – they would shout at Naftali. – Or, maybe the next Heinrich Heine? Or, perhaps, even Maimonides?

Maimonides was a Jewish philosopher, whom Naftali's father greatly respected, and whose portrait hung in their house – a man with a long beard, staring intently straight ahead. Naftali's father was always looking at this portrait, as though for approval, whenever he argued with Naftali's mom. As for Naftali, he had no intention of looking up at that stern face, because at his height, he felt like an ant, compared to this highly-hung portrait, and he only hoped the man was too far away to notice his little shortcomings.

– He was born in Spain, – Naftali's father once said, pointing at the black-and-white picture of Maimonides. – And if you learn Spanish well, maybe we'll go to Spain. We adults are too old to master a new language, so we will rely on you to help us in conversations with the locals. Young children like you grasp things so quickly... I remember how one day you were crawling right here on this very floor, spitting out any food that touched your lips, and the next day you grabbed a spoon from the shelf and held it in your hand like a grown up!

– It wasn't exactly how you describe it, – said Naftali's mother, who'd entered the room from the kitchen in a bright headscarf and a yellow *sarafan*, apparently overhearing Naftali's father's last words. Naftali knew she loved to talk about him as a baby, but she refrained from participating in the 'serious conversations' Naftali's father usually started.

– Why wasn't it like Papa described? – asked Naftali curiously.

– I spent a long time teaching you how to hold a spoon, my dear. You dropped food all over the place – our kitchen looked worse than the stable. Then one day your father came home from a long trip, and we proudly demonstrated your achievement!

Then Naftali's mother pointed to the portrait of Maimonides:

– I overheard that now your father wants to teach you something about this strict gentleman, so I'd better go to the kitchen and finish cooking my latkes...

Naftali's father hugged his wife with a smile, and continued:

– A long time ago Jewish people had a good life in Spain and got along with people of other religions. But then they were expelled from there, like Maimonides, who was about your age then... Or like the ancestors of the Spanish teacher we're going to hire for you. If you study hard, maybe we'll leave freezing Russia and go to Spain. Because I heard that now they've proclaimed to everybody who cared to listen, that they regret their past actions. Now Jews can live there again!

– Is it interesting there in Spain? – asked Naftali.

And his father, who was always very busy with his job (he had several horses and assisted travelers who had to go from one village to another on business trips or for leisure), and almost never had time for a long answer, cut the conversation short:

– I'm so hungry! Your mother's mention of latkes made me drool. Soon you'll grow up and be able to read not only newspaper headlines, but real literature. You'll read *Don Quixote*, about a naïve traveling knight and his faithful horse Rocinante... And from there you'll learn something about Spain. The book will give you a better idea about Spain, than anyone who's really been there, because good books have that very special power.

But little Naftali didn't want to wait until he grew up to learn about Don Quixote, and he began asking every peddler who passed through the town of Tulchin about the book. And all the peddlers stared at the serious, skinny little boy with dark eyes in amazement.

– Why would an ordinary Jewish boy from a tiny

town, that's barely on the map, want to know about a Spanish knight? – one bookseller asked rather arrogantly, looking at Naftali, wearing the shabby little coat he'd already outgrown.

Another bookseller from a nearby town, who sometimes used Naftali's father's horses for short trips, said rather sarcastically:

– Instead of reading about this knight's horse – "Racing Ant", or whatever it's called – he ought to help his father, who's struggling with *real* horses! His father cleans dirty stables to feed his family, and his son can't see beyond the end of his own nose – he's off in dreamland somewhere! What good does it do his parents, to have a son who cares more about paper knights and horses, than experiencing real life?!

It was difficult to decipher whether this peddler really meant what he said, or whether he was poking fun at Naftali. In addition, he wasn't completely wrong: Naftali's father did work very hard. He was a learned man, but since he couldn't make money by discussing important books – which was what he liked – he had to learn to take care of horses. At the end of the day he was so tired, he would fall asleep while writing down his thoughts about certain religious books, still holding his pen.

As if that wasn't enough, Naftali's father's business was failing. His job was to provide travelers, who were passing through Tulchin by carriage, with fresh horses that would take them to the next stop. There, another stationmaster would do the same: let the tired horses rest, and supply the traveler with fresh ones. That way, travelers always had a horse that was full of energy, and not exhausted from too much pulling and running.

But horses couldn't compete with the new railroad, which now ran through Tulchin. Trains were faster than horses, and they didn't need pastures and grass; they didn't need oats, either, or somebody to brush their tails, or remember their names. And trains weren't afraid of everything, like Naftali's father's horses, who wore large blinders, so they wouldn't be startled by something they suddenly saw on the road. And trains did not need special treatment, unlike horses, who, besides water and hay, needed a kind word, a pat on the back, a gentle rub and even a bath.

Most travelers were happy with the service provided by Naftali's father. However, once the railroad came to Tulchin, they began to favor horses less and less, being fascinated by trains and the speed and convenience they provided. Technological progress had arrived, and people were changing their ways.

Once, a traveler who'd stumbled into the stable made a face:

– What a smell, Abram! These horses are as filthy as you! But I shouldn't be too harsh on you: your days in this stable are numbered because of the train!

Naftali saw his father cringe, as though he'd been lashed by a whip.

– My name is not Abram, – was all he said. The traveler laughed heartily.

– I thought all of you people were named Abram, – he replied, – and that you all lived in dirty little hovels, where you ate your smoked herring and garlic. Maybe it's not true, because I don't smell garlic or herring on you, but this manure sure isn't pretty!

Therefore, the peddler was right about Naftali's father's business: it really was difficult – not only because of the care required for large, sensitive animals, which would be happy one day, and then would suddenly refuse to pull a carriage or simply get sick, the next day. It was also hard because of the many rude people, who thought that somebody clearing out horse dung was the lowest person on earth, and could be treated as such.

The peddler who told Naftali he ought to help his father was a well-meaning man, who always had an opinion of people and life, but his opinions changed, according to circumstances. His name was Efraim, but everybody called him Fima, and he told Naftali something that expanded his mind.

– I know it's not easy to clean manure, – he said – and deal with angry travelers, who are always late and expect your horses to reach unbelievable speeds, as though they were weightless birds, and not heavy creatures with hooves. But if you think that literature and the arts are any easier than plowing fields or laying bricks, you are mistaken!

Naftali stood back and cupped his chin in his hand: he always did this when he had to confront something new. Characters and events described in books were like a dream for him, like a path to another world, different from his own; he never thought of it as work, especially not as hard work. Not once did it occur to him that there were real people writing these books!

– So, I made you think, young man? That's great! – smiled Fima the peddler. – Let me continue my train of thought, and if you don't understand something, it's perfectly fine. Maybe I'm only saying all this for myself – I, who spend my life completely inseparable from these books. All I do is choose and buy them, keep or exchange them, pack and carry them.

– Do you like reading them? – asked Naftali. Fima laughed.

– Does your father like riding horses? You see, both your father and I are so exhausted from taking care of our businesses, that we forget that riding a horse, or reading a book, can be a pleasure! For us, it's just a way to make a living. Now I'm joking of course, but there is some truth in what I'm saying. Yes, sometimes in the evening, when I lie in bed, I pick up one of my unsold books and read it, but very carefully, so that a buyer can't tell it has been read... Sometimes the pages are still joined together, so I have to peek in between them, meaning I can only read small parts and admire the beautiful, long words... And even when I can open the pages, I only read a few pages, because otherwise I might fall asleep with a lighted candle, and set both the books, and my house on fire – that's how tired I am from all my constant walking and carrying... But let me continue my train of thought. You just listen, even if you don't understand. And when you are older, you'll think of me, and suddenly I'll appear in front of you, like I am now. And then you'll remember my words...

Naftali listened to this Fima, eyes rounded. Hardly anybody talked to him about serious things; other adults wouldn't even look his way, never mind discuss anything troubling with him. That's why he was fascinated by seeing something new in this tall, rather tidy, middle-aged man with a mustache the color of rye, and a bright red tunic, cinched at the waist with a thick leather belt.

Fima always parted his straight blond hair right

down the middle and packed his books very neatly in coarse paper, bound with strong twine, and from his clean looks and fit body, you would never think he was ever tired or disappointed. He always smiled at others and never let insults bother him. If somebody swore or called him names, or made fun of his profession, he pretended not to notice, and usually the bullies would stop taunting him and go away.

Fima continued, slowly, as though he were carefully considering every statement he made:

– It only seems like a person holding a delicate pen is doing nothing, compared to a person who loads huge barrels of water onto horses, to deliver to people's homes, for them to drink or cook with. You know, only the rich have water pipes, and get water flowing right into their kitchens!

Naftali was surprised to hear this, but he didn't care much about how water flowed into the homes of the rich, even though his family had to pay for a water carter to come and unload a barrel in front of their house once a week. He was a huge and silent man with a long beard, who scared off every child in the vicinity and won every wrestling match organized at the Sunday market.

Now Naftali was trying to imagine a person inventing characters and situations with a slender pen in his hand. He didn't know what this man would look like. Everybody Naftali knew did something with their hands, mending leather boots or sharpening knives or making horseshoes, or just going from house to house, selling things. Painting houses, making pots, or carving beef – these were common jobs for Jews in his town. Unlike a delicate writer's hands, these people's hands would be dirty or wrinkled, or covered with blisters from their work.

Fima seemed exhausted from thinking and standing for too long, because he put his heavy pack of books down on the ground and sat on it, crossing his legs, in his tall boots, which he polished routinely. Then he continued:

– Yes, some people might think writers only make air! That's because it's easy to measure a barrel's weight, but hard to weigh the thoughts that go into writing and thinking.

With these words, Fima took a blanket out of his rucksack and spread it out on the grass next to him.

– If you would be so kind, Naftali, as to watch my books while I sleep, I'll bring you the novel about Don Quixote – free of charge!

Naftali eagerly agreed and while Fima lay on the blanket, snoring, with a hat over his face, Naftali found a spot next to him and prepared to wait until Fima woke up.

He sat on the edge of the blanket, pondering how true it was, that not everything could be measured like the oats his father fed the horses. The 'thinking' that went into writing could hardly be measured, nor could kindness – like the kindness of the nice peddler, Fima, who promised to bring a young boy a book.

3

The next time Fima passed through Tulchin on his restless way to other villages and towns to peddle his books, he brought Naftali a thick volume with a cover the color of burnt brick, which looked so imposing and solemn that, at first, the boy hesitated even to take it into his hands. Encouraged by Fima, Naftali slowly moved his finger over the black words on the title page, pronouncing each syllable separately: "Printed in St. Petersburg".

– Did you have to travel all the way to St. Petersburg to buy it for me? – he exclaimed with surprise. – You came back so quickly. Did you have to ride the train to get there? Did you visit the Tsar's palace, or glimpse any ships or sailors? Did you see the *konkas*?"[1]

Fima interrupted him:

– Stop, stop! Didn't you know Don Quixote was from Spain? I went all the way to Spain to bring him to you!

Naftali looked at him in disbelief, and Fima patted him on the back:

– I'm just pulling your leg! I didn't go to St. Petersburg, or any Spanish town... "Printed in St. Petersburg" only means the letters for the words were arranged there. I didn't have to go into the print shop, even though it would be interesting to see how they take letters, made of lead, lay them out, one by one, in a row, and then imprint the pages with them... There are two parts to novel, and this volume alone cost me fifty kopecks.

---

[1] Konka – a horse-driven trolley on rails.

– Fifty kopecks! – Naftali exclaimed. – That's what my mother spent yesterday, when we went to buy a chicken!

– How many times can you feast on that chicken? – Fima asked.

– Oh, my mother makes chicken last and last! – Naftali boasted. – First she carefully separates the better parts and grills them, and gives them to my father. Then she takes some of the fatty parts and uses them to lard the potatoes, when she fries them... She also pulls out the heart and kidneys, and puts them into a soup. Then, when she pours it into our bowls with a big ladle, I pray to God the ladle will fish out a chicken heart that will land in mine – that's how much I love it!

Naftali proceeded to list everything his mother did with the chicken:

– She carefully removes the gizzard, making sure it stays in one piece, and leaves it on the window sill for the sun to dry. Later she gives it to me when I complain about stomach pains. It's like medicine, but it's so bitter, I only swallow it if I must! She also puts the neck into the soup, which I don't like, so my mother gets it, and sucks all the tender parts off, and it takes her a long time to pluck every little piece off the bones... Sometimes we'll have already finished our meals, and my mother will still be working on her dinner... And when we're still hungry, even after we've had most of our soup, we just add some boiling water and matzoth to it and keep eating! And if we're *still* hungry, we keep adding more water and matzoth, and sometimes carrots. That way the chicken can last for a long, long time.

Fima threw up his arms:

– And I was about to say that this book, even though it costs about the same, will last much longer than a chicken, because you can read it over and over again! You can read it in the morning and in the evening, when you're young and when you're old, and find something interesting every time! When a book is well-written, its heroes stay with you for a long time. But it sounds like your mother can make a chicken last forever!

Fima started laughing and couldn't stop. But Naftali didn't understand Fima's humor.

– Don't make fun of my mother, – he frowned. – You think it's easy for her to stretch every meal so it lasts and we can survive until the next time my father makes money?

Fima stopped laughing.

– Don't be upset with me, Naftali! Don't you know I always joke about everything? It's my way not to be sad. Take your *Don Quixote* and enjoy it... I got it cheaper than usual, because it's just the second volume, and the grammar school student who sold it to me thought the second volume was useless without the first! I'm sure he was too lazy to open either of them!

– Only the second? – asked Naftali with disappointment.

– So it starts in the middle, – said Fima, – the same as somebody writing about you, starting from when you turned ten, instead of the day you were born!

– Nobody would bother writing about me! – said Naftali.

– Why not? – Fima objected. – Some writer, who's just walking by, might overhear our conversation and think we are quite funny. And suddenly you find yourself in the pages of a book, or a newspaper!

– But how can I spot a writer walking by, if I don't even know how they dress or behave? – Naftali asked. – There are no writers in Tulchin, only milkmen, bricklayers and butchers… And mothers with their kids!

– Maybe you'll be a writer! – Fima winked and pulled on his black cap with the black lacquered visor. – I have to go and sell more books now, before my shoulders are ruined by the weight of this rucksack, so I'll see you in a couple of weeks…

Naftali couldn't wait to get home where, undistracted by anybody's prying eyes, he could inspect the book and look at the illustrations in peace and quiet. When he got there, his mother was washing clothes in a large basin on the table; his father was cleaning the stable, and the horses, calmed by his self-assured presence, stood quietly. Naftali grabbed a warm piece of bread from the stove, salted it, devoured it, then sat by the window with the book in his lap.

Elated by the serene effect of peering into a faraway life, he turned the pages one by one. He noticed a beautiful, lanky knight, surrounded by different characters, in every illustration. Some of the characters were ugly and coarse, and crudely dressed, while others – despite their elegant clothing – looked intimidating, even threatening. Obviously, this throng of individuals didn't suit the fine and delicate knight.

There were other pictures in the *Don Quixote* book. In one picture, this knight was addressing a giant head almost as big as he was; in another he was talking to pigs, and in yet another he was riding his exquisite horse, so different from the thickset, hard-working mares that

Naftali's father owned, and behind him, a simpler and rounder man followed.

Now, every time Naftali felt sad or lonely, or simply bored, he would take the book out from under his mattress and try to make sense of the individual sentences, and browse the pictures. Often he dreamt that Don Quixote, with his thin beard, and eyes that seemed to understand everything, and express goodwill, would step out of the pages and take Naftali with him on his never-ending travels. He dreamt that the knight in shining armor would pluck him from the boredom of life in their insignificant town, whose streets were strewn with garbage like potato peels and torn sandwich wrappers discarded by the workers, and take him somewhere else.

In Naftali's dreams, Don Quixote's powers had no limits, and people of every religion lived freely. Everyone coexisted peacefully, and were allowed to do as they pleased.

Naftali couldn't even hope that his father, always tired and preoccupied, or his mother – who spent all her time in the kitchen, trying to fill her family's stomachs, so they would have time to feed their minds by studying the Torah – could be persuaded by Don Quixote to do something totally different. But he thought Don Quixote had special powers that could breathe strength into him and his parents, and he waited for his new imaginary friend to appear on the dusty Tulchin streets.

4

Two months had passed since the peddler had given Naftali the Don Quixote book. And one day, on his way to buy soap and tea at the general store, near the newly built railroad station, Naftali spotted a towering man with a beard, who had just arrived on the train to Tulchin. In awe, Naftali decided this well-dressed man looked like Don Quixote himself! First, his physique was similar to what Naftali had seen in the pictures: he was very tall and thin, but instead of looking frail, he looked quite sporty and fit.

Second, the stranger looked very noble. Tidy and stylish in his spotless, freshly-pressed suit, he not only stood out from the rushing peddlers, ragged beggars and rowdy porters surrounding him. Indeed, he looked so distinct on that shabby Tulchin street, among the chickens and stray dogs, he even seemed unearthly.

Third, he had a refined, expensively-dressed female companion – his Dulcinea. The kind, fresh expression on her face gave Naftali the courage to get closer to the unfamiliar noble couple, who'd illuminated the dingy street with their inexplicable presence.

The man who looked like Don Quixote stood there, with his rosy-cheeked, blue-eyed Dulcinea, looking around, apparently not knowing which road to choose. Two stocky porters with thick necks and sinewy hands, who had just helped Don Quixote unload his luggage from the train, were eager to carry his huge suitcases, which were almost as big as a mare. But with a quick gesture, Don Quixote stopped them.

Naftali, in his short, patched coat and boots that were tied around the bottom with string, to keep the soles from walking away on their own, approached Don Quixote and the beautiful lady. And quietly, so as not to disturb this dream, he said:

– *Buenos días Señores!*

This was one of the expressions he had learned in Spanish.

However, Don Quixote seemed not to notice him. This was not surprising, because he was so tall, and Naftali so short, the crown of his head barely reached Don Quixote's belt. But his lady heard something, and leaned down toward Naftali, trying to hear what he just said.

Naftali was afraid to talk to Don Quixote, because if he mistook windmills for his enemies – as Fima had said – he could easily mistake a little boy for somebody else, too. But the kindness in his companion's eyes encouraged Naftali to start a conversation.

–*Buenos días!* – he repeated, his voice trembling and weak, and this time Don Quixote finally noticed him. He raised his eyebrows and said something to the lady in a language that Naftali couldn't understand.

Naftali was puzzled: Don Quixote did not seem to speak Spanish! Or was he angry, because Naftali's Spanish wasn't good enough? And was he punishing Naftali by speaking this unknown language?

Naftali tried again. He was rather ashamed that in the presence of such an important person as Don Quixote, he could only say two simple phrases:

– *Buenos días, Señor y Señora, cómo están?*

Surely, such an important visitor to their dumpy town deserved to hear more Spanish than two phrases, that simply meant: "Good morning, Sir, good morning, Madame, how are you?"

But, unfortunately for Naftali, at the very moment he was mumbling his Spanish phrases, two of Tulchin's rabbis showed up, helped Don Quixote into their carriage and rode away, before Naftali could explain himself. Nor could he speak with the rabbis, who were very busy loading Don Quixote's luggage and complimenting Dulcinea's fresh appearance:

– Ms. Clara, we'll look after things now, so you can rest after such a long trip, though you look so magnificent, it seems as though life's complexities don't affect you one bit!

Naftali thought: why Clara? Was that her name? Was she not Dulcinea? Or was Don Quixote so afraid of evil people that he came here secretly, under another name? If so, perhaps Naftali should keep this meeting secret, too, so as not to put his new hero and the beautiful lady in danger. He wouldn't breathe a word of anything to anyone!

Standing there in the middle of the street, Naftali watched the two porters, happily counting the money Don Quixote had given them. Naftali didn't care about money: moreover, he couldn't understand why the porters were so excited about it. They'd just had a chance to meet the most remarkable person, and all they cared about was some dull coins!

The first porter said to the second:

– That man is very rich.

– Who is he? Do you know his name?

– I sure do, – the first porter replied. – He's king of the railway. He builds railroads...

– Is that why he came to our town? – asked a third porter with stringy, unwashed hair, a bulbous nose and extremely red cheeks, who joined the conversation. – Because he wants to inspect the railroad here?

He'd been standing on the platform, drinking from a big bottle, just observing things, and now he was staggering a little. He was very upset that he wasn't the one helping the rich man, and he watched enviously, as the two other porters counted their money.

– I heard he came here to help the Jews, – the first porter replied, while the second stood in complete silence with a blank look on his face.

– Why are Jews always so lucky? – he asked. – They always find a way out. They'll be flush with money from the railroad king, while we rot away in this hellhole!

– Ha-ha-ha! – laughed the third porter. Then he threw the empty bottle down and belched loudly, and Naftali finally realized the man was very drunk. To avoid possible trouble, Naftali tried sneaking away, but the drunkard suddenly shouted:

– Look at this little *zhid*! He is spying on us!

And then he grimaced, trying to scare Naftali with his ugly face:

– Get lost, little *zhid*! Go to your mama and papa! And don't forget to ask them to wash you with the soap you bought, because you stink!

And two of the men started laughing and making fun of the boy. The third man, hoping to avoid conflict, motioned them to stop, but they ignored him and continued harassing Naftali.

And Naftali knew it was because their hearts were frozen solid.

He clasped the tea and soap he had just bought tightly to his chest and hurried home, trying to forget their hurtful words. But deep down, he was very happy, because he had seen Don Quixote and because, as the carriage was leaving, Don Quixote's lady had smiled, and waved at him, through the window. Unlike the cruel porters, her heart was kind, and warm.

5

As soon as he got home, Naftali rushed to the corner of the room where he hid his various treasures, and took out a fragment of a mirror. It used to be part of a large mirror that his father once purchased at the marketplace, but then it broke, and his mother was very upset because, she said, it was a bad omen when a mirror breaks. It meant, she said, that something bad would happen soon. But Naftali did not see anything bad coming, so he stole a piece.

And indeed, no major misfortunes had fallen upon Naftali or his parents since then. Yet, life in Tulchin was so boring and uneventful, that sometimes it seemed quite bad. The streets were so dirty and dull; the Russian, Ukrainian, Lithuanian, and Polish neighbors were so unfriendly; and his parents were so overwhelmed by hard work and household chores that Naftali hoped Don Quixote and his beautiful companion, Dulcinea, would change everything.

And so he stood holding the piece of broken mirror, studying his face and wondering, whether a skinny boy like him, with a big head and glasses, even deserved to be saved by a Knight in Shining Armor. He held the piece of mirror up to various parts of his clothing, as though to see himself through Don Quixote's eyes. This is what he observed: a coat of worsted wool, which his father had worn when he was Naftali's age, and fairly new trousers – still too new to have gotten torn on a fence, like the old ones, which Naftali snagged on a branch while climbing his favorite oak tree in front of his house. That was where he hid when things at home got tense, to avoid being sent to his study corner to memorize lines from the Talmud.

Naftali's schoolmates also had worn-out clothes, but their hand-me-downs were mended so neatly, you would never suspect they'd been worn before by younger and older brothers, and maybe even a cousin. Meanwhile, Naftali's old clothes were a mess – frayed sleeves and pant legs, because his coat and his pants were often too big, and nobody bothered to alter them. His clothes didn't always match the season, either: in winter he might wear a flimsy coat to *heder*, and in summer – his father's heavy jacket. Naftali didn't mind; his teachers scolded him less than they did the other boys out of pity, assuming his family was very poor, or uncaring.

But Naftali didn't like that they blamed his scruffy appearance on his mother who, they assumed, would rather study the Torah, than tend to her son's shabby clothes. Naftali knew his mother was different from other mothers. On the one hand, it kind of frightened him, because the other pupils ridiculed his family, which often ended in a scuffle: someone would try to push Naftali into a puddle, to emphasize a point, so Naftali would have to push back. Then the other boys would join in, and soon everybody would be fighting, kicking and screaming, even though they couldn't remember why.

On the other hand, his mother's uniqueness made Naftali proud and happy; he found a special pleasure in sitting with her late in the evenings, preparing for another day at the *heder*. She would shyly approach Naftali after supper, when his father was already sound asleep and snoring, and ask whether he wanted to discuss some passages from the Torah. She was a good-looking, strong woman with red hair, a small waist and able arms, but she was afraid her son would mock her, like her husband did, whenever she mentioned her interest in studying the Torah.

– I love you, Raya, – said Naftali's father, – and because I love you, I want you to be a real Jewish woman. Look at the other households. Look at Haim and Rivka, at Baruch and Liya. They live happily; they're always smiling when we see them in the street. They always nod to us politely and then continue their amiable conversation... And do you know why they are happy?

– Why? – Naftali's mother would ask, even though she already knew the answer, and that this conversation would end like all the others.

– Because in *their* homes, the men do what they are supposed to, and women do what they must.

– And what exactly do they do that makes them so happy? – Naftali's mother would ask.

– They do what the Torah instructs them to do! – Naftali's father would shout and raise his index finger in the air, as though pointing at somebody 'Up There'.

And Naftali's mother would look at him defiantly. She was rather shy and not very hopeful of ever overcoming her husband's stern beliefs, but she never changed her position on studying. Angered by her silent persistence, her husband would throw a dish or two in the air, and some would break, which made him even angrier.

– Because Rivka and Liya keep their houses in order, so that their children and husbands are happy! Meanwhile, you pretend you're too busy even to go to the market and buy a chicken, so sometimes we have nothing to eat but bread – like beggars! You can't feed a family on stale bread alone. And just look at your son! Why does he look like he sleeps in a hay stack, like a runaway? Why are his clothes torn? Because you waste hours reading my books and studying the Torah, instead of attending to your duties!

– But you study the Torah too! – Naftali's mother would object.

– I study the Torah, because the Torah says that's what all men should do. But women are supposed to cook and clean, so that their *husbands* have time to study the Torah! – Naftali's father would reply. Then he'd leave the house to calm down, and the conversation was over.

Naftali's father was actually a loving man, but his strict views on women's duties worried Naftali's mother. Young boys often tried to be like their fathers, and she was afraid Naftali would tell her she wasn't supposed to study with him.

But Naftali felt sorry for his mother. He couldn't understand why his father was so strict with her. Naftali himself was often ridiculed in school by other boys for reading too much – for reading when everybody else was playing, and even in class, during which he'd sneak peeks at the Don Quixote book he kept under the table behind the teacher's back, whenever he turned to write on the blackboard.

Naftali realized that becoming a learned man wasn't easy, and that if you really wanted to study, you had to ignore the giggles and jokes made by your peers, who were more interested in 'practical' things, like buying things cheap, or simply hanging around the street, watching the passersby. Naftali was a boy eager to read and learn, and his mother was a woman, who was also eager to read and learn. Their situations were different, but the obstacles they faced were the same.

6

Naftali was proud of his mother and happy to discuss everything with her – not just the Torah and Talmud, but everyday affairs, problems, and thoughts. She would sit beside him on their large wooden bench, hug him, and ask what he had learned that day at the yeshiva.

On this particular day, Naftali said:

– We learned that Hashem would appoint a king, who could govern as he pleased, but he had to follow several rules. For instance, he shouldn't have too much gold and silver, because that would make him proud. But it was okay to have as much money as he wanted for Beit Hamikdash.

– And what is another rule? – his mother asked.

And Naftali, glad to be so full of knowledge, hurried to share it with her:

– The second rule is that the king can't have too many wives! Our teacher said it was hard to control even one wife, never mind a whole herd of them!

Naftali's mother smiled:

– Your father complains that it's so hard for him to control me... But even ten women couldn't keep this house in order. You know how messy he is, especially after those long trips taking travelers to other cities – he throws his dirty clothes on the floor by the bed, so that, magically, they'll be clean again the next morning...

– It really is magical, – Naftali exclaimed. – I see the mess when I go to bed, and when I wake up, I see clean shirts and pants hanging on the line!

– It's only magical to those who've never washed

a huge pile of dirty clothes before... – Naftali's mother would sigh. – You don't see how I break my back washing them, because I do it when you and your father are asleep...

– Poor Mama, – Naftali said, giving his mother a hug, and for a while they just sat in silence, ignoring the loud snores coming from the next room.

– But that's not important, – she said, – let's talk about the king's other rules, instead!

– Well, the king had to have two Torah scrolls: one to keep in his palace, and the other to carry around with him, so that no matter where the king went, he would stay humble and fear Hashem.

– That's very wise, – Naftali's mother said. – I can't wait for another rule!

– Well, the king shouldn't have too many horses, either!

– If these were rules for your father, – Naftali's mother said, – he'd be very upset, though I think he really does have too many horses: we can't afford to feed them all. Hay isn't free. Sometimes your father even worries that if we buy too much food for ourselves, we won't have enough money for the horses' fodder. He doesn't tell me that, but I see it in his accounting book, where he tries to calculate how much we should spend on ourselves and on his business, and every month we spend less on ourselves, and more on the horses... Once, I overheard a customer say that one of our horses looked starved! But your father is too proud to share his calculations with me. Instead, he sees our modest dinner and then says I'm too lazy to shop at the market more often for fresh eggs, chicken or butter. He works very hard, and I don't want to upset him, so I don't tell him that the money he gives me isn't enough. Don't mention this to your father, Naftali, but his criticism makes me quite sad.

– Poor Mama, – Naftali repeated, hugging her, until she asked him to tell her more. And Naftali told her everything he'd learned, while she listened with great interest and enthusiasm. And Naftali was proud that he could help his mother to learn.

– I'm so happy you study so hard! – she said. – It brightens my days, to know I have such a smart and dutiful son. Even washing dishes and clothes doesn't seem so grim, when in the evenings you can share in the enlightenment that comes from study and books!

And this meant it was time for bed. Naftali's mother was unusual for her time, because she wanted to study the Torah. But in other ways she was like any other mother. She wanted her son to get enough sleep, because a good rest would make him even more able and eager to study.

7

And Naftali loved to sleep! His mother told him that when he was a baby, he almost never closed his eyes, because he preferred to study his surroundings. And since he was always awake, she was, too, making sure he didn't do something harmful, as babies do, like swallow a button, or put a pea up his nose.

– So isn't it surprising, – she said the next morning, as she tried to wake him, – that with so much to do and observe, now that you're grown, you'd rather sleep!

But Naftali wasn't listening to his mother – he was trying to sneak in a few more minutes of sleep. After all, it was Saturday, and on Saturdays Jewish people didn't have to do any chores. And besides, he wanted to finish the dream he was having, about a warm sea... A sea! Naftali suddenly remembered he was going to the river with his friend Syoma Dvorkin today. He was excited – this was the first time he had permission to go that far away without one of his parents! He jumped out of bed and quickly dressed, knowing that Syoma would be coming any minute.

Physically, Syoma and Naftali were complete opposites. Naftali was thin and not very tall; he had freckles on his nose and cheeks that only came out in the spring, and he wore glasses. Meanwhile, Syoma was a broad-shouldered lad with big fists, and eyesight so perfect, he could hit any bird with his slingshot, no matter how far away. However, despite his strong physique, Syoma was a lot like Naftali – he was very kind and quiet, and he didn't like boisterous games, or shooting birds, since he felt sorry for them.

Also, Syoma was famous among the other kids because he collected maps, no matter what kind – from a magazine left by some traveler, or even an old book, containing old facts. It could be a map of a town in Spain of the fourteenth century, surrounded by thick walls in case of an enemy attack, or a map of Russia's capital, St. Petersburg, with its web of cold rivers, islands, and elaborate channels. Or it could be a sailor's map of the Black Sea, indicating the depth of the water, the direction of the currents, and detailed descriptions of its coastlines.

This naval map was especially precious, because Syoma traded a piece of his father's cheese for it, to a wandering Jew, who claimed he'd been a sailor on a luxury ship the Tsar and his family used, to go on vacation. Naftali and Syoma figured the wanderer had made the story up, because they couldn't imagine that the Tsar would want a Jewish sailor on his ship.

But no Tsar could restrain Naftali's and Syoma's imagination! It was enough for them to unfold the map and imagine themselves as brave sailors conquering storms and traveling to any country, without even showing their passports – they would just board their ship (which they called the "Nadezhda", meaning "Hope", in Russian), and off they would go!

One day, when the boys were preparing for an imaginary journey in front of the rickety little hut with a straw roof, where Syoma lived with his parents, Syoma waved goodbye to his mother:

– Farewell, my beautiful Shulamith! – he shouted.

Accustomed to Syoma's flights of fancy, his mother only twirled her finger at her temple, as people do, to imply that someone 'cuckoo'.

— Your mom's name is not Shulamith, it's Haya! — Naftali objected.

But Syoma, ignoring Naftali, suddenly fell to his knees and started wailing.

— My dear Shulamith, how can I be without you, on my voyage, where only the fish, the moon and the silence of the night will hear my cries... Listen to the waves — their whisper will bring you news about your faithful sailor!

Irritated, Naftali threw his arms in the air and said:

— Why are you talking such nonsense?

— Can't you just shut up? — Syoma pleaded. — Everybody knows that sailors cry and long for the wives and fiancées they leave on shore. And if I have to choose a name for a wife, why shouldn't it be the most beautiful name, from the story about Shulamith in the Bible?

— Fine, — Naftali said, — but now I want to show you what I would choose... Do you have a map of Russia?

— Sure, — Syoma reached into a pile of maps wrapped in some faded fabric. — Which one do you want? I have one of geological expeditions, I have one of the Crimean War, and I have one that my father marked with the Pale of Settlement line... There, you can see where Jews can and can't live...

— Give me that one! — exclaimed Naftali impatiently. — Look! — he said. — According to this Pale of Settlement ordered by the Tsar, Jews can't live in Kursk, or Orel, or Smolensk, or so many other places...We can't even live in Yalta! But in my imagination, I can board a ship and sail on the Black Sea and catch a lot of fish — so many fish, they wouldn't all fit on my ship, and to unload the fish,

I would stop in Yalta... No, wait... You will sail to Yalta and see your Shulamith there, right?

– If you keep ridiculing me, – Syoma snapped, – I'll never let you sail with my maps again. You can forget about even looking at them.

– I won't do it anymore, – said Naftali. – But just think: if you went to Yalta and met a pretty girl there, who invited you to live in her home because she had lots of room, you couldn't, because of the Pale of Settlement! But because we play using our imagination, you can! You can actually live in Yalta!

And the boys looked at the map and imagined how nice it would be if there were no Pale of Settlement, and their families could live anywhere they wanted. Their imagination knew no limits. In their minds, they traveled from Tulchin to Moscow and to Orel and Smolensk, and nobody could stop them, or say they didn't belong there.

8

Today they had no time for maps. Today, what was entertainment for Naftali, was work for Syoma, who was taking his father's herd of sheep to the pastures by the local river. Syoma's father was very poor, and even though it was Shabbat, the rabbi told him he could work on Saturdays, so he could earn more money and have a nice meal on the next Shabbat. And since he couldn't afford to hire a non-Jewish shepherd on Saturdays, like some richer Jews did, he asked Syoma to take care of the sheep. Syoma was very proud of this task and referred to the sheep as "the herd".

One would imagine that there were a number of sheep in a herd – maybe twenty, or even fifty. For instance, Naftali remembered an illustration from his book about Don Quixote that showed him fighting a herd of sheep, which he mistook for an enemy army. Naftali was excited to show Syoma how Don Quixote fought the sheep, until he saw Syoma's "herd", which didn't resemble troops in shining armor at all. They just looked like frightened animals – and what's more, there were only three in this herd: two boney sheep, and a newborn lamb, which could barely stand on its wobbly legs.

– Where are the rest of them? – Naftali exclaimed, as they led the sheep out of the yard and along the road leading to the pastures.

– Well... – Syoma said. – My father had to sell the rest, because he was in debt. But still, the three we have left are so nice, aren't they? Look at the little lamb – it's so cuddly!

But Naftali was disappointed: it was one thing to promenade a huge herd that others would envy, and quite another to drive these pitiful sheep, so lean and unhappy. He also felt quite awkward, imagining everybody's disapproving looks: here they were, walking with sheep, while the other Jews rested and celebrated Shabbat, in their best clothes. Even the river, the shining sun, and the bright green pastures before them did not brighten his mood. Suddenly, Naftali felt like going back home, to be around his books and read about Don Quixote, instead of spending time with Syoma and his pitiful, hungry sheep, that had immediately started devouring the green grass.

Naftali sat down on the ground and put his head into his hands. After a short time, he saw a large herd, enveloped in clouds of dust, coming toward them from a hill. Was he dreaming? Were they just ordinary, woolly, bleating animals, or an enemy army, only pretending to be sheep? And if they really were an enemy army, should he get up off the ground and attack, or should he be weak and afraid, and maybe even hide?

What would Don Quixote do in this situation? In the book, he always attacked: no matter what others thought of him, he was sure the sheep were an enemy army, and he was proud to fight them!

But these sheep approached so noisily, that Naftali was frightened. He didn't want to play Don Quixote anymore; he just wanted to step aside, and let them go by. He hoped Syoma wouldn't guess what he was thinking. But Syoma looked worried, too.

– My father warned me to be careful, – Syoma said, – because some of the locals don't want our sheep to graze here. They think these pastures belong to them, and the last time my dad came here with our herd, they wanted him to pay! He said to watch out for a big, beardless man in a fur vest – that was the one who insulted him!

Naftali looked more closely at the approaching herd, but there was no big beardless man guiding it. Rather, they saw a fair-haired boy only slightly older than Syoma and Naftali, who could've been about fifteen. The boy saw them, too, and stopped several feet away, as though he were on the other side of an invisible border.

– Hey, – he shouted in Russian, – get out of here!

– My father told me to bring our sheep here, – Syoma yelled back, in Yiddish, – they need to eat. Can't you see how undernourished they are?

Luckily, Naftali was there to translate what he was saying.

– If you want them to graze here, you have to pay! – shouted the fair-haired boy, who started toward them as though ready to collect the money. – These pastures are for *us*, and not for your kind!

– What is he saying? – Syoma asked, reaching into his pocket for his slingshot. He wasn't going to use it; he only wanted to scare the boy, who probably thought he was reaching for money.

– These pastures are for Russians, – the boy continued, – your sheep can't just eat our grass for free. If you want them to stay, pay two kopecks for each!

– That's not fair, – said Naftali. – We have a newborn lamb – he's so small, his stomach won't hold much grass. If you want to be fair, you should ask us to pay less for the lamb.

– Don't try to outsmart me, Jewboy! Just wait till our people come to your barrel house, and spoil all the alcohol you sell to us! My father got drunk yesterday because he bought vodka from you!

– What is he saying? – asked Syoma.

– Just stupid things, – Naftali answered.

– Either pay, or take your sheep and get out of our pastures, – the boy shouted again, and he walked right up to Syoma. Afraid the boy would attack him, Syoma took out his slingshot and picked up a stone.

This made the boy so angry, he tackled Syoma, grabbed the slingshot, and snapped it in two. A scuffle ensued: Syoma and the youth rolled around on the grass, hitting each other, while Naftali looked around for help. But there was nobody around, but sheep – a lot of sheep.

Naftali tried pulling Syoma out of the other boy's grip, but the boy kicked him, hard, on the leg with his big leather boot. And since he was much stronger than Syoma, he quickly overpowered him and started stuffing dirt into his mouth.

– You said your sheep were hungry, right Jewboy? You're probably hungry, too, so eat!!! I know you would eat anything for free, because you and all your people are stingy!

The boy was young, but already he had the same negative attitude toward Jews as the adults. This attitude made him despise Naftali and Syoma, even though he'd never even seen them before. It also allowed them to say terrible things about the Jewish people, as if they felt superior to everyone else, and let the boy feel righteous and justified in his hatred. And this attitude was the invisible enemy here, in this field, disguised as sheep.

Naftali was at a loss for words. He'd never fought an invisible enemy disguised as a fair-haired Russian shepherd before, and wished Don Quixote was with him now, to advise him on how to win this kind of fight, and help the boy learn to respect Jewish people.

9

Naftali's thoughts were somewhere far away, but danger was very near.

Something had to be done right away, since poor Syoma was almost suffocating under the big Russian boy. He was trying to hit back, but he kept missing, so his legs and arms just kicked and flailed helplessly in the air. Naftali looked around frantically, over the green pastures, covered with furry white animals, like huge cotton balls scattered over a large bedspread, when suddenly he saw a black sheep! Actually, he was not sure whether it was indeed a black sheep, but it appeared to be some kind of animal, walking on the right side of the field, in the distance.

It had just emerged from the forest and seemed to be approaching the meadow where Naftali, Syoma, and the Russian boy were. Following behind the black sheep, Naftali distinguished the outline of a human figure.

– Look, look, there's a black sheep! – shouted Naftali, trying to distract the Russian boy, and it worked: the boy stopped trying to make Syoma eat dirt and looked where Naftali was pointing. Syoma tried to free himself from under him, but the Russian boy had one knee on Syoma's chest, keeping him on the ground.

– You should get yourself some new glasses, – said the Russian boy sternly, before turning back to Syoma and smearing more dirt over his tightly-closed lips, but less enthusiastically now. – That's not a sheep, it's a dog!

And suddenly, the Russian boy sprang to his feet, leaving Syoma lying on the grass, spitting out dirt.

– This is your lucky day, – he said, – I happen to know that dog, and his owner, Guedali. He's one of your tribe, but he's very nice, and I don't want him to see me fighting with you. Just last week he rescued one of my sheep, which had gotten lost and fallen into a pit, covered over with brushwood, that was meant to trap a bear. Guedali pulled her out and tended to her injuries.

With these words, the Russian boy gave a special whistle and walked away, with his herd following silently behind. A couple of minutes later he'd vanished from sight, and the meadow looked quiet and peaceful, again, as though no violence had ever occurred. Indeed, Naftali couldn't believe what had just happened to them.

Syoma quickly got up, dusted himself off, and looked in dismay at his torn sleeve. Then he anxiously checked on the sheep and the little lamb, who stood peacefully eating the fresh grass, apparently indifferent to Syoma's troubles with the young Russian bully.

– How come humans have to protect their animals, when these stupid sheep didn't even blink while I was almost killed! – he exclaimed. Then he spotted the approaching man with the big black dog and, instantly forgetting his humiliation at the merciless fists of the Russian boy, he shouted:

– What is that I see? A dog on wheels?!

– I have no idea, – Naftali said, his eyesight too poor to tell, – but I'm curious about the Jewish man, whose immense kindness can make even evil boys stop fighting, and walk away, at the very sight of him!

Once the man was closer, Naftali realized that he was pulling a rope, attached to a crude platform on wheels, on which there stood a big, shaggy black dog. The man was small-framed and hunchbacked; he was dressed simply and ruggedly, yet very appropriately for traveling in the countryside, and was carrying a canvas sack. The dog was so disheveled, you could barely see his eyes behind the mop of hair on his head; he breathed heavily, and looked quite old and tired.

– Don't go thinking he's lazy! – the man shouted, without even greeting the surprised boys. – He carried this sack of books for almost a *verst*, but then he got tired, so I took it from him.

And as though to demonstrate, the man gave the sack to the dog, who grasped the handle between his worn, yellowed teeth. It stood quietly on the platform, staring at its master with an inquisitive look, as though asking for permission to disembark.

– Lie down, Bolshoi! – the man commanded, and the dog carefully stepped off the platform and lay on the grass, placing the sack in front of him, as though guarding it from strangers and thieves.

The hunchbacked man then knelt down and put his ear to the ground.

– Do you hear it? – he asked the boys.

– Hear what? – the surprised Syoma and Naftali asked in unison. Without answering, the man said to the dog:

– I'm so sorry, Bolshoi, but you'll have to move over a little.

Looking annoyed and exhausted, the dog raised its sad eyes to the man and yawned loudly. It tried to get up, but was too worn out, so the hunchbacked man tried pushing him gently with both hands. It was hard, because the man was slight, and the dog was so heavy and huge.

Syoma offered his assistance, but the man said:

– I only moved him because I heard a grasshopper, and I was afraid that Bolshoi was hurting him. What if Bolshoi should break his legs? It's okay now.

And, paying the boys no more attention, the man took a prayer book out of his bag, and started praying, prefacing his prayers oddly.

– Oh, this wonderful field, with its grass and its crops and its creatures, with all its natural beauty God gave us! Oh, this wonderful forest adjoining the field, with its marvelous trees, stumps, birds and animals, with all its natural beauty God gave us! And oh, these wonderful boys, who are probably still too young to realize how beautiful these forests and fields are, and whom I intend to teach a lesson!

As soon as the man had finished his energetic prayer, Naftali asked:

– What's the lesson you want to teach us?

– I don't know yet! – the strange man replied, enigmatically. – I only know adults are expected to teach lessons, and that young minds are eager to learn, because they are like a sponge, – the man laughed. – So let's wait and see, whether an opportunity to teach and to learn presents itself!

10

Naftali and Syoma were surprised at the man's words, but he'd saved them from the mean Russian boy, and made them very happy. They were too preoccupied by the little lamb, who kept trying to wander away, to take seriously the man's promise about some lesson. They needed to tie the lamb to a stake they'd shoved into the ground.

Meanwhile, the hunchbacked man, obviously tired after a long trip, fell asleep next to his dog, and awoke near sundown, as the boys collected the sheep together, preparing to go home.

Suddenly he jumped up and shouted:

– The Shabbat evening meal! We need to make it home before the meal and Havdalah! I've been invited by very important people, who have a very important guest – and I can't be late! And you don't want to miss your end of Shabbat dinner, either, do you boys?

Then this Guedali slung the sack of books over his shoulder, grabbed the rope and started pulling the platform, where the dog lay daydreaming. They had only walked for half a kilometer when they noticed a horse and cart on the side of the road. The owner, a stocky man with a beard shaped like a spade, was urging his horse to go further, but the horse wouldn't take another step; undernourished and bony, it was dripping with sweat, from too much exertion. Desperate to get to his destination on time, the man started kicking the horse in the stomach with his big boot.

– Stop it! What are you doing? – Guedali shouted to

him as he approached.

– I promised my children to be home for today's evening meal, – the man replied, angrily, – but this useless piece of meat won't move a muscle. I've been on the road from the farmer's market in Nikolev for two days, now, and I can't miss the end of Shabbat – my wife is angry enough with me for missing most Friday nights, when they light candles. I have already angered Hashem for working and riding the horse during Shabbat, but I don't want to anger the wife and kids.

– How can you call this beautiful creature a useless piece of meat? – exclaimed Guedali.

– Don't you know that every little insect and flower has an angel over it, commanding it to grow?

The man laughed in response:

– You're funny. I was all mad about spending the end of Shabbat alone in these woods, instead of relaxing at home and tasting grape wine, but at least now I have the company of three crazy wanderers and a dog on wheels!

Guedali answered:

– My dog is old and sick, and I'm doing everything I can to make him comfortable on this earth. The Torah teaches us not to inflict cruelty on animals, and if you have to choose between two options, you should choose the one in which no one gets hurt, even though in your case, this will mean missing the evening meal with your family!

– But my children will be hurt – they'll cry! I'm almost never with them, because I work so hard, and I promised them to make it this time! – the man argued, but with evaporating conviction. He was calmer after talking to Guedali, who had a soothing way with words.

– Listen! Listen! – Guedali suddenly exclaimed, raising his index finger in the air. – Be quiet and listen!

Naftali looked around trying to understand what he should be listening to, but all he heard were birds chirping and the light whisper of the wind. And his own thoughts.

And he was thinking how even the grimmest situations had their wonders. Why, just a couple of hours ago, Syoma was losing his fight with the Russian boy, when suddenly Guedali appeared out of nowhere, and saved them. And now there was this man with his tired horse... Naftali knew a little about horses because of his father's stable, and this man's horse, which looked like it hadn't eaten or been bathed in ages, probably couldn't even make it across the road! If they hadn't stumbled upon this man, he might have grown even angrier, tried to force the horse walk, and then grown sad, because the horse might have died from its effort...

The man didn't expect to meet anybody on this deserted road, but now he'd heard Guedali's words of wisdom and was happier: he was consoled by the thought that, despite having to miss the Shabbat evening meal and sunset with his kids, he was going to save the horse and not make it suffer! So many unexpected events in one day!

Naftali was so lost in his thoughts that he jumped, when Guedali lightly touched him on his shoulder and asked:

– Did you hear something?

– I started listening, – Naftali replied, – and I couldn't hear anything, but then I had some thoughts...

– I did too! – the angry man blurted out. – I remembered how my five-year-old son used to tell me that our horse always complained to him, about me mistreating her... And a second ago I looked her in the eye and saw how sad she was because of my cruelty, and I was ashamed... I realize now, that my son may understand this horse better than I do. I should have listened to him...

– That's wonderful, – said Guedali. – I wanted you to listen to the voices of everything around us – to the whispers of the trees and wind, to the chirping of birds and crickets, because every creature has its own voice and its own place in this world, and all we have to do is listen, and not be cruel to them. And it seems that through your thoughts, you were able to hear some of their voices!

– Yes, you gave us a good lesson, – said the angry man. – You see, kids, even adults need a good lesson sometimes! I'll stay here and let my horse rest now, but you can still make it home in time for your dinner, so go ahead.

And Naftali, Syoma and Guedali said good-bye to the once angry man, who was now grateful for his lesson, and continued on their way.

11

Now that the danger of being beaten up by the Russian boy was behind him, Syoma realized he hadn't eaten anything today besides the goat cheese and rye bread his father had given him.

— I hope my parents didn't eat all the *cholent* my mother cooked yesterday, and left me some, — he said, sighing loudly. — And I hope it's still nice and hot... Sometimes it's only lukewarm and no matter how much I beg my mother to reheat it, she refuses, because you can't heat up food on Shabbat.

— Oh yes, — said Guedali. — Women have to know so many things! Even when they serve a dinner to guests, they cannot wash the plates after the meal, unless they have a second meal for which these plates must be used...

— We don't often have a second meal, — exclaimed Naftali, — so my mother always leaves the dirty dishes until the next day!

— Yes, many families must make do with only one meal, — Guedali noted. — Luckily, people accustomed to hunger know how to stretch a meal, like stuffing a goose neck with other ingredients, for instance. You fill it with onion and fat, or whatever else you want, and it lasts longer! I'm sure your mothers know lots of tricks like that.

— I love tricks! — Syoma declared. — My mother is used to mine. But sometimes she thinks I play tricks just to break rules, especially on Shabbat, even if I don't try to. For example, if she sees me running, or playing with my little sister, she just says, "You're breaking Shabbat rules!", but she doesn't realize I was actually running away from a stray dog that was trying to bite me, or that I was holding my sister because she was so desperately crying and begging for some attention. Instead of seeing my good intentions, she only shouts, "Don't do it!", without bothering to ask what's going on.

– Your mother once came to us on Shabbat and asked for a pinch of salt for her Cholent, – said Naftali. – And since she carried it back home, she broke a rule herself!

Syoma looked at Naftali with disbelief:

– Don't you accuse my mother! *Your* mother came to our place one Friday night, when my mother was about to light the candles, complaining about your misbehavior. She said, "Oh, Naftali is causing us so much trouble!"

– You're lying! – Naftali protested. – My father might say that, because he's never happy with me, but my mother and I get along very well, so she would never! And even if she did talk about me on Shabbat, how does that break a rule? Does the Torah mention my name?

– Because on Shabbat you can't talk about misfortunes! – smirked Syoma.

– You're a misfortune yourself! – Naftali exclaimed. He was so upset, he stopped, plopped down under an oak tree and refused to go any further.

– Let's all have a rest! – said Guedali. – Besides, your little lamb looks too tired to walk, and you can't force animals to do things on Shabbat... You know, you boys are quarreling about whose parents broke more rules, but I'm sure you've both broken several rules today without even realizing it!

– For instance? – Naftali and Syoma asked in unison.

– Look at your little lamb! – answered Guedali with

a smile. – Why is there a rope with a tight double-knot around its neck?

– We had to tie it to a stake, – Naftali said, – so it wouldn't get lost somewhere. It was a necessity!

– That's not a necessity, – laughed Guedali. – Tying a knot is necessary when you have to rope off a ditch, for instance, so people can't fall in and break their necks! That's preventing real danger, but where's the danger in a tiny lamb running away from two able-bodied boys? You see, one is allowed to help a sick animal and relieve its pain on Shabbat, like I did, once, when I pulled a sheep out of a bear trap and fixed it wounds. But you are only inflicting pain on this poor lamb with your clumsy double knot – it's too tight! The animal can hardly breathe!

Naftali went to the lamb and quickly untied the knot. The lamb happily shook his curly head and started running away, but Naftali caught him and put him in his lap and petted him.

– Let me get this straight, – Naftali said. – To tie or untie a double-knot on Shabbat is considered breaking the rule. But you're allowed to relieve an animal's discomfort and pain on Shabbat, so *untying* the knot around the lamb's neck is *not* considered breaking a rule...

– That's right! – Syoma exclaimed, trying to make peace with Naftali. – I heard that it's okay to tie a single knot, like on a shoe. So, what if one ties a single knot and then waits and after a certain time ties another single knot; would those be considered two single knots, or one double, which is prohibited?

– When I was a boy like you, – said Guedali, – I also tried getting around the rules. I used to always have a handkerchief in my pocket. But on Shabbat one isn't allowed to carry anything, so I took a big handkerchief my mother had made for me, and tied it around my wrist, instead. Since it wasn't in my pocket, I didn't carry it, so I didn't break the rule! Still, do you think my parents were satisfied? Instead of applauding me for not breaking the rule on Shabbat, they would find something else to shout at me about!

— Do you fight with them even now? — asked Syoma, regretting his question immediately, since Guedali suddenly grew sad.

— I wish I could, — he said, — but they are gone… And we can't talk about our grief on Shabbat, remember? Let me tell you a happier story about Shabbat rules. We've been talking about breaking them, without even realizing it until somebody points it out to us. But the man in my story not only knew what he was doing, he was so intent on *not* breaking the Shabbat rules, that everything around him started changing because of his inner strength and spirit! He affected events with his thoughts and will! Are you ready to listen?

The boys nodded eagerly. They were always hungry for anything new, and this unusual stranger had already captured them with his wisdom and easygoing character. They made themselves comfortable under the large oak tree, next to the sleeping dog, the snoring lamb and the sheep, and listened closely.

12

– A hundred years ago, – Guedali began – there lived a holy man on this Earth who cared about the well-being of all people and especially Jewish people, because he himself was a learned Jew. Even as a child, this holy man possessed remarkable abilities that distinguished him from other boys. Not only could he read and write at the age of five, but he was even able to compose thoughtful observation on an important religious book. At twelve, he wrote his own treatise on certain aspects of Judaism. Later, when his father took him to a Talmud teacher, the teacher was so impressed by the boy's expertise, he said he couldn't teach him anything! The boy had already accumulated so much knowledge that it surpassed this teacher's scholarship.

– I wish my knowledge surpassed the teacher's knowledge at our *heder*, – commented Syoma. – Then instead of having to go to school every day, I'd just stay home and help my mother, or rest!

– Do you think this holy man stopped studying just because a teacher couldn't teach him anything more? – objected Guedali. – Not at all! He found another teacher who was even wiser than the first, and when his skills surpassed the skills of this second teacher, he became a teacher himself. But the story is not about teachers and pupils; it's about Shabbat! Are you indeed ready to listen? – inquired Guedali.

The boys nodded again and Guedali continued:

– This man had no limitations: he cared not only about big things, but also about little things, and not only about Jews who lived near him, like friends and family, but also about Jews who lived far away. And if you studied history in your *heder*, my friends, – Guedali continued, – you would know that a hundred years ago there lived a man named Napoleon, who wanted to take over as many nations as he could! Now, what's the connection between some holy Jewish man, who sits quietly at his home while his wife looks after the household, and a violent, blood-thirsty commander, whose only desire is to conquer the world? – Guedali asked, looking inquisitively at the boys.

Syoma only shrugged his shoulders, but Naftali said:

– Since the holy man cared about Jews, I think he saw some danger in Napoleon, because by taking over the world, Napoleon would be taking over Jewish people as well!

– Not bad, – said Guedali. – Yes, this holy man warned all the Jews about Napoleon, and he became especially worried, when Napoleon entered Palestine, where a certain number of Jews lived at the time.

– I thought you were going to tell us a nice fairy tale about Shabbat, – Syoma protested – but instead you're as boring as our teacher at the *heder*! I'm better off falling asleep when you continue, I'm tired.

Guedali said:

– I apologize, everything in the world is of such interest to me that I jump from one event to another and stray off topic... You are right. My story is not about Napoleon; it's about miraculous things that happened during Shabbat.

Guedali winked at Naftali and continued:

– Who needs all this history anyway? Let's get back to Shabbat... So, our holy man heard about the plight of

Jews in Palestine and, afraid they could be hurt by Napoleon, he decided to send them some money that he and his pupils had collected. I'm sorry, Syoma, but I have to mention one more historical detail, do you mind?

Syoma rolled his eyes and waved his hand in the air, indicating that Guedali should continue. He spread his coat out on the grass and lay down, pretending to fall asleep. He even yawned when he noticed Guedali watching him.

– The problem was that back then Palestine was controlled by the Ottoman Empire, with which the Russian Tsar didn't have a very good relationship. So when the Tsar heard that a holy man in some little town in Russia was sending money to Ottoman territory, he assumed the holy man was an enemy, who wanted to support the Ottoman Empire! The Tsar didn't realize that the holy man was only trying to support Jewish people living in Palestine. Suspecting treason, he ordered his officers to bring the wise man from his remote little Russian town to St. Petersburg, and put him in jail.

– Again with the history, – Syoma groaned. – I guess we'll never hear anything from you about Shabbat!

– I'll skip the history, – Guedali winked, – and get to our hero. One day, while he was peacefully praying at home, somebody knocked on his door. Unwilling to interrupt his prayer, the holy man, Rabbi Zalman, didn't answer the door right away. A minute later, whoever had been knocking at the door, was pounding it with his fists, and even his boots! Rabbi Zalman's wife turned pale, but she stayed calm, and continued peeling potatoes, knowing her husband wouldn't appreciate it if she interrupted his prayer. Not until it seemed the door would finally crack, or simply fall apart from all the pounding, did Rabbi Zalman finish his prayer, go to the window, and see the kind of large black carriage used to transport prisoners, with sturdy metal sides, to prevent their escape.

– Open the door! – three coarse voices shouted from outside. – We have an order from the Tsar himself, to arrest you and bring you to St. Petersburg!

Rabbi Zalman hugged his wife and opened the door. Soon he was in the carriage, sitting on a stiff bench, while the three gendarmes were telling jokes and playing cards in another compartment, furnished with warm blankets and pillows.

It was Thursday, and Rabbi Zalman spent the entire day in the carriage, alone with his thoughts, not allowed to even open a window curtain and see the daylight and busy streets. The next day, Friday, the carriage continued its long, exhausting journey to St. Petersburg. When it stopped in some city for a minute, Zalman heard a clock on a tower strike twelve. He realized only a few hours remained until Shabbat, and he asked the gendarmes to stop.

One gendarme with a kind face and stout belly was ready to fulfill Rabbi Zalman's request, until the two other quipped:

– This is Russia! We celebrate Sundays in church here, whereas Friday is just another day. Change your customs and you'll be fine!

And the carriage continued on its way.

Rabbi Zalman sat in his dark compartment, living on bread and cucumbers, while the gendarmes stopped at every farmer's market and feasted in their compartment, boasting about how they'd gotten a huge jar of pickled cabbage for free from a farmer they'd scared to death, by threatening to arrest him for inflating his prices.

Rabbi Zalman waited until they had finished their meal and asked them again to stop because he had to rest during Shabbat.

Again, they only laughed, and one of the gendarmes, a piece of pickled cabbage stuck between his teeth, told the rabbi they didn't care about Shabbat: they only cared about the Tsar's order to bring him to St. Petersburg for interrogation, as soon as possible.

With Shabbat only a couple of hours away, Rabbi Zalman started thinking about what he could do, to celebrate it in peace. He waited till the gendarmes had drunk some *kvass*, hoping it would warm their hearts, and begged them a third time to stop. As before, they ignored his pleas.

Suddenly, only seconds later, they heard a loud crack: one of the axles under the carriage had broken, and the carriage tilted so heavily to one side, the gendarmes' drinking glasses rolled off the table and smashed on the floor.

This would've been a good time to stop and rest, but the gendarmes were determined to displease their prisoner however possible. They weren't interested in what he'd done – only that he'd angered the Tsar. And out of devotion to their leader, they didn't want to show any kindness to this Jewish man who, in their opinion, would surely be imprisoned for the rest of life.

Thus, one of them walked to a nearby village and returned with a craftsman, who fixed the axle, and the carriage continued on its way to St. Petersburg. And even though Shabbat was drawing very near, Rabbi Zalman stopped asking the gendarmes to park the carriage, since he realized he couldn't influence them with his words.

But shortly after they'd resumed their journey, one of the horses suddenly groaned, stopped in its tracks and fell over! And when one gendarme ran out to make it get back up with a kick, he realized the horse was dead.

Judging from all the commotion, Rabbi Zalman guessed what had happened. Still, he said nothing to the guards, knowing that his words wouldn't influence these faithful servants of the Tsar. Instead, he only listened, and overheard two of the guards ridiculing the one with the big belly:

– It's your fault that nag collapsed and died, Pyotr, – they laughed – you were too heavy for her!

With sadness, Rabbi Zalman realized the gendarmes didn't care about him, or the animals. They showed no remorse over the horse's death – all they cared about was pleasing the Tsar, by getting their prisoner to St. Petersburg as quickly as possible.

It took an hour to cart the old horse away and replace it with a fresh horse from a nearby village. But to everyone's surprise, no matter how hard the horses tried to pulled the carriage, or how energetically the gendarmes pushed it from behind, the carriage didn't move even a centimeter, as though there was magic involved.

Rabbi Zalman sat in his compartment, waiting, while the gendarmes watched their horses' useless efforts in disbelief, trying to grasp why the healthy, well-bred colts couldn't do their job. Finally, they decided not to continue to St. Petersburg, but to pull the carriage to the side of the road, instead, and stay there overnight. It was exactly one hour before Shabbat.

Thus, Rabbi Zalman was able to rest and celebrate

peacefully. Being a religious man, he didn't want to anger Hashem by rushing somewhere during Shabbat, and his commitment to achieving this was so deep, it affected the material world, and his wish was granted. And the next morning the horses pulled the carriage with ease, and the journey to St. Petersburg resumed.

– That was the nicest, most entertaining story I've ever been told! – Syoma exclaimed.

– Yes, – Guedali said. – I like this story because it shows the wonders of nature! Let me tell you a bit more about Rabbi Zalman… Several months later, one of his pupils went to St. Petersburg along the very same highway. It was autumn, and the leaves on the trees were either gone altogether, or dried up and colorless, except for one spot, where the student noticed several trees, whose leaves were fresh and bright green. And this was the exact spot where Rabbi Zalman had spent his Shabbat!

That was the end of Guedali's story. And now, on their way home to observe their own Shabbat, Naftali was so lost in thought, envisioning the wise and brave Rabbi Zalman with those stupid, arrogant gendarmes, he didn't even realize when he got home, that Guedali had been invited to dinner right there! Today Naftali's father was gathering important guests for dinner, and Guedali was one of them. This strange coincidence quickly dissolved Naftali's thoughts about Rabbi Zalman, and brought him back to reality.

He was at the doorway, preparing to listen politely as each guest greeted him, with questions like: "My, how you've grown, Naftali – how old are you now?"

But suddenly, he froze: there, among the many familiar faces in the dining room, he saw Don Quixote!

13

What a sight! Sitting next to his beautiful Dulcinea in a well-tailored city suit, Don Quixote stood out from the Tulchin Jews, whose men always wore the same long, mended dark coats and wide-brimmed hats. The locals didn't need various outfits, because you didn't need fancy clothes to look after crops, or sell fabrics or meat. Second, these were religious Jews, concerned with prayers and G-d; they cared more about having pure thoughts and a clean mind, than perfectly clean, elegant clothes.

And the delicate Dulcinea, in a silver, silk dress, with her hair falling over her shoulders in thick, soft waves, looked very different from the Jewish women, too, who favored dark dresses or extremely long skirts, and even covered their heads, so nobody would be interested in them, except their husbands.

Naftali was in shock. What a day of surprise encounters! First, there was Guedali and his dog, who saved them from danger; next, the angry man with the tired horse, who learned to avoid causing harm; and now, Don Quixote, whom Naftali had seen in the illustrations in his book, and then in real life at the train station, was right here, in Naftali's own house! From the very moment Naftali saw this unusual man at the table, he knew some very unusual things would start happening. And he was right!

He just stood on the doorstep, too shy to go inside, until one of the guests – Haim, a very poor man in dirty overalls – offered him a stool. Haim had no special trade, so he did whatever odd jobs there were: one day he'd lay bricks for somebody building a house, or cover a roof with clay shingles; the next day he might sharpen somebody's kitchen knives; and another day, if the milkman was too sick to work, Haim might deliver the milk to the houses on the milkman's horse-pulled cart. Unfortunately, these odd jobs didn't come up very often, and Haim and his shy wife had nothing to eat, so their neighbors would invite them for dinner. Yet despite his misfortunes, Haim always joked that one day he'd get lucky and become rich. "I only get small jobs for now", he always said, "because I'm saving my strength for something truly great and remarkable!"

But now Haim looked at Naftali with a very serious expression:

– Do you see the distinguished gentleman in the suit? – he asked. – He came here because of your letter!

Everybody turned to look at Naftali, waiting to hear what he would say, but being the center of attention only made him more self-conscious, and Naftali's mind went blank. He was confused: he had wished for Don Quixote to come to his house and change his life, but he had never put his words in writing! What letter was Haim talking about? Could Don Quixote have read his thoughts? Did he come just because Naftali wanted him to?

Haim continued:

– This gentleman told us the letter he received was penned by a very educated person, who speaks several languages with ease, and is concerned about other people's well-being – and we decided it must've been you, Naftali!

– It could easily have been him! – Naftali's mother boasted. – He knows Yiddish quite well, and the *melamed* has something good to say about him every time I bump into him on the street. He is also fluent in Russian, and he's even studying Spanish! Naftali is also very kind, – she continued, smiling proudly, – he loves studying maps with his best friend Syoma Dvorkin, and he's always dreaming about far-away lands... Sometimes he says perhaps a better life awaits us in one of them! So, what did the letter say?

– It was a plea to help all the poor Jewish souls here, and lead them to a better life, – Haim said. – It also said the recipient of the letter, due to his immense wealth and caring heart, was perfectly suited for such a difficult task.

Addressing Haim, Naftali said:

– Perhaps you mean Moses? He took the Jewish people out of slavery, and his words were spoken, before someone wrote them down! But I'm no Moses, so nobody wrote my words down!

Everyone laughed, including Haim, and Naftali realized he'd said something clever. Don Quixote stopped eating and raised his finger:

– Slavery! How interesting. The letter actually mentioned slavery – but you shouldn't laugh at this young man. Take him seriously. If he already knows three languages, he might indeed grow up to be an educated, and respected, man like the one who sent me the letter.

– Sorry, Naftali! – Haim said. – We were only joking with you. This gentleman came here to lead us to freedom, because some time ago a very learned man named Michael Heilprin wrote him a letter, suggesting he help the Jewish people here. Michael believed we should finally reject harassment and live on land that we *own,* so nobody could force us off.

– It's completely true, – said Don Quixote. – I would like to tell you more about Michael, because he is such a good example of what a learned individual must be... Only I must confess that after receiving his letter, I hesitated for some time, wondering if such a humble man as I should be involved in the rescue of Jews. But Michael's words, written several years ago, still ring in my mind, and I have followed his advice to do charitable things ever since!

– Please do tell us more about this Michael, – everybody said, – because we already know about you. Your fame precedes you, as they say: it arrived in Tulchin even before you got off the train! Yet, we don't know anything about the gentleman who, for some reason, cares about our fate!

Then and there, Naftali decided the well-dressed man sitting at his family's kitchen table really was Don Quixote: how else would everybody know all about him? Did they read the book by Cervantes? And if so, then why did they always look at Naftali as though he were crazy, whenever he tried to tell them about Don Quixote's adventures?

Don Quixote continued:

– As you probably know, I became rich because I was always very careful with my money. Can you guess why I decided to marry my wife?

Upon hearing these words, Dulcinea laughed and said:

– This has nothing to do with the story about the learned man who wrote you the letter!

But everybody in the room insisted Don Quixote tell them every detail about how he'd chosen his wife, and he continued.

– Once, I presented Clara with a nice kerchief, – he said, – which was nicely wrapped, and tied with a fine ribbon. Well, instead of cutting the ribbon with scissors, Clara simply untied it. When I asked her why she did that, she explained that this way, she could reuse it! I realized then that she was very practical and knew how to economize, so I figured that if I married her, my wealth would soon multiply. And the more money I had for myself, the more money I'd have to spare for others.

Naftali was still surprised that the woman's name wasn't Dulcinea, but he decided that Clara was also a beautiful name, which suited this woman, who smiled broadly at him during Don Quixote's story about her.

Clara said:

– I'm not used to being the center of attention, so I think we should talk about the letter writer, who was behind our decision to come here, and tell you a little more about what we are doing with our money and our wealth.

And after Clara's announcement Don Quixote started his real story.

14

— The man who wrote us cares about fairness and unfairness, and he became famous in America over thirty years ago, for arguing that the Torah was against slavery...

— But we are not slaves! – exclaimed Haim.

— Are you sure? – someone asked him. – I feel like a slave here, because a slave doesn't own anything. I cannot own land, or settle where I want!

— You are not slaves, – said Don Quixote firmly, – but your situation here is certainly not the best, because you are denied many rights... Michael Heilprin always concerned himself with the rights of dispossessed people – especially the Jews. He was Jewish himself; he was born in Poland, but he moved to Hungary and learned Hungarian, then to France for a while, where he picked up French. Being a typical Jew, he always learned the language of whatever country he settled in. This knowledge of different countries, customs and languages enriched his brain. He knew almost everything – he could answer any question you asked, just like that! Then he proceeded to America. There he befriended the publishers of an encyclopedia, and started writing informational articles for it. But he also used his immense knowledge to help people.

— Yes, it's a great thing to use not only money, but also knowledge to assist others! – said Naftali's father. – Knowledge is an incredible and important gift, and we have to use it wisely.

Everybody nodded in agreement, and Don Quixote

continued:

– Michael Heilprin became famous in America because he argued for the rights of the slaves, who had been brought to the United States from Africa. He felt it was morally wrong for people to own other people, and, being a writer, he used his pen, and his mind, to challenge this wrongdoing!

– Was he successful? – Naftali asked, eager to know whether a skillful writer could have an impact on others with his thoughts and words.

– Well, yes. – Don Quixote replied. – When a well-known rabbi argued that the Torah said slaves were permitted, Michael Heilprin responded, and when his commentary was published in a major local newspaper, it caused an uproar! There were other people who wrote articles calling for slavery to be abolished as well, and they all helped the anti-slavery movement.

– We were taught that there was a civil war in America to abolish slavery! – noted Naftali.

– You were taught well, then, – replied Don Quixote. – It's true that sometimes wars must be fought to achieve things; however, it also helps to argue a point with a pen, instead. Believe me, the pen can be mightier than the sword, even though it's obviously lighter in weight!

Naftali looked to see whether Don Quixote had a sword on him, as depicted in the book by Cervantes, but he couldn't see one.

Don Quixote continued:

– Because Michael Heilprin was very sensitive to people's misfortunes, he saw that other people were suffering, besides the slaves from Africa. Jews also suffered from being ridiculed and harassed wherever they settled!

And when he wrote to me, after learning about my great fortune as a railroad king, he suggested there were other countries, where Jews could settle, have peace of mind, and own a piece of land. I was very inspired by this idea... Michael wrote that he was already helping some Jews settle in America, but that other countries, like Palestine, might be interesting too.

Today was the day for not only unexpected events, but also for interesting coincidences, Naftali thought. He'd heard the word "Palestine" twice: first, in Guedali's miraculous story about Rabbi Zalman's Shabbat, and now from Don Quixote.

– What is so good about Palestine? – somebody asked. Don Quixote replied:

– It's good because our ancestors came from there... However, I've read about people who went to Palestine, but realized that life wouldn't be easy there, either. They'd have to build everything from scratch, since there aren't many Jews left there, and there is almost no housing for newcomers – only sand. They'd have to plant flowers, and even fruit trees...

– I have a complex question, – Naftali's father said. – How do we go about choosing a country to settle in? Should we go to the barren land of our ancestors, just because we know from history that they used to live there, even though others live there now? Or should we go where the land is more fruitful, so we can be sure our children are fed and our families will prosper? Or maybe to a country that would welcome us, and where our neighbors would be friendly?

– I've asked myself the same question, – said Don Quixote. – Michael also mentioned Argentina, which he said is a nice country, whose government welcomes set-tlers from different lands.

– What's so special about Argentina? – said one of the guests. – We don't know anybody who ever went there! We know people who went to America and never came back, because life in America suited them well...

– Argentina has gauchos! – exclaimed Naftali, who recently learned about Argentina from his teacher in the heder.

– Gauchos! – laughed Naftali's father. – So there must be horses, too! The only thing I know in life is how to take care of horses! Maybe we should go there and see if luck will follow us.

– Speaking of horses, – Naftali said to Don Quixote, – why did you come by train and not by horse? Don't you have one named Rocinante?

Don Quixote looked at him with surprise.

– Why would I have a horse? – he asked.

An uncomfortable silence ensued. Naftali's cheeks turned red. He was afraid to say he'd mistaken this gen-tleman for the hero from Cervantes's book. Suddenly he felt foolish. As usual, he'd gotten carried away with his daydreams and made it all up...

But Clara came to his rescue:

– This boy has such a rich imagination! – she ex-claimed. – He obviously reads too many books, but I'm sure his talent for learning new languages will help him in a new land. And I think he is comparing you to Don Quixote, because you are a dreamer, like Don Quixote, and you think you can help many people. I think it's a compliment!

Don Quixote looked at Naftali very seriously and

said:

– Perhaps I am Don Quixote. Sometimes I, too, feel I'm fighting invisible enemies. And surprisingly enough, I'm frequently ridiculed by the very people I try to help. I think it's because they're afraid to leave home. For some people it's easier to stay where they are and tolerate being harassed, than to face change. But I have a dream… And my dream is for Jews to be free and live in a free land.

On hearing these words, the guests grew silent for a moment. They realized this was a serious conversation that would affect everyone. For some families it could lead to real change, and for others – to arguments, regrets, and the decision not to leave the town where they, their parents, and even their grandparents were born.

But then the spirit of Shabbat took over, and everybody starting laughing and smiling and drinking again. And as they celebrated the end of Shabbat together, they imagined themselves living in a free country, on their own land, and the wonderful idea of freedom became firmly planted in their minds.

15

That night, Naftali had trouble falling asleep, because he was overwhelmed by the ideas the adults had discussed at the table. But there was another reason: despite his respect for Don Quixote, he couldn't believe that a person with such a big body and such big dreams really cared about a little thing like saving ribbons! To Naftali, the kindness and warmth of Don Quixote's wife, Clara, outshone her thriftiness, be it with fabrics, money, or food.

Besides, how could saving ribbons help somebody get rich? Naftali could have saved hundreds of ribbons himself by now, but how would these ribbons help his friend Syoma Dvorkin, who had to work on Shabbat because his family couldn't afford a *shabbos-goy*?

Naftali could try to save on hay, by feeding the horses less, which would stretch their food a little longer, but would it make him richer? Or would it only make the horses skinny and unhealthy, and so weak, they could die on the way to a destination and anger the travelers?

Naftali's parents could save money on firewood, too, by burning fewer logs and wearing fur coats inside the house all winter, but what could they purchase with these savings? There still wouldn't be enough to acquire a small shop, in order to earn more money, or even to reupholster the carriage, so Naftali's father's customers wouldn't smirk at the holes in the fabric!

But it seemed Naftali wasn't the only one wondering about the wealthy Don Quixote this evening: Naftali heard a noise in the kitchen, where his father and a guest, who was staying the night, were sleeping. He raised his head from his pillow trying to hear what was going on, then, careful not to wake his mother, he tiptoed to the door and looked through the crack. And to his surprise, he saw Shmuel, another odd-jobber, who didn't say a word at dinner, hovering around Don Quixote's coat, which was hung on a hook on the wall.

It was too dark to see exactly what Shmuel was doing, but it seemed he was trying to remove the coat from the hook. Naftali's father approached him and tugged at his sleeve to stop him. Shmuel pushed him away, but Naftali's father persisted.

– What are you doing, Shmuel?! – he whispered angrily, but Shmuel ignored him. – Shmuel, stop it, please! – Naftali's father pleaded. – Don't embarrass me! You shouldn't be touching my guests' belongings...

Naftali was shocked. He couldn't believe that a member of their community would try to steal something from Don Quixote, who'd come to help them, and who lay sleeping in the tiny second room. Being accustomed to the inconveniences of long-distance travel, Don Quixote had said he would prefer a modest room in his new friends' home, to his pretentious hotel room, with its stale breakfast and annoying maids.

But Shmuel kept hovering around Don Quixote's coat, so Naftali's father objected again:

– Shmuel, don't make a fool of yourself. Stop it immediately!

Instead, Shmuel pulled on the coat so aggressively, it flew off the hook and fell onto the floor. Naftali's father picked it up immediately, and hung it back on the hook. In the dark, the whole scene looked somewhat strange, and Naftali didn't know what to make of it.

Shmuel said:

– Did you think I wanted to pick his pockets? You must have a low opinion of me, then. Lazar, you are such a learned man, yet you smell horse dung and wear the same old coat every day. Meanwhile, this man does not know the Torah as well as you, but he possesses this exquisite coat, fashioned by the best tailors in France. No matter what you think of me, I'm not trying to pick his pockets or steal his stylish coat – I'm just examining it. I'm not a thief!

Carefully adjusting Don Quixote's coat, Naftali's father replied:

– I know that, but I believe one should not be so concerned with possessions – they're nothing, really. What's important is our heart and our thoughts, and how much goodness we bring to the world.

Shmuel interrupted, almost shouting:

– The whole time this guy sat at the table proclaiming his love for Jews, I had only one thought: that he almost put you out of business!

Naftali's father was very surprised to hear Shmuel's declaration.

– But how could a total stranger put me out of business? It's nonsense! You may be older, Shmuel, but it seems you're no wiser.

– Well, he built the railroad, and now your former passengers travel by train, instead of hiring you and your horses! Think about it: this guy, who has everything in the world, completely ruins you with his trains, and instead of kicking him out of your house, you gaze into his eyes with devotion.

Naftali's father was dumbfounded.

– I don't blame the man for my business troubles, –
he explained. – He didn't invent the railroads personally!
He came here to help us, so we should focus on a better
future for our children, instead of his personal wealth.
How petty it is to feel the fabric of somebody's coat, only to
fuel your envy! You see, Shmuel, I stopped caring about
material possessions long ago, after learning of the teach-
ings of Leo Tolstoy. Have you heard of him? He is one of
Russia's greatest thinkers, and a remarkable man!

– Go ahead, tell me about this Leo Tolstoy, – Shmuel
said. – But I think you should ask the visitor with the
expensive coat for money... Make him feel guilty, tell him
you're losing customers because of him! That way you
might get some money now, instead of waiting until he
sends you to... He himself doesn't where to send you –
Palestine, Argentina or America! Remember that famous
Russian saying, "It's better to have a pigeon in the hand,
than a crane in the sky..."

– Listen, Shmuel, you should know about Tolstoy, –
Naftali's father interrupted. – He is a nobleman, a count,
but a while back he realized that material possessions are
just 'things,' that don't make people any kinder or like-
able... When Tolstoy heard that Russian villagers were
starving, he and his helpers went to see these villages,
and what he saw shocked him: children crying and begging for food, their desperate mothers having nowhere to
turn for help; peasants digging in the fields hoping to find
an old, rotten potato they might've missed the last time...
Well, Tolstoy opened free canteens for the poor, gave them
logs for their stoves, to warm their huts in the winter, and
he even bought some horses and gave them to the peasants to use, all with his own money.

– I can't believe such generous people exist, – Shmuel said. – Although, this count sounds like an interesting person... Quite extravagant, I would say.

– Tolstoy isn't extravagant; it's just that he has a big heart, which hasn't been frozen by the Russian cold. And when he gave the horses to the villagers for free, do you know what he asked for in return? He didn't want anything for himself. He only asked the more able villagers to plow the fields of the disadvantaged ones: those who didn't have a strong man ink their family to plow the fields and harvest: widows with children, weak and sick women, orphans, and the elderly.

But Tolstoy didn't arrive at this idea himself. He was inspired by something he witnessed in one of the villages during the famine. The villagers had nothing to feed themselves, never mind the poor horses! So, they sent a messenger to another nearby village that had more food, and asked them to feed eighty horses over the winter. And in exchange, the horses would work for them all winter long, for free! Well, the peasants from the nearby village realized how clever this idea was, and they agreed to "host" the eighty horses.

The agreement worked out beautifully for both sides: the nearby villagers fed the horses, and in return the horses "worked" for them in the fields. And after the winter, they returned the eighty horses, healthy and well-fed, to their poorer neighbors. They helped their neighbors immensely, because if they hadn't fed these starving horses, they would all have died over the winter! And then there would have been no horses to plow the earth in the spring, in order to plant seeds and grow different vegetables... Tolstoy learned from this example of humanity, and carried out the same plan, over and over again... What he showed was that people should give up their useless possessions, because they only need what they need... Do you agree with me, Shmuel? – Naftali's father asked.

But he was met with silence. Naftali peered into the kitchen trying to see what was going on, but it was too dark.

– Shmuel, what do you think of Tolstoy's thoughts? – Naftali's father repeated, but all he heard in response was loud snoring in the room. Finally Naftali was able to see: Shmuel lay on top of a large storage trunk; he was fully clothed, his beard and hair were disheveled, but he was sleeping like a baby!

It was obvious that he only cared about simple things, such as why Don Quixote had such a nice coat and Naftali's father did not, or why a person with railroads makes more money than a person with horses. More complex ideas about giving up possessions and helping the whole village with food did not matter to Shmuel, and since he had lost interest in the long-winded discussions for which Naftali's father was famous, he had simply fallen asleep, and was probably having sweet dreams.

So, Naftali's father was interested in big ideas, while other people, like Shmuel, cared only about things they could get right away. And Naftali decided he was exactly like his father: he cared about ideas, too – small ideas, like saving ribbons, and big ideas, like Tolstoy's. In the morning, he would ask his father to tell him more about Tolstoy. And with that thought, Naftali went back to bed and fell asleep.

16

In the mornings Naftali liked sleeping late. Sometimes he was awakened by the rooster, or by the racket his mother made with the pots and mixing bowls, when she started cooking. More commonly, like most boys his age, Naftali slept like the dead, and not even a fire or a shooting nearby could wake him.

While he slept, the adults followed their own rhythm of life, which didn't always include Naftali. Therefore, by the time Naftali woke up, both Don Quixote and Dulcinea had already dressed, eaten their breakfast, kindly served by Naftali's mother, discussed some things with Naftali's father, such as keeping in touch, and organizing the next meeting about the Jewish people moving to other countries. In fact, they were ready to leave. As usual, Naftali had been ignored. As usual, the adults didn't care that he was eager to talk to Don Quixote about his own thoughts on ribbons, horses and trains this morning!

But perhaps it was just as well. When Don Quixote, in a perfect suit, and Dulcinea, in a beautiful dress, her blond hair in braids, greeted him with a cheerful, "Good morning", Naftali was overcome by emotion. The fact that these two marvelous guests were even looking at him, an ordinary boy, about to ask his mother for his usual breakfast of bread and a glass of milk, was so overwhelming, he suddenly forgot everything he'd wanted to say!

Meanwhile, Don Quixote was telling Naftali's father about his plans:

– Thanks for the wonderful visit, Lazar Evseevich, – he was saying. – Now we're going to the train station, and back to France, where we currently live. Once we rest up from the long trip, and crossing all the borders, where they stop you and compare your mug with the passport picture to make sure it's really you... When all that nonsense is over, I plan to go hunting! Did you know it's my favorite sport? We usually go to a little village near Paris, along with our dogs, and some servants who carry the guns, and carry home our fowl if the hunt is successful... We hunt for pheasant! And even for deer! Clara, do you remember those beautiful antlers I brought to you after one of those hunting trips?

— Yes, of course, – replied Dulcinea, blushing. – I'm always so worried for you when you hunt... Maybe that's why you always bring me something from the forest. Last time it was antlers, before that it was a bear skin to put next to my bed, so when I wake up, I can put my feet into the warm, thick fur... And all the dishes our servants cook with the pheasants and rabbits...

And then we all sit down for a meal, just like we did only minutes ago with these wonderful people...

— I suppose people can hunt for recreation, – Naftali's father said. – We hunt too, but since we are less sophisticated than people in Paris, we hunt mostly to feed ourselves. You know, there is a famous Russian writer, Leo Tolstoy, who is against any kind of hunting! Can you believe it? He says all animals have a soul, like people. And I cannot agree with him more. When I look into the eyes of an older horse in our stable, I feel very sorry for it... It's as though it realizes its life is almost over...

— Yes, I know about Tolstoy and his ideas, – Don Quixote replied, shrugging his shoulders. – They say he believes this so firmly, he doesn't even eat meat anymore!

– Tolstoy! – exclaimed Naftali. – That's the man you were talking about yesterday, right, Papa?

– What did you say? – Naftali's father asked, evidently surprised that his son knew the name. Naftali realized his father had no idea he'd been listening to last night's conversation with Shmuel. Suddenly he turned red as a beet, inadvertently giving himself away.

Naftali's father was also uneasy; he could only imagine what Naftali thought about the previous night's confrontation with Shmuel. But rather than make his guest uncomfortable by saying anything, he exclaimed:

– Naftali is such a bright boy! He knows about many writers and already reads in three languages... Luckily, Don Quixote was so absorbed in his thoughts about hunting, he didn't notice what Naftali had just said.

– I chanced upon an article in the local newspaper about Tolstoy's habits at home, – he continued. – His servants have to cook and serve two different meals for every dinner now – one with meat and fish for Tolstoy's wife, and then another of *kasha*, soup, mushrooms, potato puree, *borsch* or porridge, for the count himself. His wife sits at the head of the table, and all the vegetarians, including Tolstoy and his daughters, sit to her right. He may have meant to ease the life of animals by not eating them, but now the life of his cooks is more complicated! Isn't that a paradox?

– Yes, we are always trying to improve things, but by improving one thing, we often make another thing worse! – Naftali's father replied. – I've read a lot about Tolstoy's views... Apparently, some of his friends ridicule him: they say on the one hand, he's against killing animals and doesn't eat meat, but on the other, he uses their fur and their skins for his hats and shoes.

On hearing this, Naftali looked down at his own worn-out shoes and got the shivers. He imagined that the leather for these shoes had come from cows just like Zorka – the gentle, kind-eyed cow his parents owned that mooed so softly and provided the cup of fresh, warm milk Naftali had with his bread for breakfast every morning...

– And what was Tolstoy's answer? – Naftali asked, intruding into the adult conversation. Dulcinea smiled at Naftali, but his father and Don Quixote completely ignored him.

– But Tolstoy anticipated questions like these. He said everybody had their faults, and that since he couldn't fix all of his own faults at once, he would work on the most biggest ones first. And once he had fixed his most important shortcomings, he would deal with his fur hats, deerskin shoes, and cowhide belt. Tolstoy really understood animals' souls, though. I deal with horses every day, and they all have their own temperaments! I heard that when Tolstoy was a little boy, he loved horseback riding...

– And I have never liked riding horses! – Naftali interjected, again, comparing himself to Tolstoy, but as before, nobody paid attention to him.

– So, one day – continued Naftali's father, – little Leo was riding his favorite horse bareback and barefoot, like the peasant boys he'd observed. He wanted it to run faster and faster, so he kept kicking it in the sides with his bare heels. One of the servants noticed this, and when Leo came home that day, the servant told him he shouldn't kick the horse so hard. He said: "Think of the horse as Porfirii Stepanovich, the old groom you like so much, who tells you stories about his life. Since Porfirii Stepanovich is old, you help him by bringing him tea and picking up his glasses when they fall off his nose. Well, this horse is old too, so you'd better give it something to drink before it collapses." And Tolstoy later told his friends, this conversation completely changed his view of animals... Naftali listened carefully to the episodes from the life of the young Tolstoy. He was impressed that the adults were spending so much time discussing not some merchant, but a writer of novels and newspaper articles; they were discussing his life and ideas at length, and examining their own lives in relation to these ideas.

And from listening to this conversation between his father and Don Quixote, Naftali decided that a pen can indeed be mightier not only than the sword, but mightier than money and material goods.

17

– We've enjoyed the visit immensely, – said Don Quixote rising from his chair. – And now we have to leave to catch our train. But with all the gifts we received from the wonderful Jews of Tulchin, I don't know how we'll be able to carry all of our luggage!

– Don't worry, – said Naftali's father. – My son and I will load it onto our carriage, so you won't have to lift anything heavy. We'll go to the station right away, and load everything onto the train before you even arrive there – you can never trust the schedules. Once, I gave a lift to a traveling salesman, who was catching the overnight train to another city, for a business meeting the next morning. We arrived fifteen minutes early, but as we approached the platform, the train was already whistling, puffing, and leaving the station. We shouted as loud as we could and waved our arms, but there was nothing we could do about it. My poor passenger had to ask me to take him to a nearby hotel, and the next time I saw him, he told me that because that train had left early, he lost an important business contract. The conductors here hate checking their pocket watches to make sure they are on time – everything in Russia is so unpredictable!

– Your suggestion to take our luggage ahead of us is very wise, then, – said Don Quixote.

– Thanks for your foresight and for your hospitality...

– I'm not going with you, – Naftali suddenly exclaimed, addressing his father. – I'm going with our guests, in their carriage!

– You'll do as I say, – Naftali's father said, angrily. Naftali had never argued with him before. But he was growing and changing every year; eventually, he would try to be more independent and voice his own opinions. But being a very strict and rigid man, his father handled Naftali's little rebellions by being even stricter, for Naftali's own good, so he wouldn't become a lazy, aimless dreamer, instead of a serious scholar, who wasn't afraid of hard work.

But Clara could tell Naftali was eager to talk to them, and she had nothing against it; being from an uneventful small town, the boy probably wanted to learn about hunting, or life in Paris. Clara thought Naftali would benefit from learning not only from the books he apparently enjoyed reading, but also from people he met.

– It's all right if he comes with us, – she said, – he can point out the road to the station, so our coachman doesn't get lost!

– Yes, yes, – Naftali exclaimed, – I can show them the way, so they don't get lost!

– You're just being lazy! – Naftali's father said. – You don't feel like carry suitcases, am I right? But physical work is good for you, you need to build up your muscles, – he said, and Naftali knew from his father's steely voice, that this discussion was over.

Naftali looked down at his cowhide shoes, fighting back his tears. He always kept his feelings to himself, afraid to express what he really felt... He was afraid to mention Leo Tolstoy again, because his father would reprimand him for eavesdropping on his talk with Shmuel last night. At the same time, he wanted to talk to Don Quixote and Clara more about the writer and his ideas;

he was sure his kind guests wouldn't be as judgmental, or quick to form opinions, as his father, who made Naftali feel inferior in their conversations, and afraid of some rebuke.

Naftali's father always encouraged adult conversations and discussions, and he loved it when other people provoked him and argued various points in the Talmud at Shabbat. He saw it as pure sport – gymnastics for the mind – except that here, you could compete with only words and your brain, rather than a ball or a pole.

However, whenever Naftali opposed his father's views, his father took it personally; he took his son's objections for disobedience, rather than a way of sharing ideas and creating new ones, by challenging old interpretations. Naftali's father didn't understand him, so it was useless to explain that he only wanted to ride with Don Quixote and Dulcinea so he could talk to them, and not because he was lazy...

The train station wasn't very far away, so Naftali's father decided not to load Don Quixote's luggage onto the cart he used for extra-heavy loads; instead, his horse would carry all the suitcases on its back. But since there were so many of them, he wondered if he should use one horse, or two.

– Do you think Lastochka will be able to carry all this luggage to the station without getting tired? – he asked.

Lastochka was one of his favorite horses – a hard worker who could carry any load, no matter how many versts she had already walked.

– Maybe we should divide the luggage between Lastochka and Seryi?

Seryi, meaning 'gray', so named because of his color, was Naftali's favorite horse; when he was in the mood, Seryi was fast, and happy to let Naftali ride him wherever he wanted. Yet sometimes, the horse seemed so overcome with sadness, he wouldn't budge, or even let Naftali stroke him.

Naftali only shrugged in response to this father's questions. He knew that whatever he said, his father would do the opposite. If Naftali were to say, "Please load only Lastochka, she can easily carry all this weight," Naftali's father would say, "But what about Seryi? You always let him rest, because he's your favorite. But why should he be privileged?" And if Naftali said, "Let's load them both," Naftali's father would say, "If we load them both, they'll both be tired, and what if we get an unexpected customer who needs a horse right away?"

– Should we take both horses, or only Lastochka? – Naftali's father asked again. – You don't want us to be late for the train station, do you?

– Only Lastochka then, – said Naftali. – She'll manage to carry everything perfectly.

– But what if she gets tired? – asked Naftali's father. – If she stops and refuses to go on, we might be late. If we divide the luggage between the two of them, we'll have a better chance of reaching the train station on time!

– That's fine too, – said Naftali. And, piece by piece, they split the spit the suitcases between Lastochka and Seryi, and headed out.

Seryi wasn't in the mood; he walked slowly, stopped frequently, and looked very sad indeed. But Lastochka was her usual fast, and eager, self: as Seryi dragged himself along, she would stop, and look back at him, as though waiting for him to catch up.

– Horses are like people, – Naftali's father said, after a while. – And Seryi reminds me of you. When he's in one of his moods, he's stubborn as a mule. Look at him! There's something on his mind, and he just doesn't want to move!

Luckily, they still had at least an hour before the train was supposed to leave, so Seryi could have his way and be as slow as he wanted, on this beautiful day. The sun was shining over the meadow, and everything was beaming with joy! Crickets chirped in the cool green grass; birds sat happily in the trees, and even Naftali's father seemed cheerful.

But Seryi was sad. And when he stopped dead in his tracks, with that sad look on his face, as if to say he wouldn't move another inch, no matter what, Naftali's father got angry.

Naftali took some bread out of his pocket and approached Seryi. He stood next to him, stroking his big sad head, and looking into his big sad eyes. When he tried giving him the bread, Seryi slowly turned his head away.

– Seryi, – Naftali whispered into his ear, – you'd better start walking. My father doesn't like it when you behave this way... I don't like certain things either, but I still have to do what my father says... I wanted to ride with Don Quixote and his wife and discuss Tolstoy. But my father always wants things his way, so here I am, walking, and talking to you, instead!

– What are you whispering? – shouted Naftali's father. – And don't give him any bread. Give him a kick instead, so he'll get going and do his job!

– Seryi, – Naftali pleaded, – I have to do things I

don't want to, and so do you. Otherwise we'll be in trouble! Do you want my father to come and kick you? I would never kick you myself. As Tolstoy said, animals have souls too – I feel bad enough as it is about my cowhide shoes...

Seryi looked at Naftali the whole time, as though he understood every word; still, he wouldn't move an inch. Lastochka stopped too; she was well ahead, eating grass, and glancing back at them from afar. Naftali's father was standing between the two horses, closer to Lastochka, but still close enough to Seryi and Naftali to take action.

– Hey, – shouted Naftali's father, – tell that bastard horse if he doesn't start walking, he's going straight to the knacker's yard!

Naftali knew that expression – it was where animals were killed, so their skin, bones, and meat could be used for other things. Yet Naftali knew his father would never do something so heartless. He was only saying that, hoping it would make Seryi move. Naftali put his arms around Seryi's head, looking lovingly into his eye and pleaded with him:

– Please Seryi, do it for me. And when we get to the station, I'll give you an apple!

Seryi must've understood Naftali this time, because he started walking, and the rest of the journey passed uneventfully: the horses walked along just fine, and the luggage was delivered on time. Don Quixote and Clara were already at the train station, chatting with the conductor on the platform, while a baggage handler loaded their luggage into their carriage, and off they went!

Clara waved her handkerchief through the window at them; Naftali felt she understood that his life with such a strict father wasn't easy, and that was why she had been willing to talk to him and maybe give him some advice. But she couldn't – because of Naftali's father's watchful eye and iron grip on him! And now, she and Don Quixote had disappeared, along with the train, and Naftali would never see them again...

18

The platform at the station was empty; only the porters, who stood smoking by the ticket office, and a fat gendarme eating *pirozhki*, remained. Naftali was on the verge of tears again: he was so mad at his father, he didn't want to talk to him ever again. Why did he want to kick Seryi? Maybe he thought this was all a joke, but Naftali despised cruel jokes like these.

Naftali's father could tell Naftali was upset with him over their guests' departure, but he couldn't understand why. They had come to discuss which country the Tulchin Jews should move to, and at the time Lazar Evseevich thought the topic was beyond Naftali's comprehension. But now he decided to talk to Naftali about it himself, later. Naftali's father wasn't a mean parent; it's just that he had his own way of thinking, and he'd forgotten that as a child, he was always upset with his *own* father, for not letting him do things his own way. He decided to do something nice for Naftali, hoping to make him happy.

– There's a bookstore right by the train station, – he said. – Should we run over and have a look? We can tie up our horses and leave them here for a couple of minutes – I'm sure that gendarme will scare any thieves away with one look!

– Oh yes, let's go! – Naftali exclaimed, and they crossed the tracks. There was a canteen on the other side, where travelers could go for tea and hot soup, while their trains picked up new passengers. And right next to it there was a little bookstore, which carried various books, mostly in Russian.

This was Naftali's lucky day! As soon as he entered the bookstore, he took a quick look at the display counter, and saw a big red book with gold lettering, that said *Tolstoy's Stories for Children.*

What a miracle! He didn't get to talk to Don Quixote and Clara about Tolstoy, but now he would read the red book and discover everything Tolstoy had to say, from the great writer himself! Naftali jumped for joy – this tiny bookstore was the last place on earth he expected to get a chance to "meet" Tolstoy...

He pointed to the book, and told the tall, lanky youth, in a white shirt and black vest, behind the counter it was the only thing he wanted.

– Thirty-five kopecks – the clerk said, and Naftali's father paid him with some coins out of his pocket.

As the youth prepared to wrap it up, Naftali exclaimed:

– No, please don't, I'm going to read it right away!

Naftali opened the book and flipped through the pages, until the title of one of stories, "Two Horses", caught his attention. He started reading the story aloud, and the youth, who was bored to tears, seemed only too happy to listen. It went like this:

Two horses, each pulling cart, walked one ahead of the other. The first horse was doing fine, but the second horse stopped frequently, so her load was removed and given to the first horse to pull. After her load had been removed, the second horse said to the first one, "Ha-ha-ha, now you will suffer and be covered in sweat because of your double load. And the harder you work, the more work they'll give you." The first horse didn't respond, because she was occupied with pulling her load. When the horses and their master arrived at their destination, the master said to himself, "Why should I feed both of these horses, when only one is actually carrying the loads? It's better to feed the first horse with double portions, kill the second one, and make something out of her hide. At least then, she'll be useful." And despite the second horse's protest, that was what he did.

After Naftali had finished reading, nobody spoke. The youth, who didn't realize the very short story was over, sat waiting for an ending; Naftali's father was also contemplating the tale, and Naftali liked how everybody was finally paying attention to him. That morning, the adults had ignored him, and now at least the two people in the store listened to him, afraid to miss a single word. Naftali had understood the power of reading, and he was enjoying it.

– What a great story! – the youth finally concluded. – I think I get it: the first horse was rewarded for her hard work with a double portion of food; and the second horse, who thought she was so clever, when in fact she was just lazy, got her due when the owner simply got rid of her. Thank you, my dear customer, for entertaining me with your reading, and please come back soon. I can see that you know a lot about horses yourself, – he laughed, pointing at Naftali – because your jacket is covered with hay!

But Naftali didn't mind his laughter; he knew the youth was only joking around, and not being hurtful. Naftali said – Goodbye, – and he and his father left the bookstore.

On the way back across the tracks, Naftali's father said:

– Tolstoy must have seen us!

– What do you mean? – Naftali asked.

– Didn't you see how similar Tolstoy's story was to our own situation with Lastochka and Seryi? Lastochka carried her load properly, but Seryi didn't want to budge. Tolstoy described the very same situation!

– But you won't kill Seryi, will you? – Naftali asked, his voice trembling.

– Of course not, – his father assured him, – I'm only pointing out that literature, even though it seems like fantasy, often has roots in real life. In Tolstoy's story horses talk to each other, and we know that in reality they don't have human voices or use words, like the horse in the story. But Tolstoy described almost exactly what happened to us – isn't that interesting?

Naftali agreed that it was, indeed. He was reassured that despite his father's strong character and steely voice, he still cared about Naftali's interests and even proved it, by buying him the book by Tolstoy. Naftali decided that just as he couldn't tell his father everything, for fear of being misunderstood and ridiculed, his father was afraid to display his true feelings. This was the reason they couldn't get along sometimes, but in the end they always sorted things out and realized they loved each other. And so, father and son walked happily back to the train station, hand in hand. The day had gotten off to a bad start, but it ended quite well.

19

Several months later they received a letter from Don Quixote in a thick envelope; it was dirty and crumpled, after traveling all the way from Paris, so Naftali put it inside his favorite book, by Leo Tolstoy, to flatten it. Then he examined it closely, inspecting the stamp, the brown wax seal, and the address, written in firm handwriting. After that, he even smelled it!

– What are you sniffing it for? – his father asked. – That won't tell you what it says – you have to open and read it!

But Naftali was trying to detect Clara's perfume, hoping that she had written a few lines, too, and maybe even mentioned his name. If so, he wanted to know, before all the Jews in Tulchin read Don Quixote's letter. He blushed just thinking of it! But the letter smelled only of frost and paper; even if it *had* smelled of Clara's perfume once, the scent had faded during the long journey to Russia by train, then by horse, and finally, in the postman's bag.

Eventually, Naftali's father grew impatient; despite Naftali's protests, he took the letter and opened it with a sharp knife. He put the empty envelope aside (which Naftali stuck back into his Tolstoy book, for safekeeping) and unfolded the pages. Naftali's mother sat mending clothes, pretending she wasn't interested. But she was also eager to hear the contents of the letter.

– Perhaps he'll comment on our hospitality, and on how well we treated him – said Naftali's father, hopefully, – or maybe he'll mention you, Naftali! Let's see if I'm right!

And with those words, he read the first sentence, which said:

"My dear friends! I would like to share my joy with you. Today my horse Alfa came in first at the race track, and I won a large sum of money."

Naftali's father stopped short and raised his eyebrows. He couldn't believe what he was reading. Even Naftali's mother looked up from the shirt she was mending and put her needle away.

– So, – she laughed, – the gentleman starts his letter not by describing his journey from Tulchin back to France on the train, but by talking about horse races?

– His horse must be strong and well-trained, if it wins races, – said Naftali. – I bet none of our horses could run that fast. And in France the horses' nutrition is better – instead of plain hay, they probably gulp down onion soup and croissants!

– Shush! – shouted Naftali's father. – Stop joking, or else I won't read you the letter. Then he started again, from the very beginning, repeating the first sentence word by word:

"Today my horse Alfa came in first at the race track, and I won a large sum of money. She has had to work very hard to win. Your little boy might be interested to know that I have several lads who trained her when she was young. She had already won eleven races, so this one is her twelfth, and I'm very proud of her. She started out rather slowly, to make the other jockeys think she hadn't recovered yet from the injury she suffered in a previous race, but this was only a trick I devised with one of my shrewd and skilled trainers."

– He's very shrewd indeed, this baron, – Naftali's mother, interrupted, again. But after the look she got from Naftali's father, she stopped talking and continued her mending.

Naftali knew that his father valued his mother's opinion greatly and was always willing to follow her advice; however, he liked to pretend that he was the most respected, and always had the last word. Like the horse that pretended to be weak during the race, Naftali's father liked to pretend he was strong.

– Yes, he is smart, this baron, – Naftali's father agreed, – but why should poor Jews like us care about rich people's entertainment? I realize that he had fun and won some money, but is this really what we wanted to hear from him, after his visit?

Naftali had no idea exactly what his father wanted to hear, but he liked the story about the horse winning the race and wanted to know every last detail.

Just then, they heard Shmuel's voice from the porch.

– I told you this gentleman only cared about profit, – he budded in, – and that's why you should've gotten as much money from him as you could, when he was here. It's too late now!

– Why are you eavesdropping on us, Shmuel? – said Naftali's father. – Can't you stay home and eat strudel with your wife, and leave us alone for a while?

Shmuel answered:

– When you hear why I came, you'll stop being so arrogant with me, Lazar Evseevich! There's trouble again!"

– What trouble? – asked Naftali's father nervously. – You always bring us bad news!

– It's not so bad yet, – Shmuel replied, – but it could

get worse. One of the Russians who lives nearby claims his horse was stolen by thieves...

– But what does it have to do with us? We don't need anybody's horses, we have plenty of our own!

– Well, I'm just warning you, Lazar. This guy is very angry and he's trying to blame others for his drunken rage at the tavern, during which his horse either ran away, or was indeed stolen. He might come here and make trouble!

Naftali's father said:

– For now it's quiet, so let's hope everything will be okay. We're reading a letter from our former guest. He won a horse race.

Shmuel shrugged:

– Yes, he won the race, and his horse ran for the prize money. But you'll be running for your life, when this crazy Russian comes here looking for his runaway mare!

– Shut up, Shmuel! – Naftali's father exclaimed. – I've had enough of you. Thanks for the warning, and now, please, just go away!

Shmuel gave a whistle and left. Naftali and his parents looked very serious. They knew Shmuel was a joker and a liar, but the news of the Russian neighbor looking for his horse was unsettling. What if this guy indeed caused trouble? Nobody knew what to do, or say. Then Naftali's father broke the silence in the room.

– Let's finally finish this letter! – he said. – Okay, here he says that his horse won... Oh, here is what he wrote next: "Dear Lazar Evseevich, my horses are not simply beasts. They run for charity. The money that Alfa won today is going to a local hospital to help orphaned children, and I've put aside a small sum for another family to travel to Argentina and live alongside other brave

Jews... Please let me know when you decide to go, so I can make the arrangements... I realize this is a difficult decision to make, but I know you are very wise; since anti-Semitism in Russia is growing, I'm sure you will make up your mind quickly.

20

The very second Naftali's father read those lines, there was a knock on the door. Everybody in the room looked at each other in terror.

– I hope that's Shmuel again! – said Naftali's mother, and this time Naftali's father didn't give her his famous look of scorn. In times of real danger he stopped pretending; now he was serious and ready to protect his family, no matter what.

Then somebody kicked the door, and it flew wide open. Suddenly a huge hulk of a man burst into the house! Evidently drunk, he tripped over the water bucket in the corridor and crashed to the floor so heavily, a plate fell off the nearby table, smashing to pieces beside him.

– What the devil! – the drunkard shouted. He started groping around the floor, like a blind person looking for something, and cut his hand on a piece of the broken dish; now he was even angrier. When he finally struggled to his feet, the first thing he saw was Naftali, who was standing right in front of him.

– Who are you? – he shouted, staring at Naftali with surprise.

Naftali was scared; he'd never been in a situation like this before and he didn't know what to say. He thought *he* should be the one asking the man who he was, and what right he had to burst into their home, but this wasn't the time for philosophical discussions. And when he saw his father slip into the stable unnoticed, he knew there was a plan.

– My name is Naftali, – he said. – I live here.

– So, you're a little *zhid*! – said the huge man matter of factly. – Did you see my horse, little *zhid*? She's black, with a white star on her head... Or, no, white, with a black star on her head... Naftali was having trouble understanding the man; he was too drunk to speak clearly, or even stand on his feet without swaying.

– Why don't you open your mouth? – he shouted. – You got water in it, or what? Suddenly Naftali's mother was in front of him, shielding him from the intruder.

– Stop shouting, he's just a little boy. We don't have your horse, – she said quietly, as though she were speaking to a child, and not a drunken hulk, who'd just kicked in their door.

– So, you defend your little bastard! – he shouted again. He searched the room, frantically, for his horse, checking under the bed, the table, and even under the rug, in case the animal was hiding there. And if the situation weren't so dangerous, Naftali would have laughed out loud at the spectacle.

– Marusya! Marusya! – he wailed, and Naftali wasn't sure if that was the name of his horse, or a woman who'd left him. All of a sudden, the man's wild eyes rested on Naftali's Tolstoy book, which lay on the table, with the precious empty envelope still inside.

Reaching for the book, he lost his balance and almost fell onto the table, but only knocked another plate onto the floor. He grabbed the book and brought it right up to his red, puffy nose for a closer look.

– So, little *zhid*, you read our Russian books! – he shouted once again. – This is *our* book, it's not for *zhids* like you! What do you know about our Russian soul?

He raised the book in the air, preparing to bring it

down on Naftali's head, when suddenly a very stern voice boomed from behind:

– Put the book down, NOW! – it commanded.

The voice was so imposing, the hulk lowered his arm at once and turned to see whose voice it was.

Naftali and his mother also turned to look, and were instantly relieved: there in the corner stood Naftali's father, holding the whip he used on horses that misbehaved. He looked so big and menacing – the opposite of his peaceful and thoughtful self – that even Naftali was afraid of him! Clearly, he was prepared to use the horsewhip on the intruder and kick him out without delay.

And the hulk knew it, too. On seeing the whip, raised in the air and ready to land on his face, if necessary, he inched backward, toward the door, watching Naftali's father's every movement. The very idea that a family, made up only of a bookish boy, a slight woman, and a slimly built man, would actually challenge him, left him absolutely speechless. He finally made it to the door and disappeared into the cold, dark night.

After making sure the intruder was really gone, Naftali's father put down the whip, went up to Naftali and his mother, and three of them hugged each other in silence for a long time.

* * *

The next day at Shabbat, Naftali's father read Don Quixote's letter to all the dinner guests; he started with the paragraph about a man, who had been sent, on Don Quixote's money, to study Jewish life in Argentina. During his travels to various new Jewish colonies there, the man met some Jews he already knew from Russia. He claimed he barely recognized them: they looked so much healthier and happier than they had in Russia, where sometimes, throughout the course of a hard week, they would simply forget to smile.

"These Jews weren't the thin, pitiful people, with sunken cheeks and hunched shoulders they'd been here," Naftali's father read. "They didn't jump out of their skins at every sound, as they had back home, where they experienced constant humiliation and abuse. No, in Argentina, these people were proud of what they were doing – eagerly cultivating their land, and breathing the healthy air of the pampas and freedom, which had completely transformed them..."

Everybody in the room listened and watched him attentively. But when he read the part about Don Quixote winning the horse race, and donating the money to charity, to help the orphans, and send one family to go and live in Argentina, all the guests looked down, as though they were staring at a mouse under the table, or crumbs in their lap...

– Let's decide which family should go first, – Naftali's father said. – Who would like to go to Argentina?

Everybody was silent. Then one of the guests said:

– Perhaps we can stay here for a while... We have a roof over our heads, and we don't suffer humiliation *every* day, as this man writes... Sometimes everything's fine, and some of our Russian neighbors are very kind.

On hearing this, Naftali's father looked over at him without a word, but Naftali knew that yesterday's frightening episode with the drunken hulk was still fresh in his mind.

And Naftali's mother only looked at her husband and her son. None of them had said anything about it to anyone that day. But deep in their hearts they knew, that *they* would be the first family moving to Argentina.

21

The next morning was Saturday. As usual, Naftali intended to sleep as long as possible – right up until his mother pulled off his blanket, forcing him to wake up. But suddenly he heard his friend Syoma's voice in the kitchen.

– Can't you get him out of bed? – he asked.

– Naftali needs a little more sleep, – Naftali's mother replied, – he's exhausted after such a hard week.

Naftali thought he must be dreaming, because only in a dream would his mother not be trying to wake him up.

– We might be going very far away soon, – she continued, – so he should sleep as much as he can now. Because who knows how things will be during our journey?

And on those words, Naftali's mother's voice broke.

Naftali was very surprised: his parents always seemed so confident, as if they knew exactly what to do at any given moment. But at this particular moment, his mother sounded uncertain and very sad.

Since it was rude to eavesdrop, Naftali was about to announce himself, when Syoma said:

– I'm going on a trip too... And I wanted to invite Naftali to join me!

Suddenly Naftali's mother, who'd just seemed on the verge of tears, laughed out loud! Naftali found her changing moods so unusual, he threw off his blanket and rushed to the kitchen, to see for himself. To his surprise, his mother stood there, smiling, as she chatted away with Syoma.

Syoma had with him the old leather satchel Naftali's

father had given him, once, where a traveler might pack a change of clothes, a water flask, sandwiches, or whatever else he would need on his travels. But instead of food and clothing, Syoma's bag held carefully drawn roads to other countries, to their fertile lands, blue rivers, green mountains and buried treasures, because Syoma's satchel was full of maps!

– Hey, I have something new today! – Syoma exclaimed as soon as he saw Naftali. Usually so quiet, today Syoma seemed very excited.

– What's the rush? – Naftali's mother asked. – Eat something first!

She started slicing pieces of bread and looking around the kitchen to see what else to feed her tall, thin guest, who had grown about five centimeters over the summer.

– Would you like an omelet? – she asked. – It will only take a minute, our hen just laid the eggs!

But Syoma was so immersed in what he wanted to share with Naftali, he just shrugged his shoulders and said he wasn't hungry, and that they were in a hurry. Nevertheless, he grabbed a piece of bread, salted it and devoured it, as though he hadn't eaten for ages!

– I thought you said you weren't hungry! – Naftali exclaimed, as he watched all the bread disappear off the table and into Syoma's mouth, piece by piece.

– Oh, sorry! – Syoma said, embarrassed. – My parents say I have to eat a lot because I'm growing so fast...

Next, Naftali's mother served Syoma an onion omelet with a fresh cucumber, sliced in perfect little circles, and he gulped that down, too, in no time.

Naftali's mother laughed sympathetically.

– I think you're eating so fast because you're eager to show Naftali whatever it is you've got in that satchel! – she said. – In that case, drink up your tea and go ahead.

– Thank you for breakfast! – Syoma said, as he and Naftali gulped down the tea, said goodbye to Naftali's mother and ran out the door.

– Only don't go too far! And be back for dinner! – she yelled after them, but Naftali was already several meters away by then and could barely hear her. He'd be back by dinner, but he and his best friend were going far away today.

– Follow me! – said Syoma, pulling Naftali by sleeve. They followed a path past quite a few homes, until they got to an old house that was now used for storage; there was a pile of wooden planks in back of it.

Syoma climbed onto the pile; he started pulling out loose planks and positioning them one on top of the other, as though he were building a fence.

– Don't just stand there! – he yelled, impatiently, on seeing Naftali just peering at him through his thick glasses. – Take that plank and put it here; take this one and put it there!

Naftali was used to Syoma's eccentricities and followed his instructions, but he got a splinter from the first plank he grabbed, and stopped to suck his finger. Meanwhile, Syoma continued building the fence enthusiastically: he even took a hammer and rusty nails out of his seemingly bottomless bag and hammered a couple of planks to the "base". Once his work was finished, he took a pencil and a piece of paper out of the bag and wrote on it with large letters: "SHIP'S LOG".

Naftali was slightly disappointed. This wasn't anything new!

    – So, after all this work, we're sailing to unknown places again, like we always do?

    – Oh, stop whining, – Syoma replied. – Just look at this! – And he took a brand new book out of his satchel and gave it to Naftali, who read out the title on the cover: "Travels of a Naturalist Aboard the Beagle."

    – Wait, why build a ship, if you're only riding a dog? – he asked.

    – What are you talking about? – Syoma was confused.

    – A Beagle is a dog. The naturalist traveled on a dog... Couldn't he afford a nice horse?

    – Don't talk nonsense! – Syoma exclaimed. Then he took his pencil and on the same piece of paper he printed, alongside the words "SHIP'S LOG": "HMS Beagle".

    – The Beagle is the ship on which this naturalist traveled around the world! – he explained. – He went to so many countries: New Zealand, Chile, Ecuador... They hired him to go on this ship and write down everything he saw, so he could report it back to the Queen. She wanted to know everything about the people he met, their customs and habits, and their natural surroundings. What a life he led: when the ship reached a new port, he'd disembark early in the morning, go to a town or village and talk to the natives, and observe the insects and animals; then later in the day he would return to his cabin and record all the events of the day in his diary! I got a map of New Zealand and Peru, but I still need to obtain maps of the other countries he traveled to. Oh, and his name was Charles Darwin!

    Naftali impatiently took the book from Syoma and

started leafing through it...

– So, – Syoma announced, – I'm going to be Charles Darwin the naturalist, and you'll be my assistant. I'll tell you how to navigate the ship!

Then Syoma started motioning with his hands, as though he were turning a wheel. – Ten degrees right, five degrees left, now raise the sails! – shouted out. – And now we are approaching the Galapagos Islands – oh, hurray! I can see huge birds and huge turtles already, they are so happy we're visiting them. They've been so bored on this deserted island that they're waving at us with their humongous paws... They're so huge, I can ride them – like a horse!

– You're the one talking nonsense now! – Naftali exclaimed. He knew turtles were small enough to fit on the palm of an adult's hand. – You can't ride a turtle!

– Shows how much you know! – Syoma said. – Look and read here! He pointed out a page in the book, and Naftali read it aloud:

"Today we approached the shore and took a short walk during which we saw beautiful pink flamingos standing quietly in shallow waters and huge turtles weighing almost two hundred pounds. The locals eat them: they say that two days of hunting provides enough to eat for the whole week. Turtle meat is a real commodity here on the Galapagos Islands. Ships come and take turtles away to sell them. The locals told us that once, one ship took away seven hundred of these turtles, and another team of sailors took two hundred turtles, one by one, in a day. To carry such heavy creatures is a difficult task, and usually at least two men are needed to do it."

– Now then, assistant, – Syoma then said, – do you

see that huge turtle crawling on the beach? Ask the sailors for help and load it on our ship! I'm hungry! We are going to have turtle soup tonight!

But Naftali was so immersed in the book that he didn't obey. He flipped through the pages until an interesting paragraph about horses caught his eye:

"These men are perfect riders and they are not afraid of anything; the last thing they are afraid of is falling off their horse. Even when they find themselves on the ground, they stand up as if nothing happened and immediately jump back on the horse. They know how to manage an untamed colt – they are born with these skills. Moreover, they like to make bets, and I knew such a man personally: he claimed he could throw down his horse twenty times and that nineteen times out of twenty he would not fall off himself. I met these riders in Patagonia."

– Syoma, do you know where Patagonia is? – Naftali asked. – The people are described quite nicely here... Look how different these Patagonian men are from the Cossacks, who ride their horses in a way that scares both the animals and the passersby, who try to stay out of their way. Once I met a Cossack who glared at me so angrily, I jumped away, in case he wanted to lash me with his whip. Cossacks make a sport of trampling crowds with horses, but Patagonian horse riders look so kind-hearted... Let me read you more from here: "The gaucho is very polite and hospitable; I have never encountered even one instance of rudeness or inhospitality. Gauchos respect their country, which they love dearly, and they respect themselves; they are very bold and spirited."

– Patagonia... That's in Argentina! – Syoma remembered. – That's a map I still have to get. Darwin was so lucky to have been everywhere – New Zealand, the Galapagos, Argentina... And we can only go there in our imaginations, on our toy ship, – Syoma sighed.

– But I might really go to Argentina! – exclaimed Naftali. – How strange that the adults had a conversation about Argentina just yesterday and today you brought this book!

Naftali grew silent: it really was strange to think the passage he read was about the same destination that he and his parents would soon be traveling to themselves. It was giving Naftali the opportunity to learn more about what would be their new country, so that he knew what to expect. He was both surprised, and relieved by this coincidence: he felt less alone, that by providing such valuable information, things and events had somehow conspired to make him feel at ease about his future.

When he came home after his outing with Syoma, agreeing to return to their ship the next day, he noticed a new comb on his mother's night table. Unlike her dull, wooden combs, it was brownish, but very shiny, evidently polished.

– Where did you get this comb? – Naftali asked his mother.

–It's a gift, from your father, – she beamed. – Isn't it beautiful? It's made from a turtle shell! And it won't break as quickly as my other combs, turtle shells are very sturdy.

– Turtles! – Naftali exclaimed. Why, they'd just been talking about the gigantic turtles on the Galapagos Islands, described by Charles Darwin, and suddenly there's a comb made of turtle shell in the house! Another coincidence...

And Naftali sat and he ate and he told his mother about the events and little miracles of the day.

22

The next day Naftali asked his father to take him to the fair, being held in Tulchin's main square.

– Why do you want to go to this fair? – his father asked. – Every time I asked you to go with me before, you said you would be bored there and annoyed by the crowds!

– I saw the beautiful turtle shell comb you gave Mom, and I want to see if they sell any other exotic things, just out of curiosity, – Naftali replied, although this wasn't exactly true.

The truth was, Naftali had decided to start preparing for the long voyage to Argentina, and he wanted to buy everything he'd need aboard the ship. But since he wasn't sure his father would approve, he decided to keep his intentions secret – at least for now.

It was still early morning, when they reached the main square, but it was already quite crowded. There were rows of tables set up with something for everybody – food, toys, household items, and more. People could find whatever they needed, and even things they didn't need, but that they liked, and bought for fun! For the women there were crochet hooks and yarns, lipstick and rouge, and fabric for sewing skirts, scarves, and aprons. For the men, they were selling hammers and knives, saddles and horseshoes, spades, belts and pants; and for the children there were dolls, wagons, trains and boats. There were even vendors carrying large trays full of sweets – around their necks!

Every merchant advertised his goods as loudly as possible; women selling pickled cabbage and vegetables chomped loudly on crunchy cucumbers as they asked passersby to try them, and a young lass pulling a fish out of a huge wooden barrel claimed it had been "caught just minutes ago".

There were also various attractions for people to watch, such as a lad in a bright red shirt, who was feeding rolls of paper, punched full of tiny holes in different patterns, into a big, wooden music box, which then played the various melodies that were 'punched' into the paper.

And across the square there was a puppet theater, featuring a character named "Petrushka", who played tricks on the other puppets, like cheating the greedy merchant, and tricking the lazy peasant into working, and the crowd laughed and applauded every time.

After the performance, Naftali and his father ate hot *pirozhki* stuffed with boiled eggs, cabbage, and ground meat, and proceeded to a row of tables loaded with tinwork. While Naftali's father looked at the goods laid out before each merchant, Naftali looked at their faces. Some stared into space with dreamy expressions, which only changed when an adult came their way; they were indifferent to Naftali, knowing he couldn't make a serious purchase. Other merchants smiled at him, but really only hoped to lure his father to their goods. Still other merchants scowled at everybody, as though they wished they were still in bed, rather than here, at this early hour, selling their insignificant wares.

Naftali was looking for someone kind, who could tell him where to buy a compass; he wanted it for the voyage to Argentina, ever since he'd seen it mentioned in the book by Charles Darwin. Strolling past the rows of tables, he finally saw an elderly man with a big beard, selling heavy weights, scales, and various other objects, whose purpose was unclear to Naftali. The man stood stroking his beard and, on seeing Naftali, he waved him over to his table.

– Do you sell compasses? – Naftali asked sheepishly, when he was close enough.

– We sell scales and irons and metal buckets, but nobody in this town has ever asked for a compass... What do you need it for? – he asked Naftali. – To find the way home, when you visit a faraway friend? Please tell me, I'm very curious, – he said, with genuine interest.

– I'm going to Argentina, – Naftali replied, reassured by the man's sympathetic ear and smile, – and I need to make sure we don't get lost, since it's so far away. I also need a flask, and a sturdy rope, in case somebody falls overboard during a storm, and we need to rescue them.

– Well, I'll have to make a list, – the merchant said, in a serious tone, as though he really wanted to help. – I'll buy a compass, a rope, and maybe a flask from my supplier, and bring them for you next time! Only make sure you bring money with you.

Naftali was moved by the merchant's kindness, but he wasn't sure if he'd be able to come with the money for next time, so he just stood there, wondering what to do, and totally unaware that his father was right behind him.

– Are you really going to Argentina, young man? – asked the merchant, who so enjoyed talking to Naftali that he lost interest in other potential customers passing by.

But before Naftali could open his mouth, he suddenly heard his father's stern voice say:

– He's not going anywhere!

Naftali's father was suspicious of the friendly merchant; living among people who were hostile toward Jews had taught him to be cautious of strangers. But Naftali didn't think this merchant posed any threat.

– I going on a ship and I want to be prepared! – he exclaimed. – Like Charles Darwin, who went around the world aboard The Beagle!

– Well, good for you, then, – the merchant smiled, – maybe people will treat you better elsewhere, than they do here... I'd go in a heartbeat. Do you think I like guarding these stupid scales? But I'm not rich and can't afford such a long voyage... If I were younger, I could go as a deck-hand on a ship, for free, but shoveling coal and wood into the boiler requires great stamina... And since I know nothing about navigation, I can't be a captain either!

Naftali was fascinated, and even his father, realizing this merchant was just a chatty old fellow who meant no harm, relaxed.

– You know boys, – he said. – He thinks he'll navigate the whole trip from Tulchin to Argentina with his toy compass, but he doesn't even know how to use it! Besides, nobody needs his help, with a real captain on board!

His father's comment upset Naftali, who was already imagining himself, standing shoulder to shoulder with the captain and giving him advice. What if the ship's big compass broke? Naftali could use his pocket compass to guide the ship to the correct destination! What if the ship started sinking and Naftali, the only cool head among the panicking passengers, had to direct everybody to safety?

Seeing Naftali's humiliation, the merchant decided to cheer the boy up:

– I don't have a compass, – he said, – but I have something else for you!

– What is it? – asked Naftali, who didn't want to even see his father's face just then.

– Do you know about birds? – asked the old man smiling.

– What about them? – exclaimed Naftali, noticing that even his father was intrigued.

– Well, birds live on dry land, right?

– Right! – answered Naftali, still unsure where this conversation was going.

– And they don't fly out too far over the ocean, right? – asked the old merchant again.

– Right! – answered Naftali again. – Because if they fly out too far, there won't be a dry spot in the ocean to land on and rest, if they get tired.

– So, as soon as you see birds through your binoculars from the ship, you'll know that land is close by.

Naftali thought about this for a minute and immediately remembered the Bible story about Noah on his ark. For days and days he didn't see any land, but then he noticed a dove and knew immediately that land was near.

– Yes, the birds! This makes a lot of sense, – said Naftali.

– And you have to feed them! – winked the old merchant. – You can take seeds along with you to thank them for showing you where land is! You can buy some seed from the vendor in the very next row.

– Thank you for your advice, – said Naftali's father with some disappointment. – But even if we do sail on the ship, it won't be this month, and the seeds will spoil by then. So for now we'll just buy some hay for our horses... Besides, my son fantasizes a lot. I haven't decided myself whether we are indeed going on a journey, and he's already buying a compass – as if ship's captain would need help navigating from a little boy!

Again, Naftali was upset with his father. The compass could also help them locate their new home once they arrived in Argentina – the Gauchos would respect the new settlers more if they were self-sufficient and didn't ask for directions. But explaining this to his father would mean having a long conversation about Charles Darwin's travels and observations, and this didn't seem like the time or place. The old man saw Naftali's frustration, again, so he slipped his hand into his pocket, took something out and handed it to Naftali.

– What is it? – asked Naftali.

– It's a little notebook. I never sell any of them here. The people of Tulchin would rather gossip or play cards, than contemplate things and write down their thoughts. But you can use it at school.

Naftali and his father thanked the wise merchant, bought some hay and hurried home where a breakfast cooked by Naftali's mother was already waiting for them.

After breakfast, Naftali looked at his notebook: it was light brown, with white ruled pages to write on. Naftali decided he would use it to write about all the preparations for the voyage. In addition, he'd write down descriptions of his travels, like Darwin did. And he wouldn't show this diary to his parents; that way, nobody else could ridicule him for wanting a compass.

Before long, Naftali was totally immersed in writing in his new diary; he wrote in it regularly, recording his impressions, and the events of the day.

And this was the moment the future writer was born.

23

That night, Naftali lay in bed thinking about storms on the sea. He envisioned himself on the ship traveling to Argentina: the waves were rising, his mother was crying, his father was fearful, too – and Naftali was the only person on board who could save the ship. But what would he do if the boat started sinking? How would he calm the panicking children and reassure the others, that together, they would survive the raging sea?

Naftali desperately wanted to be the hero, but he couldn't come up with a concrete plan of action that would save everybody, and this troubled him to the extent that he couldn't get to sleep. And he wasn't the only one; he could hear his father pacing in the adjoining room, and his mother whispering nervous prayers. Suddenly his father was standing right in front of Naftali's bed:

– Are you asleep son? I need to ask you something.

Naftali felt very important: just a second ago, he'd been humbled by his own inability to come up with a plan to save the sinking ship, and now his father, who always looked so self-assured and strong, needed his advice!

– I'm awake! – he said. – What's going on? Naftali's father sat down on the bed beside him.

– Remember the wealthy guest we had two months ago, who believes the Jewish people should be able to live, where they can grow crops and raise their children in freedom? – he asked. – Well, he sent us an enormous sum of money, more than I've ever seen before, to buy a piece of land in Argentina, big enough for all the Jews of Tulchin who would like to move there!

– Not so loud! – Naftali whispered excitedly. – What if a thief walks by and hears you? He could steal it from us!

– You're right, – Naftali's father lowered his voice, and Naftali felt another rush of self-importance. – We won't tell anybody we have this money in our house. But right now, I need your help.

– To buy the land? – Naftali's eyes opened with surprise. – But how will we choose it? We can distinguish a fresh horse from a tired one, but how can we decide which land to buy, when we don't even know what it looks like?

– We'll have to wait and see, Naftali, – sighed his father. – All I know is that this man has entrusted us with the money to buy land in Argentina, and now we must fulfill our task.

– I agree, – Naftali said, quickly, sensing his father's impatience, – we'll just go and buy the land. But who will sell it to us?

– This is exactly the point, – his father replied. – I have the address of a Russian man downtown. But since nobody in the community speaks Russian as well as you, I'll need you to translate, to see that we understand each other, and to verify the contract. We need to be sure the seller gives us the best piece of land possible, and doesn't try to trick us!

Naftali eagerly agreed to go along to the land agent, and several days later, he and his father rode their carriage to the address in the center of Tulchin. When they arrived, Naftali's father knocked on the small door with a rusty door handle, but there was only silence. They waited outside, looking for signs of life through the window curtains; when Naftali glimpsed somebody moving behind the curtain, his father knocked again, more loudly. This time they heard agitated voices, but again, nobody opened the door. Then both Naftali and his father started knocking as loudly as they could.

The door suddenly flew open in their faces, and they saw a weary-looking little man with a black mustache on the doorstep. The top three buttons on his white shirt were open, and there was a little piece of food, maybe a beet, stuck to the corner of his mouth, as though he was in the middle of lunch.

He gave Naftali and his father a quick looking over; both had worn their best for this important visit, but even so their clothes were shabby. And on noticing the piece of straw clinging to Naftali's elbow, the little man said:

– This isn't a village, you know!

– What did he say? – asked Naftali's father, who understood the man's words in Russian, but not what he meant by them. Naftali didn't know how to answer.

– See what I have to put up with? – the little man shouted to somebody inside.

– We've came to do business, Gospodin Rykov, – said Naftali's father quietly.

– Didn't you see the sign on the door? – replied the man irately, pointing to a small sign on the door on Russian, which read:

"For the lawyer Leo Polyakov, ring once; for the realtor Rodion Rykov, ring twice.
DO NOT KNOCK."

Naftali quickly translated this into to Yiddish for his father, who said:

– Never mind. Just tell him we've come on business and that we're in a hurry to get to Argentina, so we don't have time to discuss, whether we should knock or ring.

Naftali translated his father's words, and Mr. Rykov finally waved them inside.

– If you want to conduct business, – he said, – let's do it. But since you are Jews, which is quite easy to conclude because of your yarmulkes, you cannot go to Argentina: you have no passports! Perhaps in your village, or wherever you live with your horse, who has already destroyed my favorite birch tree, you don't need a passport. Who would you show it to? Your horses? The bears in the forest? Ha-ha-ha... Besides, you cannot leave the Pale of Settlement anyway, so I'm not sure I understand what you want from me...

– Don't worry, – Naftali's father said, – our sponsor is a notable railroad baron, who visited us two months ago; he has already discussed the matter at the Russian Ministry of Transportation, and arranged for us to be given passports, to go to Argentina.

– Oh yes, I heard something about that, – winked Gospodin Rykov, and Naftali suspected he was lying, to appear as though he knew everything in the world, – I just didn't know people like you would be the first to go... But perhaps you gentlemen are actually rich, and only pretending to be poor? – Gospodin Rykov winked again. – In that case, you've come to the right person. I do indeed have land to sell to you. Just choose what you want!

– Why did you say "people like us"? – asked Naftali, sensing a hidden meaning in Gospodin Rykov's comment.

But Rykov thought quickly and said:

– By "people like you" I just meant industrious people! What I mean is, we don't often see people from rural areas buying property so far away... You know, they're not experienced enough to travel abroad.

But Naftali suspected Rykov just didn't believe that two Jews in shabby clothes could afford to buy land, and that he was only treating them nicely, because he wanted to make a sale today.

– And don't worry about knocking! – Rykov continued, chatting away. – People who mean business can knock on my door at any time, even at night! Even with their feet! Just kick it in! – he exclaimed, laughing heartily now.

Naftali's father stood quietly, waiting for Rykov to finish. The man continued laughing, but when he saw that nobody else shared his laughter, he opened a drawer and, after a long search, took out a greasy envelope, and handed it to Naftali's father.

– Look, is this the land you want? Choose your lot!

Naftali's father opened the envelope, which contained several photographs of various dried out fields; there were no buildings and almost no trees, so all the fields looked almost identical. In one picture, there happened to be a sheep staring right at the camera. In another, there was a man wearing baggy trousers with a wide belt, and an unusual hat, protecting him from the sun; he was also staring at the camera.

– This is number one, number two, number three... – Rykov explained. – Just choose the piece of land you would like to purchase, and we'll start on the paperwork!

– But they all look the same, – Naftali said.

– Do they? Then let me read you the description of each lot, – Rykov replied, and he took a pile of paper from another drawer and started reading from it.

– Lot one is northwest of Buenos Aires... Lot two is one hundred acres of land to the south of Buenos Aires... Lot three previously belonged to a rich landowner, who was later killed by lightning while he napped outside his home during a siesta... On lot four, there is a small building, not shown, where you can store grain or hay or even find cover during the rain.

– I like lot four, – said Naftali's father, – but will this land accommodate approximately a hundred families? That's how many of us plan to go, and the small building will be our only shelter from the elements, until we build our homes! I know we'll have to come up with a temporary housing solution, but for now our sponsor only asked me to negotiate the purchase of the land...

– This piece of land is so huge it will accommodate all the Jews living in the Pale! – Rykov laughed. – Isn't that your goal? To take all your brethren out of Russia, and settle them somewhere else? You could move the whole population of Tulchin onto this lot, and still have room to put me up, if I came to visit, ha-ha-ha!

The salesman laughed again, and Naftali felt uneasy, since he couldn't understand whether Rykov was amused, or simply mocking them.

– And what about the soil? – asked Naftali's father. – Is it fertile? Can we grow tomatoes and potatoes and maybe some corn there?

– Don't worry: this land is so fertile, you can even grow money on the trees! – Rykov reassured him.

Naftali's father and Rykov finally agreed on the price of the land, and signed a contract, requiring Naftali's father to leave a deposit and sign a promise to bring the rest of the money within the next six months. Afterwards the salesman said:

— I heard a funny story, once, about how much land a man needs. I don't know who wrote it, but if you have a couple of minutes, I can tell it to you.

— Well, I can't stop you; if there's something you want to tell me, you'll tell me — if not today, then tomorrow, — said Naftali's father, unenthusiastically, — so go ahead...

Gospodin Rykov launched into his story without delay:

— A governor tells a man: "I'll give you as much land, for free, as you can run across in a day." Since the man wanted to get as much free land as he could, he woke up at sunrise, and he started running. He ran all day long and throughout the evening, and didn't stop for even a second, in order to run as far as his legs would take him and get the biggest piece of land possible!

Mind you, it was summer, the sun was very strong, and the man got very tired; every second he had to wipe his forehead, and he was out of breath and very thirsty, but even then he kept running, afraid that if he stopped to look for water, he wouldn't get as much land as he otherwise could... So, he ran from sunrise until sundown and he covered a huge area of land – enough to hold a whole herd of sheep and horses and *still* have space left over... But at the end of the day, he collapsed. And when other people found him, he was dead: the man had tried so hard to get free land that he got sunstroke and died right there, at the end of his marathon.

Naftali listened open-mouthed: Rykov didn't look very honest, but he certainly knew how to tell interesting tales! Even his wife had come to listen, wearing a robe over a long nightgown, without paying any attention to the visitors.

– But that's not the end of the story, – continued Rykov excitedly, as though telling the story energized him. – The governor came to see what had happened and said to his servants: "Please bury him now." So the servants dug a hole in the ground where the man had collapsed, that was only two by four meters... When they were done, the governor stood at the edge of this grave, looked into it sadly, and declared: "This is how much land a man needs!"

Naftali's father said:

– I understand your point, Gospodin Rykov, but your story doesn't apply to us. The dead man in your story only needed a small piece of land, because he only needed to be buried there. But we Jewish people need land for living! We do not plan to die – our children continue the circle of life!

And on that note, Naftali and his father left the office, leaving Rykov dumbfounded.

24

Once he'd made the deal for the land, Naftali's father stopped talking about Argentina at home. He was absent frequently in the evenings, and whenever Naftali asked his mother where he'd gone, she only pursed her lips and raised her eyebrows. Suddenly, there were fewer words exchanged in the household, and Naftali started noticing that there were fewer objects, too: an almost brand new barrel they'd planned to use for pickling cucumbers had disappeared; two of his mother's large stewing pots, and even an old crib from the attic, were missing, too. Luckily, Naftali's possessions were safe; he'd hidden all of his books and checked his secret hiding place daily, to make sure they were still there.

But every time Naftali came home, he would notice that something else was gone. On Monday, a stool was missing; on Tuesday – an old suitcase, where his mother kept his baby clothes as a souvenir; on Wednesday, in the pouring rain, Naftali saw his father give a new bucket away to a neighbor, Yosef, who needed it for his leaky roof.

– You don't have to return the bucket! Just keep it! – Naftali's father was saying.

– Why would I need it after the rain? – asked Yosef.

– Maybe to carry water from the well, or hold a fish you catch in the pond, – Naftali's father replied.

– We don't catch fish, we only catch the rain! – smiled Yosef sadly. – Our roof leaks water like a sieve, and we need many buckets to catch it, so it doesn't completely ruin our floors, which are bad enough, I must confess!

– Speaking of fish, – Naftali's father said, – there's a

Russian proverb that says fish rot from the head down. So instead of trying to fix the tail, you should start from the head. Why don't you simply repair your roof, so you won't need any buckets?

– It's easy to say, but hard to do, – Yosef sighed. – I can't afford to repair my roof... And now, I would like to thank you for the bucket and get back home, to catch the last rain drops, if I may!

– Wait! I'll give you some clay shingles; the last time I had the same problem, I bought too many, and now I have extras that I kept just in case. But I think you need them more than me.

– Thank you, – said Yosef, – but as I said, I have no money, and even with a discount I could only afford one small shingle, which wouldn't cover even a quarter of the big hole in my roof!

– I have a couple of dozen of them in the shed behind the stable, and they are yours for free. Bring your brood and take the whole pile with you!

– Oh, that's great! – Yosef beamed. – Let me break this good news to my family! – And with the clinking bucket in his hand, he ran home, without even checking out the shingles.

Naftali's mother had also overheard this conversation, and she looked upset; when Naftali's father asked her whether dinner was ready, she only shuffled the pots on the stove so angrily, she spilled some hot soup and burned her hand.

– What's wrong with you? – asked Naftali's father, taking her hand and pouring cold water on it to relieve her pain.

– What's wrong with you?! – she answered. – We

are not rich enough to give gifts to others; if you had sold those shingles at the market, as you have everything else, we could have saved a little more money for a rainy day!

– I'd better wait till you cool down a bit before I say anything about it. – Naftali's father said. – I'll think of a story from Midrash that justifies with my actions, but in the meantime, let's sit down and eat!

And they sat down at the table and started eating chicken soup with carrots and noodles. Naftali's father took a matzot, broke it into little pieces and put them into his soup, and after mixing his soup, he began the story:

– A long time ago, during the destruction of the second Temple, there lived a Rabbi Akiva. He was very wise, but he also loved adventures. Once, he was traveling on a ship on the Mediterranean to the Italian coast... The weather was so perfect and the sky so blue that Rabbi Akiva couldn't restrain himself; he stopped reading his religious books and went on deck to observe his surroundings.

The sun was so bright that Rabbi Akiva could see deep into the water at the dolphins and colorful fish that followed the ship. Staring into the sea and studying these incredible creatures, Rabbi Akiva exclaimed: "Oh Hashem, you are so mighty and thoughtful to create these incredible living creatures. Yet you not only understand beauty and its merits; you have also planned wisely: everything is in its place. But imagine what would happen if sea creatures tried to live on land, and the land creatures attempted to swim in the sea? The fish would get stuck in the sand because their fins are not meant for crawling, and the rabbits would drown because their wet fur would make them heavy, and their little hind legs are not strong enough to paddle. But in their own element, the dolphins in the sea, birds in the air, and humans and rabbits on land, they swim, run, and fly freely! Oh Hashem, I pray to you and I'm in awe of your greatness!

Naftali's mother stood up, filled everybody's empty soup bowls with mashed potatoes and a little sour cream. Once she sat down again, she asked:

— What does this have to do with the two dozen shingles you promised to our destitute neighbor?

Naftali's father grew confused for a moment, then said:

— Sorry, I was just thinking how, perhaps, sometime in the near future, I'll see those dolphins too, and I forgot the whole point of the story...

— Just eat! Don't get distracted by telling stories... Have a loaf of bread with your potatoes, we can't afford meat today. But if you'd sold those shingles... – Naftali's mother started, but less angrily now.

— The bread! Yes! Thanks for reminding me, – exclaimed Naftali's father; he bit off a hunk of bread, finished chewing, and continued:

— So, Rabbi Akiva saw the fish, and thinking they might be hungry, he went to his cabin where he had a large loaf of bread; he wanted to feed the fish some crumbs. But as he stood contemplating how much bread to feed the fish, one of the passengers, an older gaunt man, approached him. He didn't say anything, but only looked at Rabbi Akiva with hunger in his sunken eyes. Rabbi Akiva saw that this man was much hungrier than the happy, beautiful fish and, without saying a word, he gave the man the whole loaf, and proceeded onto the deck, to once again admire the beautiful day.

However, when he looked at the sky this time, he noticed many rain clouds that were growing grayer and looking heavier, as though they were full of water and ready to burst. The wind was getting stronger, the sun had hidden, and the water was too dark to see the dolphins. That didn't bother Rabbi Akiva; what worried him was that a storm was approaching and the ship didn't seem very safe. So Rabbi Akiva hurried to the captain and suggested he approach the shore and anchor the ship, until the storm passed. But on seeing the learned, but not very muscular, Rabbi Akiva, and hearing his educated manner of speech, the captain decided, mistakenly, that he didn't have to follow Rabbi's advice.

The captain continued steering the ship away from the shore. Rabbi Akiva went to his cabin and started praying to the Almighty. Right in the middle of his prayer, a huge wave fueled by the storm slammed into the ship, and the panicked passengers ran up on deck. Within a few short minutes the ship broke apart and started to sink, taking the captain with it into the depths of the sea. Some passengers, including the older gaunt man whom Rabbi Akiva had fed with his bread, were still alive, hanging onto wooden planks from the ship. All the ship's cargo, mostly papyrus, now rested on the bottom of the sea.

In the meantime, Rabbi Akiva's wife received a letter he'd written before the storm, saying he was coming home. She rejoiced and bought herself and their children new clothes in anticipation of his homecoming; she hadn't seen him for a long time and couldn't wait for his return. Yet, a couple of months passed and Rabbi Akiva still hadn't returned, his wife started losing hope of seeing him ever again. All of Rabbi Akiva's friends and pupils also feared that, perhaps, he was already dead.

One day, when everybody gathered in the synagogue, an unfamiliar man entered and said he was the only survivor of a ship wreck. He said he'd seen Rabbi Akiva on the sinking ship, and didn't think he'd survived because of his physical frailty. On hearing this awful news, everyone was ready to cry. Then suddenly a voice said:

– But I'm telling you he is alive!

At first, nobody could understand whose voice this was, but they soon realized it was the voice of a beggar, who had been lingering outside the synagogue lately, but was now brave enough to come in and share his words with the worshippers. This beggar was very thin and unkempt, and nobody knew anything about him, but they loved him, because he always listened with great interest to discussions of the Torah.

– I also saw Rabbi Akiva on the sinking ship, – the beggar continued, – but I think he survived, because Hashem would spare the man who was so kind as to give me bread!

And that very moment a miracle occurred: Rabbi Akiva entered the synagogue! At first, people thought they must be dreaming, or that it was a mirage, evoked by the beggar's words. But then Rabbi Akiva started talking and hugging everybody, to convince them that he really was alive.

When asked what had happened and how he'd survived, Rabbi Akiva explained:

– When the ship started sinking, I grabbed a wooden plank that had broken off the ship and held onto it as tightly as you, my friends, are holding your Sidurs, and it didn't fail me. I swam to shore and met some people who clothed and fed me, and helped me get home. And I prayed to G-d.

Then Rabbi Akiva noticed the beggar, ran over to him and shook his hand.

– I wanted to be modest and not tell you the whole story, – said Rabbi Akiva, – but I'm sure this man, here, has already told you. The truth is, I gave him some bread, and because of my good deed, I was saved!

The wise men in the synagogue discussed the issue together and then concluded:

– Rabbi Akiva threw bread into the water, and it came back to him later, when the people on the island fed him. One must always perform good deeds, because their kindness will always be returned!

Having finished the story, Naftali's father poured some hot tea from the samovar into his large metal cup and, blowing on the hot beverage, he smiled and concluded:

– Rabbi Akiva prayed and gave away bread, and I gave away some clay shingles, and perhaps because of my kindness, we won't sink on the ship.

Naftali's mother opened her eyes wide; in a trembling voice she asked:

– Is it time?

– It is indeed, and I have reserved space for us on the ship, – Naftali's father replied. – We are going to Argentina!

After the story about Rabbi Akiva, and the news of their upcoming adventure, Naftali was totally overwhelmed.

25

The next months were spent in heated discussions between Naftali's parents, regarding what to take with them for their long voyage. Indeed, it was all they talked about.

– I simply cannot go without my fur hat and coat, – said Naftali's mother. – Even though the fur has lost its luster over time and some of it has fallen out, it will still keep me warm...

– You can take all your furs as long as I can take my long black coat and *tallit*, – retorted Naftali's father.

– But you won't need your long coat if you're going to live in the land of wild cowboys and untamed horses. Do you really want to stick out like a sore thumb? Even the horses will laugh at you!

– And if you think Argentinean cowboys wear fur coats or sip their mate tea surrounded by silver candelabras, you are mistaken as well! – Naftali's father objected. – I can just see you riding a horse in your heavy fur coat – you'll be the laughing stock of the pampas! As for my coat – it may be long, but it's light, and it wouldn't irritate a horse's skin!

– Well, if you intend to take your taleth, then why not our marvelous silver candelabras? – Naftali's mother replied. – Not only could we light them on Shabbat, but we could sell them to those wild cowboys in case we become desperate! Cowboys wouldn't know the value we Jews place on Shabbat and on lighting the candles, but they surely know the value of precious metal.

– They are too heavy! – exclaimed Naftali's father,

feeling quite guilty about not wanting to take the family heirloom that had belonged to Naftali's mother's grandfather. – And I'm not so young anymore, so I have to think about who is going to carry all that from a horse to a train, then from a train to a ship and then, again, from a ship back to the horse that will take us to the pampas?

Unable to hold his silence here, Naftali cried out:

– Papa, I'm almost a grown up, I will help you!

– Good, then if we take your mother's silver candelabras, we can take my shawl, the prayer book, and the long coat, – Naftali's father decided, and, raising his finger in the air, he added: – And, your mother shouldn't force me to cut my sidelocks!

– Why did you ask him to cut his sidelocks? – asked Naftali with surprise.

– So that nobody would know that we are Jews! If we are going to a new country, maybe we should be less conspicuous to the local people. If your father cuts them, they'll simply think he is just another Argentinean, who moved to the pampas from some crime-ridden city.

– What nonsense, – Naftali's father exclaimed. – As soon as I open my mouth, they will know I'm not an Argentinean!

– Aren't you going to Argentina to work on your own land? People who work their land don't discuss religious books all day long; they keep quiet and plow the fields!

– You should bite your sharp tongue, Raya, – said Naftali's father. – This is not the time for arguing. We need to come together, as a family, especially during the voyage that awaits us...

– I agree, – said Naftali's mother. – But still, you can only take your saddle and saddle cloth if you let me take my fur coat, mittens and felt boots!

– It's not like I'm taking the saddle for myself, – laughed Naftali's father. – I'm taking it for the horses I'll be looking after in Argentina! But to be fair, if I can take a saddle for the horses, you can take cages for your chickens!

– I'm not going to raise chickens on the pampas, – Naftali's mother objected. – I've had enough of them and their squawking here!

– But we all have to do something there, even Naftali, otherwise we won't survive, – said Naftali's father seriously. – So, what *do* you plan to do in Argentina?

– I have no idea, – Naftali's mother replied, also quite seriously. – But I guess time will tell. All I want now is to pack and to take my fur coat and mittens!

– You won't need them there for a while, – Naftali observed.

– So, it's two against one, now! – Naftali's mother exclaimed. – And why won't I need my furs there?

– Because when it's winter, here, – answered Naftali, – it's summer in Argentina! It will be hot when we get there, and by the time it's winter there, your fur will have been eaten by Argentinean moths!

– I don't even know if there *are* moths in Argentina, – said Naftali's mother. – And I'm not sure what *mate* is. In fact, I know nothing about the land that will be our new home...

– They have ostriches there, – exclaimed Naftali. – I read about them in Darwin's book. Maybe mom can raise ostriches, and we'll eat their eggs!

– Just so you know, Raya, *mate* is tea, prepared from the leaves of *yerba mate*, – Naftali's father explained. –

And because ostriches are not kosher, Naftali, their eggs aren't kosher either. Therefore, we won't be eating them...

– And what if we have nothing to eat there, on those pampas? – Naftali's mother asked. – If we're starving, we'll have to eat something... Now might be a good time to forget about keeping strict kosher and your sidelocks! I'm sure that after a few months you, Lazar, will be eating anything that moves, and that you'll be indistinguishable from the local cowboys and peasants... Finally we can forget about standing out. We'll have to live just like the locals!

– I doubt that! I'll shorten my sidelocks, but there is no way I will eat anything not strictly kosher! – retorted Naftali's father. – I've had my sidelocks here in Russia since I was a little boy and I will keep them in Argentina!

– You've kept them in Russia, alright, – said Naftali's mother, ironically, – and now we are escaping from Russia, because Russians don't like how we look! They call us names in the street, because we're so easy to spot!

– Not all Russians are like that, – said Naftali's father. – Tolstoy is Russian! And so many of my Russian passengers have treated me well and asked about my family, my business, and what my life is like here... Sometimes, our conversations were as interesting as the talks we had with our Jewish friends and neighbors right here, at our table, during Shabbat! And Naftali... Naftali, where are you? – he called out.

26

But Naftali didn't hear him. Tired of the constant arguing over what to pack, he was sitting on a stool in the kitchen, leafing through the volume by Charles Darwin that Syoma had lent him. He wanted to know what kinds of things Darwin took with him to Argentina, but only found out which books Darwin had read on his trip. Naftali wondered if maybe he only needed to take his books, too. But then he remembered the armadillos and other strange animals roaming the pampas, and he decided to take a knife, to protect his family and himself.

He read a description of a gaucho who had helped Darwin during his excursion into the pampas: this gaucho was so timid, Darwin wrote, that he mistook a large animal for an Indian. Once, after the sunset, he mistook an ostrich for a bandit and ran away.

Naftali wouldn't be so stupid as to run away from a bird, but the idea of an unfamiliar country with bandits, Indians, and wild gauchos, and all their antics, frightened him tremendously. Making sure his mother didn't see, he took a large kitchen knife and hid it under his bed, to pack in his own suitcase for the voyage to Argentina. He was so immersed in Darwin's diary and his own thoughts on their impending journey, that he only finally heard his father call him the second time.

– What? – he responded, as though waking from a dream.

– Naftali, you have surely met nice Russian children, haven't you? – his father asked. – Tell your mom that not everything here is bad!

Naftali didn't know how to answer. First, he never thought of the children he met as bad or good; second, he didn't focus on their ethnicity – he lived in the moment: if they hurt him, he was upset; if they fought him – he tried to escape the fight and, from a safe distance, explain why he prefers to avoid confrontations; if there was a mutual understanding – he played with them without thinking about "why" he got along with these kids, and not with others. He couldn't say he got along with all Jewish kids; similarly, he couldn't say he always disagreed with Russian ones.

– Why are you silent? – asked his father, who was trying to make a point. – Don't you remember the boy who let you hold his kite string once? Or the boy who gave you pellets?

– What pellets? – asked Naftali, surprised. As far as he remembered, he'd never been interested in any weapons, only in words.

– We were walking across the market square, when you saw a boy with a toy wooden cannon. You were so fascinated by it that you started crying, asking me to buy you one, except there weren't any for sale; the boy's father had made it for him. They were kind enough to let you play with it for a while, until they had to leave.

– And why did he give me the pellets, if I didn't have a cannon? – Naftali asked.

– Well, you wanted his cannon so badly, you started crying, but since the Russian boy couldn't give you the gift from his father, he gave you half of his pellets, to console you a little. He was very kind...

– I don't remember that at all! – exclaimed Naftali.

– Well, you were only six years old, – said Naftali's

father, and his mother laughed out loud.

– So, he met a nice Russian kid several years ago! – she said, sarcastically.

– Maybe he'll meet more! – objected Naftali's father. – He should not be afraid of them...

But Naftali wasn't interested in discussing Russian kids; he was curious to find out what he was like as a six-year old.

– What kind of a person was I? – he asked.

– The same as you are now – inquisitive, thoughtful, and you liked to write letters to me and to Mama; you had just learned the alphabet and were practicing your handwriting... You wrote on every piece of paper you saw – and even on the table cloth! It's just that you were quite unrestrained and cried easily, but only because you were so young. You are so much better at dealing with your frustrations now!

– How funny! – said Naftali. – I don't recall any of this; there must be so many things I can't remember from when I was a young kid. Maybe in a few years, when we are living in Argentina, I won't remember *anything* about my life here in Russia!

– Then make a point of remembering, – said Naftali's father. – Try to memorize everything you see, and write things down in your diary, so later your kids can read what your life was like! You know, Tolstoy keeps a diary!

– Enough of Tolstoy! – Naftali's mother cried out. – You talk about him so much, I'm starting to think he's a member of our family, maybe an uncle! Shush, now. It's time for bed!

And Naftali did go to bed, but before he went to

sleep, he opened the diary he'd started, when he wanted to be a naturalist, like Charles Darwin. Yet no words
came to him: he didn't know which would be the best
memory to write down. He decided to stay awake, until
he remembered a great episode from his life, and then
he'd describe it...

But he fell asleep.

27

Several weeks later, Naftali was standing at the train station, both excited by the new experiences he would have, and quite afraid of the unknown. He helped his father unload the huge suitcases and bags from their carriage, and said good-bye to his father's horses, which their neighbor had bought, knowing that a real adventure awaited him!

This adventure was represented by the train, by the smoke coming from its locomotive, by the uniformed conductors blowing whistles and holding colored flags in their gloved hands, by rushing passengers and well-dressed traveling salesmen, and by the excitement shared by everyone, preparing to see new places, and leaving the old behind.

Amid the general hustle and bustle in the square and on the platform, the passengers lined up in front of their corresponding carriages and began boarding the train. Naftali and his parents did the same, but when Naftali's father tried to bring all of their luggage aboard with them, one of the conductors put up his hand and stopped him. Naftali's father stood waiting for his instructions, but the conductor simply ignored him. Instead, he started fiddling with a lantern that was attached to the entrance of the carriage. He pulled it up and pressed some buttons, watching the succession of red, white, yellow, and green lights. Naftali stared at him, mesmerized, whereas his father continued to stand there, confused and overwhelmed, not knowing where to go. Then a second conductor emerged from the carriage:

– What are you doing here? – he exclaimed. – You have to load your luggage there! – And he pointed to the back of the train. – See the lad in the uniform? He'll help you!

Naftali studied both conductors: young and red-cheeked, they looked so sharp in their white uniforms, big leather belts and high boots, that Naftali felt awkward in his ill-fitting coat of indefinite color. When his parents carried the luggage to one of the last cars in the train, Naftali stayed behind; he noticed an older woman, with a fleshy but kind face, carrying a big suitcase, with a blond boy and a dark-haired girl about Naftali's age on either side of her. They were both carrying sacks, and their clothes were as shabby as Naftali's. The boy and girl looked alike – blue-eyed and snubbed-nosed – and the sad expressions on their faces made them look even more alike.

Completely out of breath, the older woman approached the two conductors and stopped, apparently unable to continue walking. She was sighing loudly, ready to share her grief with anyone who would listen. But the conductors were oblivious to her (one still fiddling with his lantern, and the other checking the passengers' tickets), and the other passengers had their own concerns. In fact, the only person who showed any interest in her situation was Naftali.

The boy and girl looked at him cautiously, at first, but on seeing that he presented no threat, they relaxed and started chatting to each other, while the old woman sat down on one of her suitcases to rest.

When the first conductor finally looked away from his lantern and noticed the old woman blocking the entrance to the carriage with her suitcase, he waved her away. But she immediately stood up and started crying:

– God, be merciful! God, watch over them! God, help these poor children!

At this point, the other passengers, who were showing their tickets to the second conductor, stared her and the kids, curious to see what would happen next. The boy turned his head away, embarrassed by the attention she was attracting, and the girl tugged at the old woman's sleeve, trying to steer her toward the baggage car.

– God, make sure nothing happens to these poor kids on the trip! – the older woman pleaded again, locking eyes with the first conductor. Satisfied that all the lights on his lantern were functioning properly, he put the lantern back into its place, and turned to the woman:

– Let me check where you're sitting, – he said – do you have your tickets?

– Please, *golubchik*, take good care of these poor orphans, – pleaded the woman, – they have no mother or father to watch over them... Please make sure they don't get lost on the trip and nothing bad happens to them! They have already gone through enough...

The boy and girl stopped chatting and just stared at the conductor, as the one now responsible for their fate, and Naftali saw the red-cheeked conductor, who'd been so snooty, become a flustered boy himself.

– You mean, you're not going with them? – he asked, wide-eyed, as though it couldn't possibly be true.

– Their mother just died, and their father couldn't bear their grief and just disappeared, so these poor souls were left alone, to fend for themselves! They are going to their grandmother, who kindly agreed to take care of them – and I'm only their old aunt...

– But you can't send them alone! What will I do with them? – asked the conductor, who was so shocked, his cheeks were even redder than before. He looked over at the second conductor, hoping for his support in the matter. Instead, his partner simply said:

– Go ahead and check their tickets... I'm tired of standing here under the sun, while you fiddle with your lantern and all your other stuff.

But the first conductor, who still wasn't convinced the children should travel alone, hesitated.

– God help these poor souls! – the older woman started crying again.

Then she gave him a folded banknote, and he got even more flustered, confused and red-faced. He quickly slipped it into his pocket and said:

– I have to ask my supervisor if he'll allow this!

But his tone was more sympathetic, now, and it seemed he was agreeing to watch over the kids after all. Picking up on this change of tone, the old woman turned to the children and said:

– Let's go find you some seats, before all the good ones are taken!

Apparently not caring much about the luggage, she left it sitting on the platform and got onto the train with the kids. Suddenly Naftali heard his mother's voice:

– We were looking for him everywhere, and here he is, twiddling his thumbs, instead of helping his parents!

Naftali looked guiltily at his parents, who'd returned from the baggage car unburdened, but out of breath.

– I've just been looking around... This is all so new!

– Let him be, – his father said. He seemed less strict

than usual, since the start of their journey, as though focusing on other, more important things, than disciplining his son. – Maybe he is collecting travel impressions to record in a diary later, so that his children will know the lengths we had to go to, to escape oppression and search for freedom!

– So far, the only length you've really had to go to was to the baggage car! – Naftali's mother quipped, and Naftali noticed that today his parents were quarreling more than usual. He figured it was because they were anxious about the trip. Naftali was also afraid of new people and situations but, at the same time, he was intrigued.

They boarded the train and Naftali almost bumped into the old woman who, on her way out, continued to cry, "God help these poor souls," while saying goodbye to her niece and nephew. When she exited the train, Naftali watched through the window as she carried their luggage to the baggage car. Since Naftali's parents had chosen seats right next to these orphans, he realized their interaction was unavoidable. Yet, he wasn't sure they would understand each other. Despite their similarities – they were all about the same age, they were all traveling third class, and this was the first train trip for all of them – their differences could get in the way of having a conversation.

For now, all the passengers were busy with their own affairs, putting luggage under the shelves, snacking, waving good-bye to their relatives who had lined up on the platform, or simply staring straight ahead, ignoring everyone else. The boy and girl, who looked to be Russian, sat very closely together, as though afraid of getting sep arated, and stared out the half-open window. Their aunt came up to it and waved at them. Then she pulled a small bag of something out of her pocket and shouted:

– I forgot to give you the *pirozhki* I made for you! Stop! Stop!

Just as she was about to pass the *pirozhki* through the half-open window, the conductor whistled and raised a flag into the air; the train lurched forward and then stopped, as though it didn't want to go. The children gaped at their aunt, who was frightened by the sudden movement and pulled her hand away from the window. She tried again, and Naftali's father managed to grab the bag from her and pass it to the boy and girl. Since he wasn't sure they would understand Yiddish, he did it without a word. Not knowing how to thank him, the children didn't say anything, either, and the boy put the bag in his lap.

Naftali saw a tear in the girl's eye. She quickly wiped it away with her sleeve, which Naftali noticed was patched. The train lurched forward again, then started moving more smoothly, and the old woman beyond the window disappeared. Just a second ago she was crossing herself and muttering something under her breath, and now she was gone. And everything else – the people on the platform, the dog house next to the train station, the little huts and the kids playing ball in the field – started moving, and disappearing from view.

28

Naftali was staring out the window: at first, there were lots of little wooden homes, with dogs, kids and women in front of them, waving at the passing train; then the houses were further apart, solitary small homes with this or that lonely figure bending and picking something up from the lawn in front. Finally, even these lonely homes disappeared and were replaced by vast green fields with crops, fences, horses, and cows. There were so many things in Russia that Naftali had never seen up close: he had never been to a traveling circus, he had no idea what the kids beyond the window liked to do best, he had never traveled to a big city like St. Petersburg. And now he had to leave Russia, without seeing any of it, and it was a pity.

His father, oblivious to his thoughts and indifferent to the views beyond the window, opened one of the bags and brought out lunch: boiled chicken, eggs, bread. Naftali noticed that the brother and sister next to them stared at the food and immediately started eating their *pirozhki*. Without exchanging a word, they all started chewing, all of them feeling uneasy.

Naftali was relieved when the conductor approached the siblings and asked:

– What are your names, children, and where do you need to get off? You have to tell me so I can warn you in advance as we near the station. The train only stops for a few minutes, so you'll have to get off quickly. And no playing allowed! – the conductor shook his finger as though in anger, but it was clear that he was joking.

– I'm Varlam, – the boy pointed to his chest, – and

she is Katya. We are going to our grandmother, Vasilisa Evlampyevna, who is going to look after us…

— And where does this Vasilisa Evlampyevna live? — asked the conductor.

The boy looked confused. He turned to his sister, expecting her to answer this question.

— Everybody knows our grandmother in her village, — she said. She is very kind and she treats local people with herbs, often for free, when they can't pay her. Our aunt said, whoever you ask, they all know her! So, we are going to stay at her place; she has a large home.

The conductor grew worried:

— I need the name of the place where she lives… Where should you get off? Again, the boy looked at his sister.

The girl thought for a moment and was about to say something but stopped. She said she wasn't sure, where they had to disembark, she had forgotten. The conductor frowned.

— I don't want to get stuck with the two of you on this train, I was a fool for agreeing to take you…

The girl started crying, and Naftali could barely understand what she was saying:

— It's not my fault, I didn't want to leave our home. I just wanted to stay with my mom! I have never seen my grandmother; she always lived so far from our town! Why didn't our aunt take care of us? Why did she send us away?

The boy tried to calm his sister down:

— But our mom is not at home anymore, she is gone, and our aunt has six kids of her own, so she can't take care of us… That's why she sent us to Vasilisa Evlampyevna!

On hearing this, the conductor clutched his head with both hands:

– What am I going to do with these orphans who have no idea where they are going! – he moaned. – I'll have to summon the police and let them deal with you. I'll be very busy operating my lantern and throwing flares behind the train when we stop, so that another train doesn't crash into us, and I'll have no time for you. I have more important things to take care of!

Now the boy was almost ready to cry:

– I don't want to go to police! I didn't do anything wrong...

– But maybe the police will find the address of your grandmother, – the conductor explained, – or, maybe I should just send you back to your aunt. Let me see: when this train stops, I'll put you on another train so you can go back home!

The brother and sister didn't know what to say to this; they looked so helpless, and Naftali felt sorry for them. The boy shifted in his seat nervously and Naftali noticed a folded piece of paper fall out of his pocket and onto the floor, without him knowing. As the boy wiped away the tears in his eyes, Naftali picked up the piece of paper and unfolded it: there was something written on it, in big, crooked letters. He read the first line and exclaimed:

– Zelenaya Ulitsa 3, Deryazhnaya Station!

– Are you traveling with them? – the conductor asked suspiciously.

– No, – said Naftali, – but I found this piece of paper on the floor; it fell out of his pocket!

The boy said:

– That's mine, my aunt gave it to me, but since I don't like reading, I never unfolded it. I thought it was a letter from my aunt to Vasilisa Evlampyevna.

– Yes, there is a letter here too, take it! – Naftali extended his hand with the letter to the boy and the boy gratefully took it.

– The Deryazhnaya station is only a couple of hours away, – said the conductor. – And how did you learn to read Russian? – he asked Naftali. – Aren't you Jewish?

– What is Jewish? – asked the boy, and Naftali was surprised that he had no idea who the Jews were. The girl looked at Naftali with renewed interest.

– We are just people, like everybody else! – Naftali's father replied. – And we are traveling on this train like everybody else, too, – he added, and Naftali's mother nodded.

– Well, everything is fine, – the conductor concluded. – Now that I know where these children are going, my job is done.

He muttered something under his breath and left.

29

The girl looked at Naftali and thanked him, and Naftali's father said to him, in Yiddish:

– Why don't you make friends with these kids; I need to pray here, alone…

– And I was just about to excuse myself and leave for several minutes, – Naftali's mom chimed in, – but how can I, if Naftali is going, too? What if somebody comes along and steals our things, while you stand absorbed in prayer?

– I don't want to go play, – said Naftali, – I don't know them, or what games they like…

– So, talk to them, and you'll find out! – Naftali's father said, sternly. After fumbling around with his shoulder bag, he finally retrieved his prayer book and adjusted his taleth; he couldn't wait for things to quiet down, so he could concentrate.

– Then I'll stay too! – exclaimed Naftali's mother. – I'll wait till you finish praying, and keep an eye on our belongings… I still remember the day I came home on Yom Kippur after visiting my girlfriend Tzipora, and found you holding one of my shoes in your hand!

Naftali smiled. He liked listening to this story.

– When I asked you what was going on, you said somebody had stolen your almost brand new leather shoes from the porch, while you were praying, and that you'd heard noises outside, but you didn't dare interrupt your prayers for such nonsense!

– Mama, why was he holding your shoe then? – Naftali laughed.

– I think he wanted to see if we wore the same size, so he could wear my shoes instead of buying a new pair!

– What nonsense you're talking! – said Naftali's father. – I never intended to wear your shoes; because of my poor eyesight, I only thought they were mine! And you should not make fun of me because I was so absorbed in prayer! On Yom Kippur you are supposed to give away things to help the poor, to forgive sins. Without lifting a finger, I gave away my almost brand new leather shoes, and then I forgave the thief for his sin of stealing!

Naftali and his mother laughed, amused by Naftali's father's cleverness. Then Lazar Evseevich said:

– But don't think I'll be parting with our precious belongings here. I'm sure that traveling on the train is a special circumstance, so I can pray sitting down, and discourage any thieves. Don't worry, it is allowed; just go about your business and come back later.

Obliged to honor his father's request, Naftali turned hesitantly to the brother and sister and said in Russian: – Would you like to go and check out the train with me?

– Let's go! – they agreed, instantly, and off they went.

After they had walked a bit, looking at the passengers and almost bumping into the conductor, who was carrying a tray of tea cups, the girl asked Naftali:

– Would you like to play hide and seek?

– Yes, why not? – said Naftali. – Your brother and I will hide somewhere, and you try to find us!

– I'm not going to hide anywhere alone, – objected the boy, looking helplessly at his sister. Even though they looked about the same age, he seemed quite dependent on her.

So the girl looked at Naftali and said: – Why don't

you hide, and Varlam and I will try to find you? Only don't go too far, or else your parents will be angry with us!

– Okay, I'll hide, – Naftali agreed, and he started thinking about the best place to conceal himself. The girl and boy turned their backs to him, and started counting to ten, to let him disappear. Naftali was glad they had no problem understanding each other in Russian.

He walked down the long corridor and was about to dive under one of the seats, next to a cage with a rooster, when he got the idea to go into another car. He waited until the train stopped at a small station, and when the conductor opened the doors, Naftali quickly got off the train and walked over to the next car. While on the platform, he saw several women with baskets, selling eggs, milk, wooden Matryoshkas, spoons, bowls and other handicrafts. As soon as they saw him, they started showing off their goods, which included wooden soldiers and a ship, but Naftali was afraid the train would leave without him and quickly climbed the metal steps into the next car. Nobody stopped him, and to his surprise, that this car looked much nicer than his own. It was much cleaner, less crowded, and instead of sitting on long benches, these passengers occupied pleasant little rooms, each of which had a door with a handle. All of the doors were closed, but Naftali spotted one that was open. It was somewhat darker inside, and he couldn't tell if it was occupied or not. As he peered inside, he suddenly heard footsteps: somebody was coming.

Afraid of getting into trouble for being there, Naftali panicked, slipped into the small dark compartment and sat down on the floor. Whoever was coming toward the compartment was singing to himself. Naftali held his breath.

Then he heard the door close, and suddenly he was in complete darkness. The man who was singing, turned out to be a conductor, who had shut the door, without looking into the compartment. Naftali was relieved that he'd gone unnoticed, but now he wasn't sure what to do. He couldn't hear any footsteps though the closed door; he didn't know if the conductor was gone or not, or if he'd catch Naftali, if he tried to get out now. He waited, listening closely to the sounds in the passageway, when suddenly he heard somebody breathing. Apparently, Naftali wasn't alone! Once he was able to see in the dark, he realized someone was sleeping on a bunk that was right next to him!

Afraid the sleeping person might wake up and see him, Naftali tried to open the door, but it was stuck. Fumbling in the dark, he tried to open it again, but couldn't find the handle. Just then, the train started moving again, and the man in the bed woke up from the noise. He sat up, lowered his legs, and opened curtains on the window, and the compartment suddenly lit up. Naftali saw a man of his father's age, in crumpled gray trousers with suspenders, who had been sleeping in his clothes. The man turned his head and saw Naftali. As though he couldn't believe his eyes, he squinted and then pulled away the curtain completely, to see Naftali better. Naftali could see him clearly, too; he had a little mustache on his round, pasty face, which looked rather kind.

– Hey, how are you? – asked the man casually, as though it were perfectly normal to wake up in his compartment and find a complete stranger right next to him.

Naftali was dumbfounded.

– Hey, are you hungry? – asked the man again, and Naftali wondered if the man thought he was somebody else, maybe someone he knew.

Naftali shook his head no, he wasn't hungry, hoping that if he kept silent, the man would continue thinking he was this somebody else.

– Do you want to sit here? The floor's uncomfortable, – the man continued, patting the bed, as though inviting Naftali to sit next to him.

Naftali again shook his head.

– Where are you going? – asked the man. Naftali was afraid to speak.

– Are you tired? Do you want to sleep? Do you want some water? – asked the man again. And again, Naftali shook his head.

– Tell me which station you are going to: if I disembark before you, you might be in trouble, because the passenger who takes my place might report you to the conductor. So, where do you plan to get off?

– I'm going to Argentina, – Naftali finally said. His voice was shaking.

– Argentina? – asked the man with surprise.

Naftali nodded. He was very uncomfortable and had no idea where this conversation was headed.

– You might be smart enough to sneak past a conductor, but you can't be that bright, because you're on the wrong train! There's no station called "Argentina" on this route, my friend! There's Deryazhnaya, Komarovyi, Serbinovtzy... But there's no "Argentina!" What do you say to that, young man?

Naftali shrugged.

– Alright, I'll leave you alone, my friend. I realize you sneaked in here because you don't have the money for your ticket. When I was your age, I did the same thing once, when I ran away from my parents... So, just keep quiet and let me sleep, I'm tired.

With these words, the man got back into bed and pulled the blanket over his head. Naftali felt really stupid, because now he didn't know how to tell this man that all he wanted was to open the door and get out.

The man started snoring almost immediately; Naftali sat there, afraid to move and wondering what to do. He thought the Russian children must have stopped looking for him by now, assuming he'd abandoned the game. His parents were probably worried, thinking he had gotten off at the previous stop and was now lost forever. Naftali was too terrified even to contemplate what his parents were saying and thinking by now.

The train continued moving, and its rhythmical and monotonous movements were making Naftali drowsy. Then he heard children's voices outside, and immediately his drowsiness disappeared. He thought that it was Katya and Varlam, looking for him, and he lightly tapped on the door from inside. Apparently, they didn't hear him; they were loudly discussing something.

Naftali knocked louder; the man shifted in his bed, but didn't wake up. Naftali knocked once more, and suddenly the door opened.

And there stood a conductor, staring straight at Naftali, with two unfamiliar kids peering out from behind him, none of whom Naftali had seen before. The conductor was dumbfounded, and Naftali tried to sneak out under his arm, but the conductor was quicker. He grabbed Naftali by the ear, and shouted: – Your ticket!

30

Meanwhile Varlam and Katya really were looking for Naftali. After he'd run off to hide, Katya finished counting to ten and, turning to Varlam she said: – Let's go find him!

Suddenly Varlam sat down on the floor and burst into tears:

– I don't want to! – he wailed. – I want Mama to be with us... I don't want to do anything unless she is here...

– But she is gone, Varlam, – Katya tried to explain, – and we have to manage without her somehow... She would be happy, if she saw *us* happy. Naftali is such a nice boy: remember, he helped us when the conductor wanted to send us back to our aunt?

– I want to go back! – cried Varlam. – Maybe our mom has come back, and she's waiting for us at home...

– But no, Varlam, it isn't possible, – Katya tried to console him. – I'm telling you: she wouldn't be happy seeing you in this pitiful state... If she could see us now, she'd rather we were like all the other kids, playing and laughing... Let's go!

Katya took Varlam by the hand and started walking through the car, looking under the benches. Varlam bent down next to one of the benches and saw a rooster in a cage. Without thinking, he tried to pet it, but the rooster bit him. Startled, Varlam started to cry again.

This time, Katya was upset with him:

– What's the matter now? – she asked impatiently.

– The rooster bit him! – explained a burly man who was sitting on the bench across from the vicious rooster. –

Is he your brother?

— Yes, we are brother and sister, — explained Katya, — and we are looking for a boy approximately our age and height, with a round black cap on his head and side curls...

— So, this boy tricked you and ran away? — asked the burly man. — Why am I not surprised?

— We're just playing! — Katya explained, patiently, stroking Varlam's hair. Varlam stood silently with his wounded finger in his mouth, waiting for Katya's conversation with the man to end.

— But you said the boy was different from us, right? If he was wearing a skullcap and sidelocks, he's Jewish...

— Yes, he wore sidelocks and a skullcap. Perhaps you've seen him, he would be easy to recognize! — Katya said. She didn't understand what the burly man was getting at.

— So, why are you looking for him? — the man insisted. — I'm sure this boy cheated you somehow, and that's why he's hiding. You'll never find him!

— We are playing hide-and-seek! — Varlam finally explained.

Suddenly a funny-looking man with little tufts of hair at his temples, who was sitting by the window, spoke up:

— Can't you just leave them alone? — he said, addressing the burly man. — These children are playing with their friend, and they don't need to hear your nonsense.

— Show me a Jew who isn't rich, or hasn't cheated somebody! — the burly man laughed.

— A rich man wouldn't be traveling in this filthy, uncomfortable car, — retorted the man with the tufts of hair, shaking his head emphatically. — He'd be in traveling first class, with all its comforts!

– Ha-ha-ha, – laughed the burly man. – Maybe that's where he is hiding! Jews know of various tricks to cheat people.

The funny-looking man was wearing two different-colored socks, a strange checkered hat, an oversized pullover, and his cheeks were as red, as though he'd colored them with women's rouge.

– Don't listen to him, – he said, – I don't think your Jewish friend tricked you, or anybody else in his life. But since I am a clown by profession, I am definitely the one who knows lots of tricks!

Varlam was suddenly very interested:

– Show us a trick! Show us a trick! – he pleaded.

– We can't stay here, – said Katya, – we have to look for our friend! But the clown quickly replied:

– If you let me show you my skills, I'll help you find him!

And before the children knew what was going on, he grabbed the handkerchief that was tucked into Katya's sleeve, waved it through the air a few times, and made it disappear!

Next he took a large black hat that was lying beside him on the bench, and started pulling something out of it. Katya and Varlam stood mesmerized, as he pulled and pulled what seemed to be a never-ending scarf.

After this the clown said: – Now let's look for your friend!

– And the handkerchief? Where is it? – asked Varlam.

– I almost forgot! – exclaimed the clown guiltily and pulled a handkerchief out of his pocket. – Here it is!

– This isn't mine! – frowned Katya.

The clown looked confused; he started pulling all kinds of handkerchiefs out of his pockets, one after another, and showing them to the kids. It seemed the number of handkerchiefs he had in his pockets was endless. Apparently, this was another trick. Finally, Katya spotted hers, took it back and the clown and the children proceeded to look for Naftali.

They passed all kinds of travelers, doing all kinds of things: some were eating, some were talking amongst themselves, while others kept a grim silence. They passed travelers who were playing cards, or sleeping on their benches, and travelers who were reading newspapers, or untying their shoes to get more comfortable during their trip. One traveler was feeding chickens in cages, and another – a small dog with sad eyes, who barked at the kids, causing Varlam to jump back (having already been bitten by the rooster, he was afraid of being mauled by a dog, now, too). They passed mothers calming their infants, and children, who were much more interested in looking out the windows of the moving train, than listening to their parents.

But Naftali was nowhere to be found: he was not sitting on a bench, or lying under one; he wasn't standing, and he wasn't crawling; he wasn't hiding behind this or that passenger's back, or even behind a door. It looked like he had disappeared completely!

– Are you sure he is on this train? – asked the clown. – Or is your friend with the black yarmulke and sidelocks just a product of your imagination?

Katya looked at the clown with surprise:

– Surely not, – said Katya, – we sat next to his parents, who are probably worried sick over his disappearance... We have to tell them what's happened!

Varlam started crying again: – Nobody would care about our disappearance, because we have no parents! Our mother died and our father got so sad that he simply left us... He said we reminded him of our mother, whom he loved so dearly, so he just couldn't stay with us anymore!

The clown said to Varlam: – I can show you another trick to make you happy, if you let me... Give me something of yours, and I'll make it disappear completely!

But Varlam was inconsolable: – Nobody needs your disappearing tricks; make things appear instead! Make my mom appear right here, in front of us!

The clown got visibly upset and said:

– I'm sorry my tricks are so limited... I can make certain things appear again, like objects and maybe some people. But not those who have died... I guess I'm just a lousy magician who cannot make children happy...

And now the clown sat down on the floor, like Varlam had just minutes before, and covered his face with his hands, as though he might cry. He continued:

– I lost my parents when I was very young, too, and because I wasn't interested in any trade, like carpentry or gardening or blacksmithing, I learned some tricks from a clown in a traveling circus. I joined the circus so I could make people happy! But now I see that I cannot console this little boy, no matter what I do!

Katya said: – Please don't cry! What can I do with two crying people? Come with us! The clown stood up, wiped his eyes with his sleeve, and they went to Naftali's parents.

31

When they got back to their bench, Naftali's father was just finishing his prayers. Katya and Varlam stared at him, and Varlam asked:

– Does God know many languages? Surely, this prayer is different from the ones we learned at school...

The clown explained:

– I think he is praying to a different God, but I'm sure all parents pray for their children's well-being.

– There can be no other God! – exclaimed Katya. – There is only one, and I believe he really is omnipotent and able to understand everybody, even those who don't speak Russian!

– I'm sure any God will understand the parents' pain when their child is missing, – said the clown, and looking at Varlam he added, – and the children's pain, when their parents are missing! But let's talk to this man and hope he'll understand us. Can he speak Russian?

– What happened? – asked Naftali's father, having finished praying. His Russian was not perfect and had a heavy accent, but the children and the clown were able to understand almost every word.

– We can't find your son, – explained the clown, – I think he was supposed to hide, so that they could find him, but he just disappeared.

– I see no reason to worry, – said Naftali's father. – There is nowhere for him to go, so I'm sure he must have hidden himself very well somewhere on this train...

– But we've been looking for him for quite a while, – exclaimed Katya, – it's as though he's fallen through the floor!

Naftali's father shrugged his shoulders and said:

– I don't think we should worry; he is a smart boy, he'll come back on his own, once he realizes nobody is looking for him anymore...

Upon these words Naftali's father tried to stand up, but just then the train suddenly came to a halt, and if the clown hadn't given him his hand, he would have fallen over.

– This train stops so often, – said Naftali's father, – I'm not sure we'll ever reach our destination!

– I'd rather it didn't go anywhere, – said Varlam. – I just want to go home to my mom.

Katya looked at him sternly, and Varlam, who was about to start crying again, changed his mind.

Suddenly the clown shouted:

– Isn't that your friend? Quick! Look out the window!

They all looked out the window, and to their surprise, they saw Naftali being pulled along the platform, by a tall, strict-looking conductor.

On seeing his son being led away from the train, Naftali's father exclaimed something in Yiddish, and rushed off the train.

– Wait! This is a very short stop! – warned a passenger who was standing by the open door, smoking a cigarette. – The train will leave without you!

But Naftali's father paid no attention. He was running so fast, he bumped into the conductor. He grabbed Naftali's arm and pulled him toward the train. The conductor grasped Naftali's other arm and frowned:

– What's going on here! Let me deal with this "fare-jumper"!

– He is not a "fare-jumper", – retorted Naftali's father in Russian. – He is my son! The conductor stopped and looked at him in disbelief, yet he didn't let go of Naftali's arm, and now Naftali stood in between his father and the conductor.

Katya, Varlam and the clown had also gotten off the train and run onto the platform, after Naftali's father and the conductor, who looked skeptically at the strange group gathered around him.

– I'm taking him to the police! – he said. – Nobody can ride a train without paying!

– He has a ticket, – said Naftali's father.

– He is traveling with his parents! – interjected Varlam and Katya. – He didn't do anything wrong, we were only playing hide-and-seek! Please let him go!

– I'll show you a trick if you let him go! – the clown volunteered. Suddenly the conductor turned to him:

– How come I keep seeing you on this train? Almost every week you ride back and forth, as though you have nothing better to do! Maybe I should take you to the police, too?

While the conductor stood arguing loudly with the clown, he loosened his grip on Naftali, and Naftali started inching away from him. At this point, Naftali's father pulled him away from the conductor, and they quickly got back on the train, followed by Katya and Varlam. Seconds later, the train started moving. Katya, Varlam and Naftali got into their car and looked out the window at the platform. The conductor was holding onto the clown, while the clown tried in vain to get away, because he was so slight in stature. The train picked up speed and soon Naftali's unfortunate adventure, as well as the clown, and the tall, thin, conductor were in the distant past.

That evening, Naftali opened his diary. As his father had instructed him to do, he wanted to write down his impressions of the trip, so that whoever found this diary in the future would know what Naftali's life was like. He hesitated for a bit, unsure about the topic his future readers would be interested in. Would they want to know what trains looked like in the past? Would they want to learn how to get to Argentina from Russia along the shortest route possible? Would they want to know what Naftali wore, or what games he played? Unable to find the answer, Naftali decided simply to write down the most important thing on his mind at that moment:

"Today I met two wonderful friends – Katya and Varlam. They are less fortunate than I am, because they have no parents, but, despite their misfortunes, they are very kind. They helped me when I got into the trouble and warned others that I had disappeared. If not for them, I would now be in a police station and my parents would be desperately trying to find me! If not for Katya and Varlam, I may not have reached Argentina... These children are Russian. Before, I didn't know many Russian children where I lived, and when my father asked me if they were good or bad, I didn't know what to answer. But now I see. Despite the fact that they are Russian and I am Jewish, we played games and chatted together. It does not matter what a person's nationality is. What matters is the person's heart. If they are kind and willing to help..."

Naftali stopped after writing this. He thought he should end his diary entry with something very important and his conclusion about people's kindness seemed very good to him. But since he was only a boy and wouldn't be very "adult" in his thinking for a long time, he finished his diary entry with this instead:

"I hope that in Argentina I'll meet nice children… children whose parents are gauchos, children who spend all their days riding horses! I hope they don't care that I'm Jewish and that I read a lot; I hope they'll teach me about the pampas and that we'll have a lot of fun together!"

Naftali saw there were still two lines left on the page and, to make sure the page looked complete, he added:

"I already know some Spanish, so I hope that Argentinean horses will understand my commands!"

32

While Naftali scribbled in his notebook, the train moved on. It moved loudly and relentlessly that evening and the next, and then another evening, and after that they switched trains, and then the other train, very similar to this one and even more crowded, continued moving forward throughout the day and throughout the night, and then one more day and one more night... And on the second train, there were no Katya and no Varlam. They had disembarked the previous train and now were probably getting to know their grandmother... On this train there were other kids with their parents, but Naftali could not understand what they were talking about amongst themselves, because they spoke a language that somehow resembled Yiddish, but was not really Yiddish, so Naftali could understand only occasional words but not complete sentences. He missed his new friends, and he knew he'd probably never see them again, just as he would never see Russia again.

And once they got off this train, they boarded one more train, and after they disembarked that train, they finally boarded a ship, called "Pampas" because it was to take them to the Argentinean pampas. On the one hand, Naftali was very excited that with every second they were getting closer and closer to their destination of choice; on the other hand, the conditions on this ship were so bad that he wasn't able to daydream about any beautiful, far-away land; he had to stand in the long line to the bath-room, always be hungry because the food on the ship was inadequate and tasted either bitter, unsalted, or just funny, and listen to his mother's complaints about not being able to bathe every day, as she could at home.

Once a week, a muscular, thick-necked deck hand would fill up several large basins with heated ocean water and people would use it to wash. For Naftali, once a week was enough, but he noticed other children, who got so grimy from running around in the steerage, jumping over sleeping people and watching sailors shovel coal into the boiler, that it was impossible to tell them apart – that's how black their soot-covered faces became!

Once, when he was just strolling around the ship carrying his favorite book, *Don Quixote*, in his knapsack, he saw a girl sitting on the deck, mending her skirt. One of her cheeks was smeared with soot, her face looked oily, and her hair – unkempt.

– Hi! – she addressed Naftali in Yiddish. – are you going to Argentina with me? Her beautiful, lively voice didn't match her tattered appearance.

– Hi! – Naftali replied, timidly. – I'm going to Argentina with my mother and father.

– What do you have in your sack? Maybe some food? – inquired the girl. – Give me some bread, and I'll fix your coat right before your eyes! It's too big on you. My father is a tailor and he taught me how to sew and how to mend. I'm sure that with his skills, he will never be without work in Argentina!

– I'm hungry myself, – answered Naftali sadly, – and all I have in my knapsack is a book I like reading when I don't know what else to do on this ship...

– Read me something from it! Are there any stories about princes and princesses and hidden treasures?

Naftali hesitated: he was afraid that once the girl

learned what his *Don Quixote* was about, she would laugh at him. This book was his secret: something he liked to enjoy when he was alone, and he didn't want to share this secret with somebody he had just met a second ago.

– Let me make up a story, – said Naftali.

The girl agreed. It seemed she hadn't talked with anybody for a long time and was eager to continue the conversation.

– Once I came home from school in the rain, and my feet were soaking wet. When I got there, I saw my father talking to our neighbor Yosef …

– Yosef? – the girl raised her head from her mending. – In our village there was a boy named Yosef – Yosef Rybkevich – who was tall and handsome as a prince… Was your Yosef like that?

– Oh no, – said Naftali. – This Yosef was short, old, and balding, and as far as I remember, he was missing his two front teeth. I think he lost them when he fell off a horse… His horse was pretty old, too, so they were a perfect match. The only difference was that the horse was limping because of an injured hoof, and Yosef was not…

The girl laughed, and then seemed disappointed, but she let Naftali continue his story.

– When I saw Yosef, I jumped over a big puddle and then onto the porch, and I hid, so as not to disrupt the conversation… Yosef needed help – his roof was leaking, and there was water dripping onto his newborn in his cradle!

– Wait, wait! – the girl interrupted him. – You wouldn't believe how many neighbors in my village had leaky roofs. Even ours… Listen, I want to hear something completely different from my life. Who wants to hear about their own gloomy existence all the time? It just makes me think my life will never change, that even when I'm old and toothless, I'll still be on my haunches, wiping up pools of water on the floor... No more of these stories! I'm not moving to Argentina for more of that! I'm hoping to meet a handsome young man there, who will serenade me with ballads under the stars!

Naftali realized there was nothing he could tell this girl about his life in Russia that she didn't already know – and even better than he did, because she was older. For her, he'd have to make up a story, but it wasn't easy to tell of romantic princesses and treasures, when you were looking at an unwashed girl in a tattered skirt, sitting on the dirty deck of a ship, who had asked him for bread because she was hungry.

He pretended to hear his parents calling him and left quickly.

Then he found a secluded corner, opened his book in the middle, and started reading. To his surprise, the randomly chosen paragraph described a dirty girl in unkempt clothing who was riding on a mule – it was as though the events in the book mirrored his encounter on the deck just minutes earlier! In the book, Don Quixote asks Sancho Panza which road will lead him to the beautiful Dulcinea. Reluctant to admit he doesn't know, Sancho suddenly spots a peasant girl riding a mule and proclaims that *she's* Dulcinea, only that she's been "disenchanted", perhaps by an evil magician, who has turned her into this ugly and dirty creature on the donkey!

Naftali thought he was almost like Don Quixote: he wanted to believe that the dirty girl who didn't like his story about living in Russia was somebody else, that sometime in the past she had been attractive and clean. Then something happened, and everybody, including her, started looking uglier... Naftali stood up and looked around at the passengers. Some were sleeping right on the deck, barely covered by their tattered blankets; some were playing cards; others were quarreling and scowling at each other. Perhaps they were under the spell of an evil magician, who had grouped them all together, here, on this uncomfortable, filthy ship, where they couldn't wash decently, and only a magic wand in the skilled hands of another, good, magician could turn them back into beautiful creatures...

Perhaps they were all meant for another, more uplifting and meaningful life. But somebody had to break the spell!

33

Walking around the ship, Naftali imagined he was Don Quixote, who could transform everything, and make people noble and happy, with the wave of a magic wand. Yet, he was distracted; his stomach began to growl so intently, that he couldn't ignore its callings any longer.

Naftali knew it was almost dinnertime; he looked around and saw the lineup of people, standing with their bowls and pots, while a sailor poured soup into their dishes. A sweet and somewhat rotten smell emanated from the large pot the sailor was dipping the ladle into, and Naftali realized that he would be served "vegetable" soup, again, which was basically a few yellowed cabbage leaves, swimming in unsalted, murky water.

The day before, Naftali had lowered a bucket into the ocean on a rope, and managed to scoop up some salty sea water, which he added to his soup, to make it tastier. He noticed an improvement, so he repeated the process, but unfortunately, not even the sea water could enhance the flavor of the soup today.

Still hungry, Naftali walked around the ship some more, trying to occupy himself somehow, when he saw a pretty young woman, who was trying to fall asleep on top of a beautiful antique table with pearl inlays.

Naftali watched her, moving this way and that, on the table's hard surface. But no matter how she tried, she just couldn't get comfortable; her eyes were puffy and red from crying.

– You see how silly I am?! – she exclaimed.

Since Naftali didn't know what she meant, he only

shook his head.

– We had a pogrom in our village, – the young woman started to explain, – and the Cossacks were after us, even whipping people with their quirts! They were approaching quickly and I started to run, but I didn't want to leave this table behind, because it's an expensive antique, – she continued. – Can you imagine?

– Well... – Naftali uttered, still unsure about where this story was going.

– There I was, running with this table, and the Cossacks almost got me, because I was so stupid and wouldn't leave it behind. I had to wade across the river with this piece of furniture on my back – it almost cost me my life! Imagine a life lost for the sake of a piece of wood inlaid with pearl?

– But why are you crying now? – asked Naftali.

– Well, I was almost killed because of this table, and when I decided to emigrate to Argentina, I insisted on taking it with me because of all the effort I'd invested in keeping it. And because I was so concerned with this table, I forgot to bring even the most basic things, like a blanket, so I have to borrow other people's blankets, or sleep on the deck and risk getting a splinter. Now, imagine me sitting on the pampas, with all the wind and dust and horse dung, drinking mate on this antique table! The locals will laugh at me, and they'll be right to do so!

Naftali thought how a noble knight in shining armor could save the young woman from the cold and discomfort, and he exclaimed:

– I'll bring you my blanket, so you won't ever be cold!

– But you need it yourself, – objected the young woman and smiled.

– I have two! – lied Naftali. – Two blankets and no antique table!

He knew his parents would be angry when they found out his blanket was missing, but he wanted to help.

Suddenly he felt weak: his palms felt sweaty, and everything before his eyes started swimming and growing dark, as though it were evening and the sun had already set. He tried to say something else about the blanket, but couldn't. He felt the Earth falling away from under him, and he collapsed. And that was the last thing he remembered, before slipping into a dream.

He was flying over the ship on a big wooden horse. The wind was blowing into his ears, and the horse was flying so fast, it took a tremendous effort to avoid sliding off; he was afraid that if he let go, he'd fall, crashing down onto the deck. From above, the ship's passengers looked small and insignificant, and even from so high up, Naftali could see the dismal condition of the ship and the filthy deck.

Carefully, so as not to fall off, Naftali touched a peg in the horse's large wooden head and the horse started to descend. Naftali could hear what people were saying now, though despite his proximity to them, they seemed oblivious to his presence. They were expressing their fears of the unknown. A short man said to a woman of the very same height, "And what will we do there?" And the woman answered, "Let's take one step at a time, dear husband; when we come to our destination, the circumstances themselves will show us what to do next."

Naftali touched the wooden peg once again and descended even lower. A terrifying crackling sound surrounded him, and he was afraid the wind would tear him off the horse. Now he was able to see himself on the deck. He was lying on a bunk bed his parents had set up for him, and they were asking him how he was feeling; they looked worried. Naftali didn't want to answer them, and he pulled on the peg in the horse's head. The horse started going higher and higher in the air and was about to fly away from the ship, but their voices stopped it. Naftali's mom and dad were crying out desperately: "Naftali, Naftali, please come back to us!"

Naftali didn't want to disappoint his parents, so he pulled on the peg and lowered the wooden horse again. It landed on the deck quite gently, and Naftali opened his eyes. He realized he'd been dreaming. Now he was lying in a bed and his parents were calling out to him. His mother touched his forehead: "He is getting better! He is not so hot anymore!" His father exclaimed: "Finally, he's opened his eyes! Naftali, can you hear us? How are you feeling?"

Naftali moved his right arm, trying to find the peg on the horse's head and show his father how to ride it, but he remembered that the horse was part of the dream. There was nothing beside him but blankets, his worried parents, and the same filthy deck. Then he remembered a chapter he'd recently read in his *Don Quixote* book, in which two bearded ladies tell the Knight in Shining Armor that their ugly beards would disappear, if he and his servant Sancho Panza flew on large wooden horses. The horses were provided by some peasants, who asked Don Quixote and Sancho to close their eyes, and then blew into some bags, producing a whistling sound and some sort of crackling. On hearing these sounds, Don Quixote and Sancho believed they were actually flying on the wooden horses, unaware that the peasants had fooled them.

Naftali wished that on his return from the sky, the ship could've changed to one with white sails and clean, happy people on its freshly washed deck, the same way that Don Quixote hoped that once he came back, the two bearded ladies would be beautiful again, without a hair on their faces. But, alas, the ship was the same, they were still on the high seas, and the foul smell of unwashed bodies and rotting food still surrounded him.

Yet, Naftali was happy to see his mother and his father, who announced:

— You were so sick for several days, we were afraid you'd never make it to Argentina!

— Stop talking nonsense! — Naftali's mother quickly interrupted him. — I always knew nothing would happen to my beloved child. He just got a bit sick — but he appears to be much better now!

Naftali suddenly remembered the pretty young woman with the antique table, who was crying. — Was there a young lady looking for me? — he asked. — I think I promised her something. I wonder if she is still waiting!

— Oh yes! — nodded Naftali's mother. — A young lady was walking around, asking everybody if they knew a boy in an ill-fitted coat... I think I need to fix this coat for you, because everybody's always mentioning it to me!

— Yes! — seconded Naftali's father. — When she approached us and asked us the same question, we immediately understood that it was you she meant! Then she led us to you. You were unconscious, so we brought you here and took care of you.

— I put some sea water into my soup, ate it and talked to her, — said Naftali. — Maybe the awful soup made me sick!

He decided not to say anything about the blanket to avoid making his parents mad.

– Sea water? – exclaimed Naftali's father. – Now we know why you almost perished! It's not meant to be drunk – our bodies are not used to it and it's very unclean.

– Aha! – It's all your fault, – said Naftali's mother to her husband quite angrily. – You never taught him about ocean water! You knew it all along and you didn't tell either him or me. Our son could have died just because you didn't warn him!

– Wait, – said Naftali's father calmly, – didn't you just say you always knew he would be alright? It seems that you change your mind every second! Whereas I believe that everybody has his own destiny, so whatever is meant to happen, *will* happen, no matter what actions we take.

– Yes, and I'm sure, – Naftali's mother said, – that Naftali's destiny is to safely arrive in Argentina and lead a happy life, a much better life than we all had in Russia!

– So you are not angry with me anymore? – asked Naftali's father. – Let's make up and stop quarreling. Thanks to God and our efforts, Naftali has recovered. And because seeing him well again has put me in such a good mood, I'll tell a nice story that I remember – about destiny!

– Please, tell me, please! – Naftali pleaded from his bed, and his father started the tale.

34

– Once upon a time, in a little village, there was a poor man named Joseph, who led a decent and honest life, but who was not very lucky. Even though Joseph woke at sunrise and went to bed late at night, when it was too dark even for cats to see anymore, he had almost no money and frequently went hungry. Despite his misfortunes, he continued working hard, and he made sure that he and his wife always had nice food on the table on Shabbat.

Even though their diet consisted of kasha and vegetables, and sometimes chicken and eggs, they often had to sustain themselves only on bread, and the potatoes they grew themselves in the tiny yard by their rickety house. Right next to their yard there was a huge and luscious garden, belonging to their rich neighbor, who was so greedy, he once tried to move the fence separating their gardens, just to get a few more inches of land. This neighbor didn't need to plant any tomatoes or potatoes to survive; he could easily purchase them at the market. Yet, he was always accusing Joseph of stealing his land.

The rich neighbor's wife was so nasty, that when she peeled potatoes or cleaned fish, she threw the potato peels and fish scales over the fence into the Joseph's tiny garden. The next morning, Joseph would wake up and go to water his tomatoes, and they would be covered with fish scales. He would get upset, but what could he do? His affluent neighbors were such bad people, nobody could convince them to behave differently, so Joseph decided not to waste his time arguing with this arrogant couple. Instead, he consoled himself by feeling the warm sun, smelling the freshly cut grass, drinking warm milk and talking to his modest and good-natured wife.

Meanwhile, the rich neighbor was never happy, despite his wealth. He did everything possible to get richer, but instead of making him happier, his prosperity only made him even greedier. Every week, and before making any business deal, he went to a fortune teller for advice. He'd ask questions like:

"Will I make a big profit if I buy fabric at the market in the city of N. and then go to the far away city of L. and sell it there at much higher price?" or, "Will I make a profit if I buy-up all the hay in the area, so people can't feed their starving horses, and then sell it to them at a much higher price?" or, "Will I make a profit if I dig a well on my property and charge people who want to get their water from it, instead of going to the well at the very edge of town?"

And the fortune teller would answer "yes" or "no", and the rich neighbor would act accordingly and reap a fine profit.

One day, when he went to the fortune teller to hear his next prediction, the fortune teller didn't want to tell him anything and only remained mysteriously silent. But when Joseph's rich neighbor insisted, the fortune teller announced:

– I see somebody quite poor but decent by nature... do you know anybody who fits this description?

– I have a neighbor who is quite poor, – the rich man replied, – but I don't think he is so decent by nature... I think he and his wife are obnoxious, and I wish they would move away.

– Well, the man I see is hard-working, but poor, because he hasn't had much luck in his life... – continued the fortune teller. – I also see that this man lives very close to you – it's somebody you see every day. Does this sound like your neighbor?

– Maybe, – answered Joseph's rich neighbor hesitantly. – But I don't think his poverty has anything to do with the luck; Joseph and his wife are just fools! Can you make them disappear, so I never have to see them again?

– I can't make things happen, – retorted the fortune teller, – I only can predict. And I can warn you that your possessions will soon become this man's possessions.

– What?! – shouted the rich neighbor. – Are you kidding me, you useless fool?! Are you telling me, and in such a casual manner, no less, that this idiot, Joseph, and his stupid wife are going to get my luscious garden and perhaps even my mansion?! This is not a prediction – it's a delusion, and I'm not paying you for your mad ravings! I simply refuse to believe you, you demented old fool!

And indeed, Joseph's rich neighbor rushed out of the fortune teller's house, without paying her. He was so mad, he swore he would never visit that fortune teller again, that he'd find one who would always have something pleasant to say, and not make up stories.

Yet, as time went by, the well-off neighbor started worrying that the fortune teller had told the truth. "And what if this old fool really saw something bad happening to my home and to all my possessions?" He thought to himself. "What if he *wasn't* lying just to upset me? What if Joseph really *is* meant to get all my wealth? I must prevent this from occurring at all costs! Now that I know my destiny, I will try to change it!"

And to make sure that Joseph did not get his estate, the rich neighbor sold it.

One morning, Joseph woke up and went to check on his tomatoes. They were pristinely clean and had no fish scales on their leaves. Joseph started looking around for a stray cat that might have licked them off during the night. But there was no cat around, so Joseph thought that maybe his rich neighbor and his wife had changed and stopped doing nasty things like throwing garbage into his garden. Joseph looked over the fence, but instead of the rich neighbor and his wife, he saw another family moving in and found out that his rich neighbor had quickly sold his estate to this new family. Joseph was puzzled, but he decided it was for the better.

Meanwhile, the rich neighbor used the proceeds from selling his estate to buy a huge diamond that his wife sewed into his turban. They moved as far away as possible from the impoverished Joseph, spent what money was left on two tickets aboard a ship, and embarked on a leisurely journey around the world.

Just as this journey began, the rich neighbor stood on the deck smoking his cigar and thinking how cleverly he'd managed to fool his destiny. He couldn't have cared less about the beautiful dolphins and birds following the ship, or the warm rays of the sun. Enveloped in his own greed, he only saw and thought about material wealth.

Indeed, he was so focused on money, that when the sun hid behind the clouds and the winds suddenly picked up, he didn't even notice. "I fooled everybody," he was saying to his wife, "I didn't pay the fortune teller who warned me, yet I took note of his prediction and moved away from Joseph, so he would never get my possessions! How can he reach my turban now?! All my possessions are hidden here, right on my head!" Laughing, he pointed to his turban, where his wife had sewn the huge diamond.

And that very second, a gust of wind blew the turban off his head and overboard, into the water below. The rich neighbor wanted to jump into the ocean to save it, but luckily he remembered that he didn't know how to swim. His wife couldn't swim, either, so they both started shouting and begging the captain to stop the ship and fish out the turban. But the captain just laughed and said he couldn't do it, just for the sake of a useless piece of headgear. He didn't know the turban had a huge diamond in it!

– And what happened next? – exclaimed Naftali. – This is such a great story. We are on a ship right now, and you are telling us a story about a ship! I can't wait to find out how Joseph could inherit all the possessions of his well-to-do neighbor. Was he on the same ship, and did he dive into the ocean to retrieve the turban?

– No, things are more complex than you think! – Naftali's father laughed. – Remember I told you that Joseph was flat broke yet he tried to create happiness for himself and for his wife? He also was very religious and he dutifully followed the Shabbat rules... To make his Shabbat even better, he tried to purchase seafood before every Friday, and always thanked God that he still had food on his table, and that he and his wife were still in good health, because he believed that as hard as life seemed, things could always be worse.

And on Thursday Joseph went to the fish market and bought a fish – the very same fish that had plucked the diamond from the turban after it had fallen into the sea.

And when Joseph's wife cut it open to stuff it with carrots and onions from their tiny garden, she saw the huge shining stone and called Joseph. And Joseph was astonished at his unexpected luck: out of the blue, he was as rich as his rich neighbor had been! But despite being one of the wealthiest men in the village and even in the whole area, he stayed humble. The next day, on Shabbat, and on the following Shabbat, and on the Shabbat that followed that Shabbat, he still bowed his head in prayer and thanked God for letting him enjoy fish and stay healthy.

– Just as the fortune teller predicted, Joseph ended up with his rich neighbor's possessions, – concluded Naftali's father. – Thus, this story proves that there is such a thing as destiny, and that whatever happens, happens, and that if we are meant to reach Argentina safely and have a prosperous life there, then we surely will!

35

On the day the passengers were informed that the ship was approaching land, and they would finally disembark, after their grueling voyage to Argentina, Naftali was still weak, but happy. He couldn't wait to run on green grass and feel the earth under his feet, again, instead of the unstable and unpredictable ocean. He had already finished packing his sack with the *Don Quixote* book and his diary, when he heard a commotion on the deck and ran up to look. Since the vessel had already reached the shore, there was a long line of passengers eager to get off and leave the inconveniences of travel and their sea sickness behind. Tired of being confined in their cramped quarters, some passengers, red-eyed and disheveled, were shoving each other, trying to descend the ladder as soon as possible.

– Let the women and children disembark first! – a shrill voice shouted.

– That's only if the ship is sinking, and we're still afloat! – a raspy voice shouted back. Naftali, who was at the end of the line up, saw the pretty young woman who had alerted his parents when he had fallen ill and lost consciousness. She was descending the ladder with her antique table, which she carried on her head, along with some sacks; there were two more sacks on her shoulders. The crowd behind her was very impatient: one older couple was following so closely behind, they were stepping on her heels, so that she turned around a couple of times and said something to them. Finally, she disembarked, put the antique table down and sat on it. That very second, somebody shouted:

– Everybody go back! Go back! We are going to another port!

– What are they saying? – Naftali's mother asked him. – I thought we had finally arrived, after so many days on this filthy ship! Isn't this Argentina?

She looked somewhat confused – without her home, her kitchen and her female friends, she had lost her composure. On the other hand, Naftali's father seemed energetic and well-organized.

– Don't worry! – he said. – We'll be perfectly fine!

– Everyone come back! Come back! – shouted the captain, and Naftali saw the pretty young woman get up off her table and start looking around. There were locals congregating not far from her, but despite their curiosity about the newcomers, they kept their distance.

The young woman approached one of the local men, who was wearing wide pants and a big hat, and asked him something. Apparently, he didn't understand and tried pushing the table away from him. The young woman took something out of her pocket and showed it to him. The man stopped pushing the table away and hesitated; Naftali realized she was showing him Russian banknotes. The man reached toward her and tried to grab the banknotes, but the woman put them back into her pocket and again tried to hand the antique table to him, gesticulating. By now, the others passengers, grumpy and disappointed, were back on board, and the young woman was the only one remaining on the shore.

In terror, Naftali saw one of the sailors preparing to pull up the ladder. He cried out:

– Come here, come here! We are leaving! Please come! – But the woman didn't heed him. She was still gesticulating and pushing the table toward the local man in the large hat, without noticing that the ship was about to leave.

Naftali dropped his sacks and ran down the ladder. The passengers on board the ship gasped. As he approached the young woman, he heard her begging the local man in Yiddish:

– This is an expensive table, but I'll sell it to you for almost nothing... You give me money, and I'll give you this precious piece of furniture.

Naftali thought he could translate this for her into Spanish, but just then he noticed his father rapidly descending the ladder and waving at him fiercely.

– The ship is leaving! Please, forget about the table! – Naftali pleaded, tugging the woman by the sleeve.

– Oh my God! – shouted the woman. – We'd better hurry!

She picked up the table and her belongings, but stumbled on the wooden ladder and dropped one of her sacks into the water.

– My documents! – she cried out in desperation. – I can't go without my documents! Naftali looked down and saw the little sack with her documents slowly sinking to the bottom. The water was only about waist-deep here, but there wasn't enough time to fish out her sack.

– We have to go! The ship is leaving! We're going to a different port! – Naftali insisted, still tugging on the woman's sleeve.

– I can't go without my documents! – she pleaded. – And my expensive jewelry is there too. What will I sell when I have nothing to eat?

She looked around, spotted a bush and broke off one

of the branches to fish out the sack, without getting her dress wet. Naftali saw his father at the other end of the ladder waving at him, and he tried to grab the antique table, to help the woman climb the stairs, but she stopped him:

– I'm staying here... I don't care... I'll get my sack and make my way here, alone... Naftali noticed that the local man was still standing close by, watching them with natural curiosity. He seemed to want to start a conversation with the young woman, but he wasn't sure if she would understand him.

Naftali realized he couldn't convince her and left her alone. He said goodbye, and, climbing back up the ladder, he saw the woman hand the branch to this man, who eagerly started trying to fish the sack out of the water for her. Apparently, the language barrier was no longer a problem for them. Standing next to the water together, they seemed to be discussing something, though Naftali had no idea how the local man could understand Yiddish.

As soon as Naftali was back on deck, the sailor pulled up the ladder, and almost instantaneously the ship left the shore and headed back out to sea. For a while, amused passengers could still see the abandoned antique table on the shore and the pretty young woman in a hat decorated with bird feathers. She had raised her skirt with both hands and was attempting to step into the water, while the local man in the wide pants tried stopping her. Pulling her back to the shore, he started undressing, apparently eager to dive into the waters himself. Soon, the woman, the man and the antique table grew smaller and smaller, then disappeared completely.

Once again they were on the open waters.

36

The problem was, the hotel that was to accommodate them was not ready yet, and they were advised by the local authorities to sail to another small city, where other arrangements would be made.

– Other arrangements? – asked Naftali's mother skeptically. – I hope we are not going to sleep on the floor!

– As long as there is a roof over my head, I'm happy, – retorted Naftali's father optimistically, even though he was looking less and less optimistic, every time there was new "news." Preoccupied with their journey's difficulties, he became less strict with Naftali. Now it was Naftali's mother who became more agitated and often showed displeasure. Their move to Argentina was definitely taking a toll on everybody.

– But I'm so tired, – Naftali exclaimed. – I can't stay on this ship any longer. After all this time I've made no friends, and even the young woman who saved me is gone. My stomach hurts, and I can't stand any more of this dirty soup with cabbage leaves – I can't even stand how my coat smells... I'm fed up!

– So am I, – said Naftali's mother. – And I'm not even sure this move to Argentina was a good idea... Maybe if we had stayed in Russia, the Cossacks wouldn't have touched us! After all, some people were able to survive the pogroms. To be honest, I'm even starting to miss our home, after so many days on this ship...

– Let me share a snippet of wisdom with you, – Naftali's father chimed in, – that will raise you spirits...

– I've had enough of your snippets of wisdom! – Naftali's mother snapped, turning away. She covered her face with her hands as she always did when she was about to cry. Naftali felt sorry for her and rushed over to give her a hug. Meanwhile, Naftali's father continued:

– How many pockets have you got? – he asked Naftali.

– Two, in my pants, – a puzzled Naftali replied.

– Imagine that your pockets are filled with words! – Naftali's father exclaimed. He looked energized, as though the anecdote renewed his will to live and explore. Naftali kissed his mother on the cheek, saw that she was not going to cry anymore, and looked at his father attentively. His mother didn't look directly at them, but she was listening too.

– Now, the words in each pocket are different. For example, the words in your left pocket say, "You are the most precious, since you were created in the image of God." And those in your right pocket say, "You are only ashes, you are one of many." When you are feeling bad, you should reach into your left pocket and remember that there are miracles awaiting us and that we are His creation... And when you feel on top of the world, you should stay humble and reach into your right pocket, to remind yourself that you are just ashes and dust...

– I don't know about the ashes, but I can tell you, I'm completely covered in dust! – exclaimed Naftali's mother sardonically. – I don't remember the last time I washed properly.

– Which pocket should we reach into now? – Naftali asked.

– Neither you, nor your mother, are very happy right now, and you're probably discouraged after such a grueling journey. But just remember that there will be a ray of hope, and that He is looking down upon us, and that should lift you up! – Naftali's father concluded, trying to sound optimistic. But he looked quite sad, and Naftali knew that despite his dad's best efforts to cheer them up, he was completely exhausted.

Another day passed, before it was announced that they had reached their new destination. This time, there was no shoving among the passengers to descend the ladder first, in case this was another false alarm and they had to go back. And even after they'd disembarked, their journey continued: all the passengers had to present their papers, after which they were taken, in a procession of carriages, to a quite deserted rural area next to a dilapidated train station.

Upon seeing the train cars lined up on the tracks, Naftali exclaimed:

– Do we have to board a train now? I thought we had already reached our destination!

– There must be some mistake, – his father replied. He looked confused, as did others in their group. They were standing in the middle of an empty field, with their sacks and their dreams, with their kids and new plans, not knowing what to expect but still hoping for the best for themselves and for their offspring. Several men approached the official, who had met the ship and accompanied them to this train station, and started gesticulating: apparently, they didn't like the area they'd been brought to.

Naftali looked around at the barren steppe, with its dry, yellowed grass and nothing in sight besides the succession of old-looking train carriages on the rusty railway.

Suddenly he noticed that one of the tracks simply ended in the middle of nowhere, in whitish sand, and pointed it out to his father:

– Look! How can we continue if the railway lines are destroyed? – he asked.

– I guess this means we've arrived, – answered his father, even more confused. – But since this area is pretty far from the land we purchased, I'm not sure how we are going to reach it from here.

The official, having refused to speak to the men who were still gesticulating around him, addressed the larger group:

– This is where you are going to live. Choose the train car you like best, and start making yourself comfortable... This is your home!

– Are we going to go somewhere in these cars? – asked Naftali, not having understood what the official meant. – I see that the railway is broken...

– This is not a train, – smiled the official. – It just looks like one. You can imagine you are traveling in it, of course. When I was a boy of your age, I imagined all kind of things... In your mind, you can go anywhere you want on this train – to Brazil, to Africa, to the North Pole... But in reality these are just abandoned train cars that we've decided to let you live in for a while, until we find other accommodations for you.

– We own a large piece of land somewhere south of Buenos Aires! – exclaimed Naftali's father, proudly. – This means we won't be here for long. Very soon we'll go to our own land and start farming!

One of the men standing close to Naftali's father said bitterly:

– We thought we were going to our new home – not to another train station!

– This *is* your home! – repeated the official. – You were probably promised many things back in Russia, but this is all we can offer for now… Eventually, we'll move you to real houses, but they're not ready yet, so be happy that you have a roof over your head.

With these words, the official patted Naftali on the back, smiled at him broadly and quickly departed. After the long journey on the ship and the ride in the uncomfortable crowded carriages, the travelers were worn out. So, without too much arguing, they carried their luggage onto the train, lay down on the cold, stiff benches and, forgetting about supper, fell asleep.

37

The next day Naftali's mother stayed "home", unpacking suitcases and arranging their new place, while Naftali and his father decided to take a walk into the countryside. They filled a tin canteen with water, in case they got thirsty, made two walking sticks, and off they went.

They walked for a long time, observing the nature around them and commenting on how different the trees, grass, birds and even the sky looked here, compared to Russia. As they neared the forest, they spotted four boys who, as Naftali immediately realized, with his good memory for faces, had arrived with them on the ship. Absorbed in what they were doing, the boys paid no attention to them, so Naftali could watch them without the fear of being scorned.

The boys ranged in age from eight to thirteen, and they all wore long dark shorts and hats with visors. Naftali noticed a commotion and saw the boys throw their hats on the ground and start crawling around on all fours. It appeared they were trying to catch something on the ground with their hats.

Naftali approached them and noticed a large bird, sitting on a tree stump, squawking nervously. She would run toward the boys, as though trying to say something, then pull back, terrified, but the boys didn't seem to care – the eldest boy, his hair and eyebrows bleached by the sun, kept shooing her away. Naftali realized only then that was a little nestling, squeaking and shivering under each hat, and another nestling hiding under his mother's wing. Out of a total of five tiny birds, the boys had caught four.

– This is terrible! – Naftali's father exclaimed. – The Torah says that one shouldn't take nestlings away if their mother is present.

– What? Why? – asked Naftali.

– I'll tell you, – his father promised, – but first I must ask the boys to release the poor little creatures. You, boys! – he exclaimed, approaching the group. – Let those nestlings go! Can't you see you've upset their mother?

The boy with sun-bleached eyebrows looked over at Naftali's father, but didn't let go of his hat, which was jiggling around on the ground.

– Why are you trapping them? – Naftali's father asked. – They're too small and bony to eat, so why bother them? Let them go, you're breaking their mother's heart and they're of no use to you, – he pleaded, hoping to convince the boy.

But the boy just shrugged his skinny shoulders and grinned:

– They're ours. We caught them, and we'll do what we want with them.

– Well, if they won't listen to me, what can I do? – Naftali's father said, turning to Naftali. – The Torah teaches us that if we need to take an egg or a little bird from its nest for food, we must either move the mother elsewhere, wait until she goes off, or at least until she isn't looking. This is to prevent causing the mother unnecessary distress.

– Then maybe it's better not to take the nestlings at all, – Naftali surmised. – These boys are only taking them to play with, not because they are hungry...

–You're right, they shouldn't have taken the little creatures at all, – Naftali's father sighed. – Maybe they'll understand when they grow up...

On their way home, they walked in complete silence. Naftali's father seemed preoccupied with something, while Naftali wished they had said something more compelling to the boys, who ignored his father's advice. Unlike them, Naftali was sensitive to the power of words, because he never forgot what his father had told him that day about birds and their nestlings.

Several weeks later, misfortune struck the immigrant colony living in trains at the defunct railway station. One day, on his way home from a makeshift school organized by the officials, Naftali saw two horses pulling a cart. The boy with the sun-bleached eyebrows, who had refused to set the nestlings free that day, lay in the back, accompanied by a gaunt, mustachioed man in sandals and gaucho pants. He was the local doctor, a familiar figure in the colony, known for his eccentric clothing and constant joking. However, the doctor's face was uncharacteristically grim today. The boy looked very pale, his eyes were closed and his breathing was labored: his rib cage rose and fell, now rhythmically, now erratically. His restless body twitched.

– Will he be alright? – asked Naftali.

But the doctor only looked at him, without replying...

When Naftali came home, his father told him some sad news.

– Two children from the colony have died recently from a disease, and two others are sick. The doctor, odd as he is, visited every colonist here and warned us that this deadly disease is spread by birds, and that children can die, because they are weaker than adults. Be careful, Naftali, don't touch any birds...

– I just saw the boy from the forest, who wouldn't let those nestlings go, lying in the back of a cart! – Naftali exclaimed. – He must be one of the sick kids. Maybe God punished him with the disease because he ignored what the Torah says... He looked very pale, and the doctor was with him. When I asked about the boy, he ignored me!

– Maybe he didn't want to scare you with the truth... Are you talking about the rude little fellow who... – Naftali's father cut himself off. – We shouldn't speak ill of him now. We should just pray for his recovery... He may survive the disease, as he's older than the others.

Naftali saw the connection clearly: the Torah prohibited touching nestlings in front of their mother, and this boy broke the rule, so perhaps the Almighty punished him.

But the next day, he happened to see another boy who had also been in the forest that day, who was perfectly fine, with his rosy cheeks and swarthy complexion. He was holding a giant slingshot, taking aim at something.

– Do you remember me? – asked Naftali. – What are you doing?

– Don't you know what's going on? – asked the boy in his turn. – We have to kill these damn birds... Exterminate them from the face of the earth! Yakov got terribly sick and had to be taken to the hospital. They say the birds are spreading a disease. I'm going to kill them in retaliation. And nobody will get sick or die anymore, because there won't be any birds left!

– He was punished because he snatched nestlings

away from their mother in her presence, – said Naftali. – The Torah says it's prohibited.

– So I will get sick and maybe die too? – asked the boy. He put the slingshot into his pocket and picked up a stone. He started tossing it in the air and catching it, over and over. And then he added:

– I think I'll throw this stone at your head so you'll stop talking nonsense... I'm still alive and I'm not going to get sick! Whereas with your glasses and tiny fists – you're the one who looks sick!

Naftali realized he'd said something he shouldn't have, and stopped talking. The boy picked up another stone, took the slingshot out of his pocket and aimed it at Naftali. Naftali covered his face with both hands and stood there, frozen and shaken. The boy took a shot, but not at Naftali, and a big bird flew out of a nearby tree. The boy spit at Naftali's feet.

– What a coward you are! – he shouted, and walked away.

38

Several days later Naftali learned that the boy who wouldn't listen to Naftali's father had died. He'd seen a funeral procession and recognized, among the other kids, the boy with the slingshot, except he didn't have it with him this time; he was just walking slowly behind the horse-drawn carriage with his sisters and parents. The boy's face was very solemn and sad, and even though Naftali didn't see whom they were ready to bury, he guessed it was Yakov, the older boy with sun-bleached eyebrows.

Naftali was overcome with emotion. It didn't matter anymore that Yakov had ignored what Naftali's father had said to him, or that he had upset the defenseless mother bird and her weak-legged offspring. He remembered Yakov's longish, sun-tanned face, his narrow, steely blue eyes, and delicate chin vividly, and he couldn't believe that now the boy couldn't even open those eyes and see the world, let alone rise from his resting place and start talking or running.

Why did this happen? Was it indeed because Yakov had disobeyed the rules in the Torah? If that's why he'd died, then why was his friend with the slingshot still alive and well? Why did other children get sick and die? They didn't try to catch nestling, or even go anywhere near the forest...

It didn't seem to matter whether these kids had behaved badly or well, if they'd observed the rules or not — they'd died despite their exemplary, or naughty behavior. Naftali asked his father, who said:

– Maybe some of them were not perfect, but they

did not pass away because of a flaw in their character... The doctor said they died because certain birds in this area are spreading an illness. Therefore, in addition to observing the rule of the Torah, we need to establish *other* rules to help us survive in this train-car settlement: we must boil our water, wash our hands frequently, and avoid touching any birds. Then, once we've taken these precautions, we will pray to God, in the hope that He will protect us from illnesses and misfortune...

That night Naftali had the urge to write in his diary again, after many weeks of complete silence. On the ship, especially after his illness, he didn't feel the need to record his thoughts. But now, pondering the recent events, he was anxious to write something. Yet he didn't know where to start. There was such a jumble of words in his head, such as "gaucho", "pampas", "bolas", and "colonia", which described things that didn't really exist in Russia. And there were words like "work" and "death" and "illness" and "rules", that seemed to have a different meaning here... For instance, what was work, when you lived in a train? How could Naftali and his parents survive without facing death? How could they avoid illness? Was it enough to follow rules, like washing your hands three times a day with soap, or should they remember their prayers? There were so many words in his Naftali's head, but he didn't know how to arrange them on paper... He decided that if he wanted to become a writer, he should let them run free, because all of these words were present in life, and he couldn't choose which ones should be written down, or which ones should never be mentioned... And that all the words he had learned here, or become acutely aware of, could be gathered together in a book he would write, one day, about his experiences in this immigrant colony.

He remembered what his father had said about the two pockets full of different words and jotted down the following: "There are so many words around us. Some of them scare us and some of them lift up our mood. 'Mother' and 'father' are good words that remind me that I am loved. 'Pampas' and 'gauchos' are new words that compel me to explore. 'Death' and 'illness' are not too scary, since they are not very clear to me yet. Some words make me feel sad – for example, a 'sick child' or a 'lost puppy'. And some words point out the beautiful things surrounding us – a 'forest', 'water', 'green grass' and 'fresh air'.

My father said that the words in the left pocket remind us that we are a creation of God. When we are in bad spirits and things do not work out, we reach into this pocket. And when we are full of ourselves and think we are more special than others, we should slip our hands into the right pocket, which contains the words 'ashes and dust'. These words remind us that we are only human and therefore we make mistakes and that we should work even harder to achieve our goals. Reaching into the right pocket reminds us that we are just one of the billion people who inhabit this earth. And I think that a writer needs all these words to describe people's lives. We can't sort them out, because one day we are so high we feel like we are floating in the sky, and another day we slide down so low that we need somebody's help and consolation... And since I like all kinds of words, I think that I will indeed become a writer.

— 222 —

39

Just when Naftali was finally used to the idea that they would be living in the old abandoned train car permanently, his father announced:

– We own the land we bought, and now we only need to claim it. But remember that dozens of other people, besides the generous philanthropist who visited us back home, contributed money to the pool, so we have to be fair and divide the land evenly.

– I didn't know that moving to another country would mean moving every few months! – Naftali exclaimed. – Why can't we just stay here?

– Because we devised a better plan for ourselves, than the others did, – Naftali's father explained. – Here, the colonists association will always be watching over us. But there, on our own land, we'll be governing it ourselves, like kings!

– And where is our land? – Naftali's mother asked.

– I have all the information here! – announced Naftali's father, unfolding a piece of paper. – It says: "In between Rio Natales and Rio Turbio, there is a plot which was previously owned by Sylvio Gallegos and is now owned by a collective of Jewish farm laborers. Signed, Gospodin Rykov, and Lazar Evseevich Smushkin."

– Rio Natales? – Naftali's mother repeated. – Is it near a river? That would be nice: Naftali could swim there and I could wash clothes.

But Naftali raised his eyebrows:

– You may say we're not learning anything at our temporary school, but I think I heard of Rio Natales in one of my geography lessons. Isn't it a stream in Chile? – he asked.

– Wait, wait… – Naftali's father hesitated, with a worried look. – I don't remember seeing any river in the photograph we were shown. Do you, Naftali?

Naftali looked at the piece of paper. The words "between Rio Natales and Rio Turbio" were written very clearly and under them there was an official stamp. A hand-drawn map at the bottom of the page indicated two roads.

– This map shows that the land is between two main roads, – he said, – not between two rivers.

– Gospodin Rykov mentioned two big roads. He said they were built by the Argentinean government to attract more settlers to those lands. I thought that Rio Natales and Rio Turbio were the names of the roads.

– Even I know that 'rio' means river, – quipped Naftali's mother. – Did we buy an island?

– I'm confused myself, – admitted Naftali's father guiltily. – When we bought this land, we hardly knew any Spanish, so I assumed this address was correct. But now we must ask an official about the location.

The next day, after traveling on horseback for two and half hours straight, Naftali and his father arrived at the local land claims office, to ask about their land.

– Rio Natales and Rio Turbio? – repeated a fidgety, middle-aged clerk with a colorful necktie, who peered at them from behind his glasses. – There are no streets named after rivers in that area. The only roads there are 'Estrada Nopales' and 'Estrada Torinda.' You need to verify your address.

– How can I verify the address from here? – Naftali's

father asked, desperately. – There is an ocean separating Russia from Argentina. If I had wings, I'd fly there, grab the man who sold us the land by the lapels and shake him! Maybe then I'd get the truth out of him!

– Perhaps we can identify your land another way, – proposed the clerk, trying to be helpful. – Can you describe it?

– I saw it in a picture! – Naftali exclaimed. He couldn't bear seeing his father so helpless.

– And what exactly did you see? – asked the clerk and, with his long fidgety fingers, he checked his necktie, making sure both tails were aligned properly on his chest.

– It was a vast territory with weeds...

– That could be anywhere! – the clerk interrupted.

– There was also a white sheep staring right into the camera... The clerk laughed and checked his necktie again:

– We can't take a single step around here without bumping into a sheep! Was there anything distinctive in this picture?

Naftali thought for a moment and said:

– I think there was a gaucho, wearing bombachas and a wide-brimmed hat... Suddenly the clerk became very agitated.

– Please, don't talk to me about those ignorant gauchos! – he exclaimed. – Can't they go somewhere else and stop giving Argentineans a bad name, with their drinking and fighting?

– We are trying to live with them in peace, and to learn from them, – objected Naftali's father. – Some even call us *gauchos judéos* – Jewish gauchos!

– You'll never become a gaucho! – the clerk retorted, as though he knew this for a fact.

– We have to, – Naftali's father insisted, – otherwise, how will we survive on this land?

– Gauchos have no families, they roam the pampas freely, whereas you're talking about land that you own, – said the clerk, lowering his voice, and checking the buttons on his vest, now, making sure they were properly fastened. – Speaking of which, – he continued, – I have no idea where your land is located.

– Couldn't you look up the name of the previous owner, Silvio Gallegos? – Naftali's father suggested.

– Wait a minute, – said the clerk, suspiciously, – did you just say Silvio Gallegos? Naftali's father nodded.

– Oh my! – the clerk responded. Suddenly he unbuttoned his vest, picked up the piece of paper Naftali's father had given him and, to everyone's surprise, started fanning himself with it.

– What's the matter? – Naftali's father asked, growing impatient.

– What a coincidence this is, gentlemen, what an incredible coincidence – things like this only happen in novels! You won't believe what I have to tell you! You just won't believe it!

– What is it?! – Naftali's father asked, banging his fist on the table. – We're talking about everyone's savings, not to mention the money given to us by a great philanthropist!

– Unless you lower your voice, sir, I won't tell you anything, – the clerk snapped back, straightening the tails of his necktie again. Next he opened the drawer, took out a comb and started parting his hair down the middle with it.

Suddenly he threw down the comb and got up off his chair.

– But it's such a remarkable coincidence! – he exclaimed. – Wait 'till you hear what I have to tell you!

– As long as I can still claim ownership of the land, or recover the money... – Naftali's father started to say.

– I doubt you'll recover your money, – the clerk replied. Then plopped back into his chair, crossed his legs, and picked up a folder from his desk.

– Have you ever heard of a 'chicken machine'? – he asked out of the blue.

Naftali's father banged his fist on the table again. – Now, listen here, – he said, – my livelihood depends on this land, so you'd better start talking sense, before I lose my temper!

At this point a heavy silence blanketed the room. The clerk sat stroking his necktie for a minute, again, before finally opening the folder.

40

He cleared his throat and started reading from the folder, out loud, in Spanish:

"This is regarding a certain forty-two-year old Yizya Weissman, a native of Russia, who came to Argentina only three years ago from the city of Kiev and soon became known to the local police. Yizya is of medium height, with dark hair and no visible scars. His clothes are impeccably clean and well-pressed. He usually wears several gold rings on his fingers. If you see him in the street, arrest him or report his presence to the sheriff."

– I have never heard that name, – said Naftali's father, – and I don't think this Weissman's bad reputation should cast a shadow over me and my son.

– I have no doubt that you are honest people, – the clerk replied, – but listen! Not only did this Yizya swindle money from several newcomers to Argentina, but he also enraged a local chicken farmer, who shot him. But since the bullet went right through Yizya, he quickly recovered.

Naftali and his father listened, without even asking about what this Yizya had to do with their land, in case the clerk threatened to stop talking again.

– One day, – the clerk continued, – Yizya was relaxing on the steps of his house, looking across the street at the home of the local chicken farmer. The farmer was looking for a wife, and all he cared about, was finding one who wouldn't mind being surrounded by chirping creatures all day long. He didn't even care if she loved him, so long as she loved his chicks! The neighbors laughed at him behind his back, except on weekends, because that was when he put on a crisp white shirt, and invited a different young lady and prospective wife, to a wonderful brunch of *asado* and other delights on his patio.

His poorer neighbors would come by his patio to say "hi", hoping for an invitation to try one of the dishes, but the farmer would ignore them. Instead, he'd show his newest female friend his beloved chickens, for whom he was always making up names. There was Chicken Alfredo, and Chicken Gustavo, and even Chicken Karl Maria, in honor of one German immigrant, with whom the chicken farmer played poker.

On this particular day, the farmer was introducing the lady to Chicken Gustavo, when Yizya Weismann showed up at the farmer's fence, smoking a cigar. Assuming this was just another beggar attracted by the smell of *asado*, despite his polished appearance, the farmer ignored Yizya, and so did the young lady: she was too interested in the chickens, since her parents were chicken farmers, too. Indeed, it seemed the farmer had finally found the right girl for himself! She sat holding Chicken Gustavo and stroking him, as the farmer served her a plate of *asado*, while lovingly describing Chicken Gustavo's temperament, as though it were his own son.

Out of the blue, Yizya blurted out:

"I know how to make your chicken farm even more prosperous than it is!" Instantly, both the young woman and the farmer stopped talking, and even Chicken Gustavo stopped chirping, waiting for Yizya say more about chickens and farms.

Yizya could tell he had their undivided attention and that he had to put his best foot forward right now, or never.

"I have a machine that will collect and box your eggs," he said, as though in passing. But his casual comment made quite an impression.

Chicken Gustavo suddenly slipped out of the woman's hands and fell onto the ground, squawking, while the chicken farmer stood up abruptly, dropping a piece of *asado*.

"I've heard of it," he said, "bring it tomorrow and I'll pay you what it's worth." Yizya was very surprised that the farmer had heard of the machine to collect and box eggs, because he'd only thought of the invention that morning: how could he have heard of something that didn't even exist yet? It was a mystery, but whatever the case, Yizya said the machine was still in Russia, that he had to go fetch it, and he'd back with it in three months' time.

– Three months later, – the clerk continued, – Yizya returned, pushing a cart, on which there stood a weird contraption on wheels, with a long arm that had a hoe attached to the end. Yizya explained how to use the machine: "First, you put the machine on the ground next to the chickens. Then you crank the engine by turning this handle. The machine will move forward, locate the eggs, pick them up and place them into the attached bucket, and then load them into these boxes." Yizya then opened up the top of the machine, and revealed a stack of empty boxes ready to house fresh eggs.

"I want to try it out first," said the farmer, "and see whether it really does everything you claim. I heard about this machine a long time ago, because I keep on top of all the news in our field, but I want to see if your machine is as fast as the others."

But Yizya objected: "If you try it out and then don't want to buy it from me, the machine won't be new anymore, so nobody else will want to buy it. Plus, if you use this machine without paying me first, it will have picked up and boxed your eggs for free, and that wouldn't be fair to me. Please pay me first, and then you can test it as much as you want."

So the chicken farmer paid for the machine, and Yizya left. The farmer rushed inside the house to show the machine to the same young lady as before, who was now his wife.

Together they cranked the engine, and after jumping off the floor, twice, the machine advanced loudly toward the chickens, who were resting on their nests. The farmer and his wife clapped joyfully, imagining how much faster they'd now be able to collect their eggs, while the machine moved from nest to nest, collecting eggs and scaring the chickens.

"But when will it finally start boxing the eggs?" The chicken farmer wondered, after some time.

But his wife didn't know either: she was just trying not to get run over by the machine.

Suddenly the machine fell over on its side, and the couple noticed a trail of broken eggs behind it. As it happened, in all the excitement over the invention, they hadn't realized the machine was simply crushing the eggs under its wheels.

The chicken coop was a disaster. The machine had run over some chickens, who were now gasping their last breath; the ground was covered in egg shells; not one egg had been boxed. Thus, the chicken farmer and his wife realized they had allowed themselves to be fooled.

The clerk paused, trying to gauge whether Naftali and his father were impressed.

– And what does this have to do with us? – Naftali's father asked.

There clerk looked concerned. Hesitating to reply, he stroked the ends of his necktie a few times, before he continued:

– Because of his other criminal exploits, Yizya hid from the police by going under fake names. One of them was "Gallegos", the last name of the man, who supposedly owned the land that you purchased. I'm sorry to say, you have been deceived.

In time all these facts proved to be true. Naftali's father was so shaken by the experience that he never mentioned this land again.

41

Just when Naftali and his parents had gotten used to the stiff cots and confined space of the train cars once again and even learned to call them "home", the immigrants were moved somewhere else. The new place looked very similar to their previous settlement: they were surrounded by dry grass and unkempt weeds, the only difference being the freshly built, tiny structures made of clay they would be living in.

The day after they moved, the same official as before showed up and asked them to join him in a larger adobe structure, which for now served as a communal building. Once everyone had congregated, the official energetically started:

– Look around yourselves! For now, all these fields are bare, but this is because they've been waiting for you! They've been waiting for strong hands and clear minds to come to Argentina and succeed and become prosperous! Imagine a proper school here, with smart and obedient kids, a dairy farm with a separate store, where you will sell cheese and butter, a communal bath and a cattle-breeding business – with your persistence and hard work, this will all soon be possible!

Naftali looked around and saw a glimmer of hope on the normally sad, gloomy faces of the settlers. A small wrinkled man in broken glasses exclaimed:

– I was a tailor in Russia, and I lost my eyesight from sewing clothes for the arrogant rich, but I won't mind milking cows now! And milk will improve my health, and my wife's too!

Another woman in a dull-colored kerchief seconded him:

— In Russia, I was just à homemaker, but now I'm eager to help my husband and sons breed cattle, I only need to know where to start. I hope somebody will train us to do things "the Argentinean way!"

Still another, younger man, in a torn shirt, asked:

— When do we start? We've done nothing for so long in the train, that we're hungry for work!

The official hesitated for a second and said:

— If you are ambitious, you'll want to get a large farm, where you will grow wheat, alfalfa, and barley, and to acquire this farm, you will have to pay for it. If you want cattle, to start your breeding, you'll have to purchase them, too. Don't be stingy with the savings you brought from Russia – because if you invest them into this fertile Argentinean land, you will become well-off very soon!

The hopefulness on everyone's faces disappeared instantly, giving way to worry. Two men spit on the floor and left, while others began angrily gesticulating:

— We *have* no money! – they objected. – We've already spent everything to buy food when we lived in the train, because what you gave us wasn't enough for our children. They're so thin, one gust of the Argentinean wind could blow them away. Moreover, we must repay the cost of our fare from Russia to Argentina. After paying off the debts, we'll have nothing left!

— Quiet! Quiet! – said the official, holding his briefcase up against his big belly, as though for protection. – You should consider yourselves lucky, because we understand how difficult it is for you to come here and start a new life. So we'll give you something for free!

The room fell silent, and the faint glimmer of hope returned.

— What is it that you will give us for free? — the young man in the torn shirt asked, skeptically.

— We will give you free tools, to work your land with, and, as a start, we'll give the head of each household a patch of land, so you can grow vegetables to feed yourselves, and become independent. You will also be able to sell these vegetables at the market. Now, stand in line and I'll assign a plot to each of the heads of the households!

And the eligible men from the audience lined up, so as not to miss their chance to get whatever they could.

Soon after the land giveaway, Naftali's parents began walking to their plot daily and tending their garden, where they had planted corn, potatoes, and wheat. They'd wake up early and leave before sunrise, to reach the plot as soon as possible, since it was at least a half-hour walk away, along the dusty, stone-covered road. Naftali would go to his occasional lessons in school, which was often closed, because the only teacher was frequently ill, and afterwards he'd make a lunch of tomato or cucumber sandwiches and take it to his parents.

Today, as soon as his mother saw him, she complained:

— I have no idea why we came here! We barely have enough grain to feed ourselves, never mind giving to the widows and the elderly as a mitzvah!

As usual, Naftali didn't know how to respond to his mother's complaints. Since their arrival in Argentina, his parents seemed to be engaged in a never-ending argument, during which his mother would blame his father for bringing her to this "bare and infertile land". On the one hand, Naftali liked this new country and was excited by his new surroundings, and eager to make new friends. On the other hand, he was homesick: he felt he wasn't learning anything in school, he missed their old home in Russia and realized that living in a rural area without any books, or anything, really, besides sand and grain fields, didn't exactly suit his character. He longed for the Shabbat gatherings they had back home, when everyone discussed the Torah, and he was about ready to write a letter to 'Don Quixote' (who lived in France with his hunting dogs, servants, and the beautiful Dulcinea) and suggest he build a library and a proper school in the colony.

– What about the mitzvah? – inquired Naftali.

– Yes, – his father said, – the Bible instructs us to leave some grain in the field, for the widows and the poor to gather... Remember the book of Ruth, Naftali? Well, she harvested whatever the plot owners left behind, for desperate widows like herself. It's true that at this time we can't leave anything to the destitute, because we've become poor ourselves, but there are other things you can do for your mitzvah!

– Can't we just go back home and forget about this barren land?! – Naftali's mother exclaimed. She plopped down on the grass and covered her face with her hands, as though ready to cry.

– You are tired, Raya, take a rest! – commented Naftali's father quietly. – We have to be strong for our son.

Then he turned to Naftali again:

– Since your mom bought up the mitzvah, I suggest the following to you: share the lunch with us and go home. And on the way, just look around and see if anybody needs your help!

Naftali ate half a sandwich and then returned home, following his father's advice.

As he approached their settlement, with its many tiny clay huts, he noticed one hut that had never attracted his attention before. Now, since he was on a mission, his eyes were open and his mind was focused on every little detail. Like most of the huts in the settlement, this one was newly built, but it already looked somewhat tired and tattered. The cheerful yellow paint on the outside was already chipped in some places, as though someone had been throwing stones against the outer walls, and the front door was almost falling off its hinges. The area around the hut was unkempt, too.

As Naftali approached the entrance, something hit him on the forehead, then fell onto the ground with a metallic sound: he'd stepped on a rake. As he stood rubbing his throbbing head, upset that his desire to be helpful had almost turned into a disaster, a strange man ran out of the house to see what had happened.

Before Naftali could even take a closer look at him, the man tripped over the rake and fell down. When the man stood back up, grinning sheepishly from embarrassment, Naftali decided that he looked like a peculiar cross between a Jew and an Argentinean cowboy. Like most of the Russian Jews in the colony, he was wearing a long black coat, a tall black hat and a taleth. But he also wore a pair of bombachas, the wide pants favored by gauchos, a cowhide Argentinian belt, and a pair of the soft, leather boots the gauchos wore to ride horses, even though Naftali suspected that if this man jumped onto a horse, the animal would buck and throw him off immediately.

– Are you ok, young man? – asked the man meekly. Naftali nodded and asked him in response:

– And you? Did you hurt yourself?

– Never mind! – the meek man answered, – I'm always stepping on that rake. Since I settled here, it's probably happened at least a hundred times. I'm so used to it that I'm surprised when a day goes by and I haven't tripped over it. Thank you for reminding me that I should keep it somewhere else, so it won't be in the way. I'll do it right now!

The man bent down, picked up the rake, and then he walked around the hut with it, muttering:

– But where should I put it? Let me think... Maybe right under the window? Or next to the shed? Or maybe in the hallway inside my house? No, I could trip over it there...

With these words the man took the rake inside the house anyway, and a second later Naftali heard a thud and a crash: the man had stepped on the rake again, in the hallway.

– Just as I thought! It doesn't belong in here! – the meek man yelled out. – I'll just put it outside, somewhere nice and safe.

When he came out of the hut, he invited Naftali to have some tea, and Naftali readily accepted. And, putting the rake right back where it had been just minutes before, the meek man welcomed Naftali into his hut.

42

The minute Naftali entered the man's kitchen, where there were books, newspapers and sheets of paper strewn everywhere, among the pots, dishes and cutlery, he remembered the mitzvah he was supposed to do.

– Can I help you somehow? – he asked the meek man. – I can put your papers aside so that we don't spill mate on them.

– No, no, don't even think about it! – the man exclaimed. – I'm a poet, I don't care about my disorganized kitchen; all I care about is words! Words need to be in the proper order, not useless utensils!

– But how do you put words in the proper order? – asked Naftali, genuinely interested.

– All I have to do is to tell a fluid story, where all the characters are in place and the action unfolds step by step, so that my readers or listeners can follow it. Let me tell you the story... Oh! I forgot about the tea! – the poet exclaimed and he grabbed the teapot.

Suddenly Naftali heard a crashing sound. Turning his head, he saw the poet standing there, startled, holding only the handle, while the teapot itself lay broken on the floor. Apparently the handle had come off in his hand as he prepared the mate.

– Too bad! – he said. – It must be a sign that instead of mate, I should offer you something to eat.

But when the man opened the wooden bread box and brought out the loaf of bread, he got another surprise:

– My God! – he said. – It's moldy again! Why, I just bought it yesterday from the baker next door! Oh wait...

That was last week… This week I almost forgot to eat, because I was composing a new poem… Sorry, young man! How about listening to a story instead? The real artist's meal is his creation!

Naftali agreed enthusiastically, and the poet addressed him not as a lone boy sitting before him, but as a large audience:

– Ladies and Gentlemen! *Damy i gospoda!* – he exclaimed. – Before you stands the famous poet and writer Favel Bavilsky, who will tell you a story of glory, excerpted from Jewish history!

Having introduced himself, Bavilsky bowed to his imaginary audience and began:

– Many, many centuries ago, – he said, – there were Jews with so much dignity in their blood, they revolted against the improprieties they'd seen… They lived in the Roman *guberniya* of Judea, under the governorship of a certain Gessius Florus. He was chosen to govern that *guberniya* by the Roman tsar, and he was a real tyrant.

One day, while the Jews prayed in the synagogue for prosperity and happiness for themselves and their children, they noticed a strange odor coming from outside. Assuming that it was a fire, they looked at each other and sniffed the air, trying to understand what was burning.

The synagogue's walls were intact, and no one's clothes were on fire, yet, now, in addition to the strange odor, there was also smoke coming in from outside. Alarmed, one of the worshippers ran out, and saw something before his eyes that was much worse than fire by arson. What he saw made him sick to his stomach, and he had to sit down on the ground immediately, because if he didn't, he would faint – not because the smell was so bad, but because what he saw before him was improper, disgusting, and unacceptable! – Favel Bavilsky exclaimed, shrilly, even standing up off his chair and shaking his fist in the air.

Then he paused dramatically and lowered his voice, so that Naftali had to lean toward him to hear what he was saying:

– Sitting on the ground, – he continued, – the man closed his eyes and opened them again, hoping it was all a dream. But alas, there, before him, in an earthenware vessel, he saw the remains of several large birds, with brightly colored feathers. Just hours before, they'd been chirping away, and pecking here and there with their strong beaks. Whereas now, the birds were lifeless. Their feathers were strewn all over the earthen container and their heads...

Favel covered his face, as though to banish the images, before exclaiming again:

– Ladies and Gentlemen, not only had these birds been beheaded, drained of their blood, and gutted, their intestines and organs had been burnt in the very doorway of the synagogue, making it unclean! This was one of the worst possible situations these praying Jews could encounter!

And what do you think these God-abiding Jews did? They rebelled against the unclean pagan ritual performed at the entrance to their place of worship! They sent their delegation to Gessius Florus, informing him of these unclean actions by some local Greeks to antagonize them. Knowing that, as a Roman, Florus didn't care much about their traditions, the Jews strengthened their argument with a purse full of gold coins. When they went to him they held the purse up to his ear and shook it, making sure he understood their point! And they asked him to prohibit these pagan rituals at the entrance of their synagogue.

Unfortunately, Florus only heard the coins. He took the purse and hid it away in his treasure chest, and let the Jews' request go in one ear and out the other. And he ordered his troops to raid the markets in Jerusalem and catch and kill all the Jews who were there. As it happened, there was an old, graying rabbi, buying tomatoes at the market, who suddenly found himself surrounded by crying women and children, trying to escape the horse-riding Romans, on one side, and on the other by Jewish rebels, trying to protect their families, by throwing their bolas at the Roman's horses legs, entangling them, so the horses would stumble and fall.

– Bolas? – someone asked. Naftali was so immersed in the story, he didn't notice the two boys, roughly his age, who'd come into Favel's kitchen to hear his story.

– They're those metal things the gauchos use to catch ostriches and guanacos, – the other boy said. – But did the Jews have bolas, too?

– What did you say? – Favel asked the boy. Apparently, the storyteller was so involved in the events of the past, it took him a minute to return to the present and realize he wasn't in ancient Judea, but in a contemporary Argentinean village.

– Bolas... Did the Jews have bolas so long ago?

– Who cares! – Favel shouted, with irritation. – Of course they didn't! But how else could you visualize these strong Jewish fighters?! Just imagine them as muscular, horse-riding gauchos, swinging bolas over their heads, because that's what they were like! And they fought like lions to protect their families and their dignity! Now, let me continue, before I lose my train of thought...

Favel collected himself for a moment, then carried on:

— So, surrounded by helpless women and children, Roman legionnaires and rebellious Jews, the old rabbi started looking for a place to hide. But what to do with the four tomatoes he'd bought? There was only room for two in his pockets! So, instead of diving under a counter to save himself from the chaos at the market, he was worried about saving his tomatoes, when suddenly a shot rang out: one of the Cossacks had taken a gun and fired it into the crowd!

And the rabbi saw something red on his pants! At first he thought that it was tomato juice. But when he felt the sharp, burning pain in his leg, he realized that the Cossack's bullet had entered his left calf!

— Cossack?! — asked the first boy in disbelief. — A Cossack in the Roman legion at the Jerusalem market? And with a gun?

Favel was angered by this latest interruption:

— Why did you come here? To question my story? — he asked. — Didn't I tell you to 'visualize' these events? Well, if you have never seen Roman soldiers, you cannot even imagine how they look. But since you've seen and maybe even been harassed by Cossacks in Russia, you can imagine that these Roman soldiers were as vicious as our Cossacks!

— And they had guns with bullets? — the second boy, skeptically.

— Just get out of here! — Favel shouted in response. —

Why are you here at all? I didn't ask you to come! I'm telling my story to this quiet, smart gentleman, who hasn't interrupted me even once! Go! Go!

– But we brought you mate, – said the first boy, grinning, – maybe you should drink it while it's still warm.

And the second boy said:

– His parents asked him to bring you some mate, and mine parents asked me to take you some bread and cheese, so you don't go hungry...

– What fine young gentlemen! – Favel said to Naftali, suddenly changing his tune. – I don't even have to have bread in my home! These kind people take such good care of me... But *I* only care about *words*, and not food, so the biggest mitzvah you can do for me is just to listen to what I'm saying.

Favel looked at the boys very sternly, took their offerings, bit off a piece of bread, quickly drank up the whole teapot full of mate, and continued:

– The rabbi looked down at his leg. It hurt immensely. He saw another man beside him, who also had the red liquid on his pants, and seconds later, the rabbi lost consciousness... When he opened his eyes again, it was already evening: several hours had passed since he'd been shot. He was lying in a shed, with a group of people around him. There was another man lying beside him. The rabbi recognized him as the man he'd seen at the market, and finally understood that these people had saved him from the Cossacks – er, the Roman soldiers – by carrying him into this shed and away from the turmoil.

"We are waiting for the doctor to come and remove the bullet from your leg," said one of the people. "He will also attend to this other man we saved, who was also shot in the leg. Hopefully his bullet can also be removed…"

– And the Rabbi thanked everybody, and said, "That would be nice, hopefully it will ease the pain."

"Yes," said another of the rabbi's saviors, "and afterwards we'll have a joyful Shabbat celebration with the doctor, to thank him!"

"Shabbat?!" exclaimed the Rabbi. "I forgot it was Shabbat eve! No, the doctor can't extract my bullet before the Shabbat ends. Don't you know one cannot do anything at all during the Shabbat? I'd rather suffer and wait till the end of Shabbat to have the bullet removed…" he said.

"Are you sure?" the people asked. "You look very pale and the sooner we remove this bullet, the better for everybody, because the doctor cannot sit and wait until the end of Shabbat for your sake."

"I'm sure he'll wait to help a person who is willing to suffer pain during Shabbat. I refuse to do anything on Shabbat, and so should this doctor!"

– Since the doctor had already arrived, – Favel continued, – he rushed to the other man, who'd been shot. He'd been silent, so nobody paid much attention to him, but when the doctor came, it turned out that the man was unconscious. Without asking his permission to remove the bullet on Shabbat, the doctor simply removed it, then showed it to everybody.

The man moaned and opened his eyes, but before anyone could even try to feed him, he lost consciousness again. The doctor said:

"He'll be okay, he is only sleeping. Now, let's attend to the other patient." "Not on Shabbat!" shrieked the stubborn rabbi, to which the doctor replied: "If you want to have a long healthy life, it's better to extract the bullet now."

– But again, the stubborn Rabbi refused. Instead, he had the Shabbat meal with everybody and went back to his rug for a rest. That night he developed a terrible fever: he had contracted an infection from the bullet that was still lodged in his leg, and his fever worsened with every second. Since it was night-time, nobody noticed how delirious the rabbi had become: he tossed and turned on his rug, flailed his arms, moaning and even crying. Sometimes he prayed to God and sometimes he muttered incomprehensibly. Eventually, he succumbed to the infection. His speech became slurred, he moved less and less, and by the following afternoon, he was dead.

The man, whose bullet had been extracted, survived. Since he was unconscious at the time, he couldn't express his religious convictions, and afterwards, he didn't mind that the doctor had worked on him during Shabbat.

Whereas the rabbi, knowing his life was in danger, should've done something about it, instead of being overtly and unnecessarily righteous.

And with these words, Favel bowed, again, to his invisible audience.

43

The two boys exchanged glances.

– I fired a gun once! – one of them said. – It was when I went to the woods and saw a gaucho hunting for ducks. He let me shoot once, but I missed. He said it was okay, since it was my first time, and that next time I'll do better!

– And I saw two gauchos fighting over my older sister with long knives! – the second boy said proudly. – When one of them wounded the other, my sister ran to him and brought him home, to tend to his wounds. It was Shabbat, but she did it anyway, because he was bleeding profusely. And since he knew nothing about Jewish Shabbat, she didn't even bother telling him she was breaking the law to help him.

– What happened after that? – asked Favel with interest. – Did this gaucho marry your sister? I would love to hear a romantic story and write a poem about it!

– I think she didn't like them fighting over her, because she stopped seeing the one who was wounded. And his attacker got into some other trouble a couple of months later and ran away, so she never saw him again, either... She's so stupid.

– What's so stupid about her? – asked Favel. – If she were to start a family with one of those gauchos and they got into a bar fight, with knives and guns, she would end up having to take care of her household and children alone! Listen – if they didn't show up on her porch after their fight to serenade her and bring bouquets, they were not worthy of her...

– Girls know nothing about hunting and fights! – the boy who'd hunted ducks with the gaucho objected. – They scream when they see a bat, even when it's just flying around minding its own business, not even going for their hair. They're even afraid to approach game after its dead... It's better to send a dog to retrieve it, than a girl! – laughed the boy.

– Girls are right! – Naftali suddenly burst out. He didn't like these boys' cockiness, but it took him a while to get up the nerve to comment. – The Russian writer Tolstoy even stopped eating meat, because killing animals is a bad thing! No living thing should have to experience pain and suffering!

Startled by Naftali's passionate statement, the boys stared at him.

– What's your name? How did you end up here? When you're hungry, you'll eat whatever your parents put in front of you! – said the boy whose sister had tended to the wounded gaucho. – I eat everything: potatoes and butter and soup and if I get a duck on my plate, I'm very happy, only it hardly ever happens.

– I eat everything too, – sighed Naftali. – But I don't think animals should suffer, or that girls are so dumb... My mother is smart!

– So is mine! – exclaimed one of the boys.

– And mine! – the other youngster agreed.

– And your mothers were girls, once, – Favel chimed in, – so they couldn't have been stupid, if they grew up to be as smart as you say. Let me introduce you to each other, my friends. Naftali lives somewhere around here, he said, and surely he needs some new companions, isn't that right, Naftali?

Naftali nodded.

– And these young gentlemen are Syoma and Lyova. Now shake each other's hands and let's have some more tea. And once we've had tea, I'll tell you a second story, which is a continuation of the first one, *khorosho*?

All three boys smiled. Naftali smiled because of the familiarity of the name 'Syoma', which was also the name of his best friend in Russia, whom he dearly missed. And the boys' pleasant demeanor (even though they tried to argue, they still looked at Naftali with nice expressions on their freckled, tan faces) made him feel welcome. He thought maybe he and they could indeed become friends. And the boys smiled because they liked hearing the familiar Russian word 'khorosho', which meant that everything was alright, all important questions had been discussed, and that now they could peacefully have more tea and hear more stories.

– I don't care for duck, myself, – said Favel, warming up the tea and giving the boys some of the bread that one of them had brought earlier, – I prefer simple things, like this tea and bread, and I can tell you, my friends, that even the simple boiled potatoes we eat with sour cream and chives can be a dinner fit for a king, if our spirits are lifted! And when you hear my next story, even our difficult life in Argentina as newcomers and foreigners will appeal more to you, and you will get by from day to day with more happiness in your hearts. And with these words, Favel started his second story.

44

– Remember I told you about the Jewish revolt and how the Romans stormed the city and attacked everybody, making them hide under the tables or run for their lives? Unfortunately, the Romans didn't stop at this... They wanted to completely destroy all the Jews who lived in the city and they made sure that nobody could get out of it! They surrounded the city, placed the guards at each gate and each entrance, and waited for the people to die of illness, hunger and thirst. After several days of the blockade, the children were crying, asking for water, the adults were desperately looking for food, and there were men in the streets, boiling straw and eating this as soup.

– That reminds me of the soup I ate on the ship! – exclaimed Naftali. – It was runny and tasteless and there were only a few cabbage leaves floating in it.

– Yes, – continued Favel, – first these Jews shared and ate all the food that was left in the market, which included fresh vegetables. Then they started picking up whatever had fallen on the ground, perhaps some cabbage leaves, and cooked a soup similar to the one you were served on the ship. But once they'd consumed these scraps, they had nothing else to eat. They were on the verge of starvation! The Romans had said that no living people could leave the city, only the dead, and soon there were quite a few corpses that had to be taken out... Some died of starvation and some of their wounds. Others died because they were so desperate and their hearts couldn't bear such difficult times...

– Can you die just because you are desperate? – inquired one of the boys.

– Surely you can! – answered Favel. – These people had lost all hope of survival. Their minds had grown unresponsive and their bodies numb. They just lay on the ground with their eyes closed. But there was one resourceful man left, a teacher by the name of Yochanan Ben Zakkai, who didn't want this suffering to be in vain. He was determined not only to have his life spared, but also to ensure the future of the Jewish people. This man understood that even if he couldn't replenish the dwindling food supplies, he could still lift people's spirits.

And he went to his pupils and asked them to bring him a coffin him…

– A coffin?! – exclaimed Naftali. – How can a coffin lift human spirits? When the children were dying here from the bird disease, every time I saw a coffin, I got very scared…

– My dear boy, – Favel hugged him, becoming quite serious. – Life in this country is surely not easy for you, and I can't even imagine how much you've already gone through if you saw those sad things… I pray you will have no more difficulties, but I know you will, since we are foreigners here. And perhaps this is why I'm trying to lift your spirits, and also my own, with these stories of the heroic events of the past! Therefore please listen and stop interrupting.

And with these words, Favel drank a little more *mate* tea and continued:

– When the coffin was brought, Ben Zakkai lay in it and told his pupils to take him out of the city. They put the coffin on a horse and went to the gate, which was guarded by a soldier, who grew suspicious because the pupils didn't look very sad... "These young men," thought the guard, "claim they're carrying the body of their friend, without shedding a single tear! Maybe I should investigate..."

But since he didn't like asking questions, he decided to verify their story physically, so he simply grabbed his sword and pierced the coffin with it. The students screamed in horror, and their screams muffled Ben Zakkai's own cry at seeing the sword pierce the coffin! Luckily – some say it was a miracle – Ben Zakkai was not hurt. Satisfied, the guard grinned and let the group pass.

They carried the coffin right to the camp of the commander whose name was Vespasian. This brutal man was highly skilled in military operations and giving orders to soldiers and servants. He didn't hesitate to punish anybody or send more troops into the city that was already blockaded, and whose people were on the verge of extinction.

The students set the coffin down before the commander, and Ben Zakkai climbed out, and, squinting his eyes, he looked into the sun to enjoy its rays, after being in the coffin for so long. On seeing the commander, he stood up straight and greeted him very respectfully:

"Ave Caesar!"

"What did you say?" – shouted Vespasian, raising his right arm as though to strike him. "Ave Caesar!" – repeated Ben Zakkai meekly and more respectfully still.

"You should be killed twice for your words!" – shouted the commander again. "The first time because I am not the emperor, and the second time, because if the real emperor had heard you, he would've put you to death instantly!"

"I've almost been killed three times already today,"

– exclaimed Ben Zakkai. "Once by a sword that narrowly missed me, and twice by your threats to have me murdered. But perhaps my destiny is to continue living."

– And just as Ben Zakkai said this, a messenger, whose shoes were covered in dust and who was out of breath, appeared before Vespasian, informing him that he had just been appointed emperor!

Vespasian was so shocked and happy at the same time that he turned to Ben Zakkai and joyfully said:

"You seem to have special powers that enabled you to escape the well-guarded city, and even predict the future. Because you brought me such good news, even before the messenger arrived, I am going to grant you three wishes."

And Ben Zakkai's head started spinning. His original plan was to ask Vespasian to negotiate an end to the siege, or at least a truce, so that food could be brought in and people's lives spared. But then he thought: instead of straw soup, they would eat cabbage soup and even stew, but would this really lift their spirits? Would better soup really help the Jewish people to survive and withstand the Roman oppression?

The boys laughed on hearing about cabbage soup again, and Favel said:

– You care too much about the soup, boys, but what do you know about the Romans?

The boys continued laughing, jostling each other with their elbows and almost falling off the bench on which they were sitting. Naftali said:

– Roman oppression? Coming from Russia, we understand very well. We too felt the heel of oppression, and had to leave for Argentina. And these Jews probably felt the same way under the Romans.

– That's true, – nodded Favel. – Yes, the Romans ruled the Jews with a heavy hand. And sensing their resistance, they wanted to wipe these Jews off the face of the earth. That's why Ben Zakkai doubted that Vespasian would grant his wish. Knowing Vespasian was determined to conquer the Jews and end his military campaign victoriously, Ben Zakkai suspected it was useless to ask him to stop the assault. So, after thinking it over, he said:

"I would like you to let a doctor examine the health of the Rabbi Tzadok, who has been fasting for forty years and seems to be failing now..."

Vespasian laughed:

"Your friend, Rabbi Shmadok or whatever his name is, made the decision to fast, so I made all of your people 'fast' too. I will surely let a doctor through to examine him – but I don't understand why you think that a person, who decided himself not to eat, is any different from other people who starve. The result is the same: they are all hungry!"

Vespasian laughed once again. He thought he had cracked a good joke. He didn't know that the Rabbi Tzadok was a very special man and that his fasting had a very special meaning: he was fasting in an attempt to stave off the destruction of Jerusalem!

– And what about the other two wishes? – asked Naftali.

– After the wish to let a doctor examine Rabbi Tzadok had been granted, Ben Zakkai asked Vespasian to free all the Jewish judges from the Synedrion, and for permission to build a Jewish school outside Jerusalem.

"What? You're asking for a school?" Vespasian laughed again. After hearing that he had been appointed emperor, he was relaxed and quite happy. "What kind of wish is that? It means nothing! I will grant you this stupid wish, too, but you are an old fool!"

– The irony of the situation, – explained Favel, – is this: while Vespasian thought he was granting nothing to Ben Zakkai and the Jews, he'd actually granted them everything they needed to survive and to continue their Jewish tradition. Thanks to Rabbi Ben Zakkai, even though the Temple in Jerusalem was completely destroyed by the Romans, the Jewish people were able to carry on their tradition and continue to study the Torah in the school Vespasian had allowed, which flourished outside of Jerusalem, in the city of Yavneh!

– Memory is very important for carrying on the tradition, – added Favel. – Ben Zakkai wanted the Jewish people to remember the Second Temple, so he established several rules to serve as a reminder. Do you know them?

– No, we don't, – shouted the boys. – We only study Argentinian history at school. The teacher speaks only Spanish and says we need to understand the country we live in.

– That's why you need me! – exclaimed the old poet. – Even though we live in Argentina, we should not forget our forebears, so let me tell you about the memory devices that Ben Zakkai came up with. The first one has to do with music in the synagogue! In the Temple there was always a full orchestra, but now, to remember what we lost with its destruction, we only have cantors who sing. And when things are good in our lives, we remember that there had also been bad times. So after the bride and groom enjoy themselves at their wedding, they throw a glass on the floor and stomp on it so it breaks, to remind us of the Second Temple's destruction! And see this unpainted square on my wall opposite the entrance? Do you know what it means, boys?

– That you ran out of paint! – exclaimed one of the boys. But Naftali said: – It reminds you of the destruction?

– Correct! – Favel patted Naftali's back. – Some Jewish people prefer not to have a full meal and serve no dessert when they celebrate somebody's birthday, to remind us that something is missing. Others leave a small square on the wall unpainted, so we always remember what took place in the past. Now, my friends, I'm a bit tired, so I would like you go home to your wonderful parents.

– But I need to do a mitzvah! – said Naftali. – Should I help you clean your yard or put your kitchen utensils in order?

– No, no! – Favel objected. – As I said, the only order I care about is the order of words. If all the trees in front of my house just fell over and dried up, and weeds started growing on my roof, I wouldn't mind – as long as they don't interfere with my writing. To be honest, I'm not very fond of milking cows or planting the seeds... I prefer to plant ideas into young minds!

Lyova and Syoma looked somewhat puzzled, even a little offended.

– Don't misunderstand, – Favel continued, sensing their mixed feelings, – there's nothing wrong with helping your parents, working with them in the fields and threshing the wheat, it's what we are supposed to do in the colonies. But I just like to observe. If I could, and had the money, I would move to the city. But while I'm still here, I soak up everything that happens around me. At night, when the owls and I are the only creatures around who are awake, I write my poems... And as long as I can do that and tell children about the glorious past of the Jews, I'm quite satisfied.

And, on hearing these words, Naftali decided he wasn't so enamored with the rural life either... The first few weeks, when everything was new, were exciting. But he'd gotten bored and lonely and, even though he continued helping his parents grow some wheat and potatoes, his interests lay elsewhere. He still joined in when they talked about starting a cattle-breeding business, but Naftali knew it wasn't something he really wanted to do. He wanted to go to a library and to read books and to write in his diary and, when he heard that even Favel dreamed about moving to a city, he decided that was his dream, too.

45

The next day, as usual, Naftali had to go to school, but there was a rumor circulating that at a relative's wedding the night before, their teacher had gotten so drunk, he forgot his own name. The jovial, kind-hearted Don Miguel had been assigned by the government to teach Spanish, and Argentinean history, at Naftali's makeshift school for the immigrant children from Russia.

On hearing that classes had been dismissed for the day, Naftali's mother said:

– I don't think you're learning anything from that foolish drunkard. You're better off staying home, or helping us with the harvest… Anything is better than staring into that idiot's mouth all day long without any results!

– It doesn't matter if Naftali learns from Don Miguel or not, – Naftali's father said. – But he must be respectful of those who try to pass their knowledge on to him.

– He can learn more from the local children and gauchos! – was her reply.

Back in Russia, Naftali's mother enjoyed discussing his lessons when he came home from the rabbi's school. Whereas now, when she asked him what he'd learned, Naftali would often just shrug his shoulders and then repeat some Spanish phrases they had memorized that day, such as "love for your new motherland", or "the welcoming Argentinean government". They learned a few other phrases, too, about gauchos and the wildlife inhabiting the pampas, but Don Miguel didn't know much and was absent-minded, too, so he often repeated himself, telling the pupils to memorize the same phrases they'd learned a week or two before.

One day his mother asked what they had learned about Argentinean history.

– In 1810, Napoleon gained control of Spain! – Naftali said.

– That's good to know. And then what? – Naftali's mother asked.

– Well, that affected how things were run here, in Argentina! – answered Naftali.

– And then what?

– And then… Then Napoleon lost a battle in Europe, and when the Argentinian people found out, they got very excited and decided to take action… – Naftali replied, but he couldn't think of anything else.

– And then what happened? – Naftali's mother asked again.

– Then Don Miguel gave us a copy of the Declaration of Independence and told us to copy it into our notebooks from start to finish and then he left for a long time. We wrote until we got tired of writing, but Don Miguel still had not returned. Then a few boys started roughhousing. One of them overturned an inkwell on the teacher's desk, another drew a caricature of Don Miguel on the chalkboard, and when the other boys tried to take the chalk from him, they all ended up wrestling each other on the floor.

– I see, – Naftali's mother said, raising her eyebrows. – And did Don Miguel ask what you remembered from the declaration when he came back to class?

– He never came back, – Naftali admitted, hesitantly. Naftali's mother shook her head in disapproval.

– You don't need to write out The Declaration of Independence to learn Spanish, – she said, – you can just go into the fields and talk to the gauchos or farm hands. They may not be educated, but I'm sure they will be more useful to you than your Don Miguel.

– I'm not sure I agree with you, Raya, – said Naftali's father, – but we'll discuss it later. In the meantime, Naftali, – he said, pointing to the window, – there are some local boys playing outside. Why don't you join them?

Naftali looked out the window hesitantly. He was afraid he and the local boys had nothing in common, and that they would make fun of his awkward mannerisms and accent. Yet, choosing not to argue with his father, he put on his shoes and coat and went outside.

46

He saw three boys playing a strange game in the grassy field. One of the boys was tiptoeing around with his arms raised, apparently imitating something. Sometimes he'd drop to the ground and lie on the grass, hiding his head between his arms. The other two boys would sneak up and toss something at him – some wooden or leather balls, on a rope, and the boy would jump up and start running. The other boys would chase after him, swinging their ropes with the dangerous-looking balls attached.

The shorter boy in bombachas noticed Naftali and ran toward him, swinging his contraption over his head. Afraid that the boy wanted to hit him, Naftali prepared to run away, but the boy shouted out:

– Wait! We need another rhea, otherwise it's no fun! Do you want to play with us?

– Yes, – Naftali nodded, uncertainly, – but how does one play a rhea?

The boy in bombachas pointed to the boy who was lying in the grass again, covering his head with his arms. – See him? – he asked. – He is a rhea! To be a rhea, you have to be strong and run fast, and we'll try to catch you. We'll put *bolas* around your legs so you fall and then we'll throw a sack over you. Watch how we do it! – he shouted and, before Naftali could protest, the boy threw something at him. Naftali felt a sharp pain in his right leg and fell to the ground, grimacing and holding his knee. The boy ran over to him.

– This is a bolas! – he exclaimed. – Do you see how well it works? I made it myself! Ignoring Naftali's discomfort, the boy crouched next to him and showed him the leather ropes he held in his hand. One leather rope was divided into smaller ropes, each with a little leather bag at the end, filled with sharp objects. Naftali took one in his hand. It was heavy.

– I filled them with stones I found here! – explained the boy. – Do you like it? Naftali's pain went away and he was no longer upset at the boy.

– Why did you throw it at me if you're only playing? – he asked.

– It's how we practice our bolas skills. And then we go and hunt for real rheas. Have you seen the rheas here? They are so huge, you can't miss them. They are quite tasty, but my father almost never lets me eat them. He sells the meat to other people. Would you like a taste? We can hunt for one and then light a fire and cook it!

– No! No! – protested Naftali. – I'm not hungry!

– Not now! We'll do it later, if my father will help us, – answered the boy. – My name is Estancio, which means 'farm,' but don't laugh. My father gave me the name because he wanted to be a farmer and have his own piece of land. Unfortunately, he never got his wish so he still roams the pampas on his horse. He is different from other gauchos, because he has a family, but we're always alone, because our parents are busy. We try to help them put food on the table, but so far, I've never caught a rhea. Do you have them where you come from?

– We have roosters and pheasants, – Naftali said. – They're big, but we never heard of rheas in Russia...

– You came from Russia? – asked Estancio. On hearing this, the other boys gathered around to listen, too. – How did you get here? What did you do in Russia? And why would you want to come here and not go somewhere else?

Naftali hesitated to answer. There were so many questions, and he was afraid he couldn't explain what brought him here. He said:

– We traveled by horse and by train and by ship and then by horse again...

– So you are rich! – exclaimed one of the boys, and he spit on the ground as if showing his disapproval.

– No we're not, – objected Naftali.

– So where did you get the money for the train? We don't even have any horses. If we did, our father would sell them immediately, so obviously we don't have any carriages either. We can't even go to school, because nobody will take us to another little town several miles away... We three are brothers, and our parents struggle, so we have to make our own toys and always be on our own, because our mom helps our father...

– I'm not sure where we got the money for our tickets, – Naftali said. – I think it was a wealthy man and his wife who helped us, so we could have a good life. I only know that many of us came here from Russia and we are not rich. When we first arrived, we lived in abandoned train cars, with stiff benches and bedbugs that wouldn't let me sleep...

– That sounds like fun! – one of the boys said dreamily. – I'd love to see the inside of a train carriage one day. They talk about building a railroad here, but it never gets built... And nobody cares if we have a good life or not. If we fell into a wild boar trap tomorrow, nobody would even look for us except our parents!

– Be careful! – said Naftali. – When the railroad

came to our town, my father couldn't make money from his business... Nobody wanted his horses, everybody wanted to ride the train!

– So you moved here for business! – concluded Estancio. – You couldn't make money in Russia so you came to make it here... Well, there isn't much money here, only grass and these clay huts, and one small store. Many of your people who arrived here from Russia left very soon afterwards... There was a boy named Adam and he taught us to play the flute, but as soon as we got to know him, he disappeared. We ran to his hut, but it was empty, except for a huge metal pot...

– A samovar? – suggested Naftali.

– Maybe, – the boy replied. – Apparently, they didn't need this 'samovar' in the city... You Russians *must* be rich. You paid your way to come here from Russia, but then you don't like how things are run here, so you leave for the city. Meanwhile, our parents can't afford to move to the city! Even if we could, what would we do there? You speak Russian and Spanish, and we don't even know how to read and write!

–Yes, I went to school in Russia and I learned how to read there...

– Maybe you can teach us to read, – another boy suggested, – and we'll teach you to throw bolas?

– I would love to! – said Naftali, though he couldn't believe these rough-looking boys, who almost knocked him down with their bolas, really wanted to study.

– Don't judge us by our ragged clothes, – Estancio said, as though reading Naftali's mind, – or because we play in the sand throwing bolas all day... We have nowhere to go! We'd like to see trains and to visit a large city – just to know how people live there... We'd love to read like you, but nobody wants to teach us! Why don't we exchange skills?!

Suddenly Estancio threw his bolas high into the air, and when they dropped to the ground, he picked them up swiftly and ran into the middle of the field. Then he shouted:

– Here it is! A rhea! Come here!

– Stop shouting, – warned his younger brother, Sebastiano, – or else you'll scare her off!

– It's very young, – Estancio continued, – because it doesn't even know how to run fast!

– But rheas are tall, – said the third brother. – Let's go check, in case he's only fooling! The boys ran to their brother, and Naftali followed behind.

47

As they approached a little meadow in the field, Naftali saw a bird on strong legs, which was the same height as the boy standing next to it. The bird was suffering and unable to run, yet Estancio continued throwing the bolas at its feet, to entangle them, even though he could now grab it with his bare hands.

— What are you doing? You can't make it suffer! – Naftali exclaimed, trying to stop the boy from practicing his bolas skills on a defenseless creature.

— He is right! – exclaimed Sebastiano, while the third and youngest brother said nothing.

— It's not even full grown!

— But it's so huge! – said Naftali. – It's almost my height!

— You should see a grown rhea! – answered Sebastiano. – Sometimes they are even taller than our mother, and she's even taller than our father, so you can imagine how huge they are! This little weakling probably got separated from its mother, and does not know what to do without her... And look, look! There's something is wrong with its leg... It's limping and that's why it can't run away!

— I broke that leg with the bolas so I could catch my prey! – boasted Estancio. – Our father says a hunter should forget about any kind of pity, otherwise he won't be successful.

— Poor bird, – said Sebastiano, coming closer to the bird for a closer look at its wound. – Maybe we should take it home and treat it with medicine. Our mother probably knows how...

– We should take it home, alright, but to show everybody what a great hunter I am! And our father'll know how to fry it!

– You're not being very nice! – Sebastiano said and took a swing at him.

– Are you trying to hit me? – shouted Estancio, and he pushed his younger brother to the ground. The youngest boy joined Sebastiano. In seconds all three brothers were kicking and screaming on the ground, while Naftali was left standing there with the bird, which just stood there, too, quietly looking back at him.

Estancio finally threw his younger brothers off and stood up. He grabbed the bird by the neck and started tugging at it, but the bird wouldn't budge.

– Come on! – Estancio shouted and pulled the bird one more time, – we need a nice dinner today! – He grinned at his brothers, who were not happy with what was happening.

But still the bird wouldn't move. As Naftali and the younger boys stood dumbfounded by the rhea's silent resistance, Estancio tied a leather rope around its neck and tried to pull her toward him. But the bird suddenly started pulling in the other direction, attempting to escape.

– Why are you standing there doing nothing? – Estancio shouted, enraged. – Help me! The brothers felt sorry for the bird, but they couldn't stand up to Estancio, so they started pushing the bird from behind, while he tugged on the leather rope attached to its neck. Not knowing whether to help the bird or the brothers, Naftali stood silently aside, feeling sorry for both the rhea, and himself.

– Don't even think about touching it! – warned Estancio. – It's ours! Catch your own and then you can do whatever you want with it. You can even make it drink tea from your samovar, ha-ha-ha!

Naftali was hoping the younger boys would defend him, but they didn't want to disobey their older brother, so he quietly left them and walked back home.

Later that night, as he and his parents sat eating their dinner of boiled potatoes and chives with sour cream, they heard a commotion at the door. Imagine Naftali's surprise when his father opened the door to see what was going on, and the rhea stuck its small, ugly head into the room, and stared him in the face with its sparkling eyes!

Horrified, Naftali's father tried to shut the door, but somebody was pushing from the other side, and suddenly the creature's legs were inside, along with its strange impish head.

– Oh my God! What is it? – screamed Naftali's mother, frightened half to death. Grabbing a kitchen towel, she ran toward the intruder, trying to chase it back outside.

– I have no idea, – Naftali's father said, shrugging his shoulders, – but it sure knows how to knock on doors!

He stepped out onto the porch to see if anybody had accompanied this weird animal to their door.

– I think I saw somebody running away, – he reported. – But why bring it here? And Naftali said: – I think it's the rhea I met this morning.

– I see, – his father replied. – And it just dropped by to say hello to you... You must have made quite an impression on it!

– What nonsense you are saying! – exclaimed Naftali's mother; she'd dropped the kitchen towel, but continued to block the creature from proceeding into her kitchen. –

Oh no, you don't! – she said, standing her ground.

– I don't think it understands Yiddish, – said Naftali's father, smiling, before turning his attention to Naftali.

– Seeing as you're acquainted with this feathery creature, – he said, – perhaps you can explain what's going on.

– You told me to go play with the local boys and I tried, but they only wanted to hunt rheas, – Naftali explained. – They wanted to take this one home for supper, but maybe they felt sorry for it and brought it here instead...

– Whatever happened to this ugly bird, it can't stay in my kitchen! – announced Naftali's mother. – I won't have it anywhere near my gefilte fish and latkes!

– Let's take it outside, and feed it some dinner scraps in our little yard, – Naftali's father suggested. – But first, let's see about its leg. It looks injured...

And this is how the rhea ended up staying with Naftali's family.

48

They named the bird Tulchinea, in honor of the town they were from.

Naftali fed her fruit and seeds and alfalfa in the yard, and sometimes he'd let her out of the yard, hoping she'd to return to the pampas and rejoin her mother. However, the stubborn rhea would always come back. She'd sneak into the kitchen and eat whatever food was left on the table: bread, feta cheese, potato peels – all of it would disappear into the rhea's big beak, and Naftali would watch the bulge pass through her skinny neck to her belly. Its inquisitive eyes were always searching for something else to devour, no matter what it was.

And this made Naftali's mother very angry.

– Kick her out of here, – she'd say, – she's stealing my things! Where is my thimble? It was just here... I need it to mend your clothes, Lazar Evseevich. And my ball of wool has disappeared, too! Have you seen it? The red one...

– Raya, maybe this creature wants to learn how to sew and knit, – Naftali's father replied, – in which case she could be a great helper!

– Stop talking nonsense! – Naftali's mother said, angrily. – Not only my thimble and wool have disappeared; so has a silver spoon I was so fond of! I brought it from Russia because it was the one I fed little Naftali with when he was six months old!

– What a wonderful bird! It wants to eat with utensils, like a civilized human being!

– You should quit joking, Lazar, – said Naftali's mother, – and do something. Things are disappearing from this house left and right. Or do we have thieves here?

– Maybe it's Indians! – Naftali exclaimed. – I heard they sometimes attack the farmers here! I brought a knife from Russia, and from now on I'll sleep with it under my pillow to protect you!

– Thank you, my dear, – Naftali's mother hugged him. – Only be careful not to mistake your darling Tulchinea for an Indian, when she comes in to steal my sewing accessories!

Naftali's father couldn't contain his laughter listening to them.

– Well, whoever our thief is, let's catch him, or her, before we blame anyone!

And so, Tulchinea continued living in their yard. When Naftali came home from school, now, he had somebody to talk to. He used to be afraid of being home alone, in the dark, if his parents were out; he'd jump at every sound. It may have been only mice, or dry leaves on the porch, but Naftali imagined wild creatures descending on his family home. And he wouldn't light any candles, in case of fire. He always imagined the worst: the flame from a candle near the window could engulf the curtains, or if it overturned on the table, his notebooks could catch fire!

But Tulchinea's squeaking made him less lonely. He would let her into the house, secretly, and she would make herself at home and go after whatever food or shiny objects she saw.

Like today: as soon as Naftali came home and put

his notebooks and house-key on the table, he let Tulchinea in and started petting her. She immediately tried to swallow another ball of wool, which Naftali's mother had prepared, to mend his woolen socks. Naftali quickly took it away from her and went to get her some bread. When he turned around a second later, he saw a piece of a candle sticking out of her mouth!

– Give it to me, if you eat that, you'll die! – he shouted in terror and started pulling the candle out of Tulchinea's beak. She tried to run into the yard, but he held her by the neck and managed to pull half of it out of her beak, whereas the other half had forever disappeared into Tulchinea's bottomless pit of a stomach.

While Naftali tried stowing away what was left of the candle on a shelf, and out of Tulchinea's reach, he heard the sound of something metallic hitting the floor. Turning around, he saw Tulchinea grabbing his house-key.

– What are you doing?! – Naftali shouted, waving his arms. – Get away!

But Tulchinea snatched the key with her beak and ran out into the yard. Naftali ran after her, almost stumbling on the porch, and suddenly the door behind him slammed shut. And he remembered how proud his father was of the new, English, self-locking device on the door, for which he'd traded a couple of coats he had no use for on the pampas.

Naftali chased after Tulchinea, hoping she would stop at the temporary fence they built just for her. However, Tulchinea managed to squeeze through a hole in it and was now out of Naftali's reach. She stopped to look at Naftali, as though challenging him to another race, and he went after her again, but Tulchinea didn't let him grab her and ran off toward the pampas.

Exasperated and out of breath, Naftali realized he couldn't enter his home without the key. Afraid to face his parents and shivering from the cold and from shock, he went to the home of the old poet, Favel Bavilsky, instead.

49

Naftali heard the poet's voice, even before he reached his door. Low and intriguing, then suddenly rising in pitch, it was telling another story.

From outside, nothing seemed out of the ordinary, from the yard, strewn with gardening tools, to the humble dwelling – dimly lit and overgrown with weeds that were now growing even between the floor boards inside.

Yet, with every twist in the plot, his listeners inside the hut realized that both the events of the story, and the old poet's storytelling talent, were extraordinary. He seemed like a magician to them, and they always anticipated the continuation on the following day of his tales about the mysterious inhabitants of the pampas, their readiness to demonstrate courage and perform honorable deeds.

Afraid to interrupt, Naftali quietly opened the door: Lyova and Syoma were sitting on a bench, peeling potatoes, while the poet sat cleaning mushrooms. Separating the mushroom caps from the stalks with a knife, Bavilsky was just concluding a sad story about a young Argentinian soldier and his faithful war horse, Lily:

– And in the same way her master had never deserted her in life, the horse remained loyal to him in death. She stood over him for a long while, as he lay wounded on the battlefield, but unfortunately, there was nothing she could do to save him this time. Unable to bear his demise, she lay down by his lifeless body and never got up again.

The poet stopped and wiped his eyes with his sleeves. Looking up, he noticed Naftali in the room. – Ach, my boys! – he sighed, sadly. – Yes, you, Lyova, Syoma, and you, Naftali! I hope you will never have to fight in any war.

The boys were speechless for a moment, then Lyova said:

– We often play soldiers! Syoma is the general and I obey his orders. We run over to that hill and practice military exercises there, rolling down the slope and aiming our guns at enemy troops.

– Children often play soldiers, – the poet said, – but these are just games. A real war has nothing to do with rolling down that hill and shooting at imaginary enemies. The horrors of real war are unimaginable. When I was your age, I didn't like playing war games. Yet I was almost drafted into the Russian army! And this was a real army, not some kind of joke. I was only twelve!

– Twelve years old? – exclaimed Naftali. – And you had to serve in the army together with grown-ups? Could you even lift a rifle onto your shoulder?

– As I said, – explained the old poet, – I was *almost* drafted, but it never happened. And I only escaped the Russian army because I was always such a good story-teller!

– Tell us about it! – shouted Lyova and Syoma in unison.

– If you promise not to get tired of yet another story, – Favel agreed. And without wasting a minute, he began weaving his next tale.

– In Russia, they drafted Jews at a very young age. This is because they didn't want these children to become too immersed in the Jewish way of life in their shtetl. Otherwise, they would have trouble adapting to the Russian lifestyle. Therefore, Jewish kids were drafted at twelve, and Russian kids at eighteen.

– And they would live without their parents, at such a young age? – exclaimed Naftali.

– Oh yes, – answered the old poet. – In some areas of Russia they would draft Jewish children as young as eight into special, so-called canton schools to prepare them for the army, and even there the parents were not allowed. Luckily, the Tsar permitted these Jewish youngsters to practice their religion. This was not easy, because they were surrounded by Russian youths, and that's why Jewish kids and Jewish soldiers tried to stay together in the army. It made them feel more secure and closer to home.

– And you? What about you? Did you see the army? – asked Lyova impatiently.

– Be patient, Lyova, – answered Favel Bavilsky, – and listen to the whole story. And so he continued:

– In those days there was one prominent person in our community, whose duty it was to recruit two Jewish youths into the army, from a population of approximately one thousand people. But nobody wanted to send their kid to the Russian army – not because they didn't want a Jewish kid to defend Mother Russia, because they didn't think their little Boruchs or Isaacs were ready for adult life in military barracks at such a tender age. And that's why this gentleman – his name was Meir – had a lot of trouble convincing parents to send their children to the military!

Meir had no sons himself, so he had no idea what it meant to send your beloved child to a training camp or a battlefield. He had five daughters of a marriageable age, and all he cared about was earning enough money to provide all of his daughters with decent dowries.

First, he went to Nathan, who owned a lumber company that cut down trees in the forest and sold the wood. Nathan had never even held an axe – he was so rich, he had over a hundred lumberjacks working for him! And he was not only lucky in business, but also in his family life, having four sons and two daughters.

Since he had so many sons, Meir thought Nathan wouldn't mind sending one of them to the army. So on the day Nathan made a successful deal, selling one ton of wood to a wealthy landowner, who wanted to build another home on his huge property, Meir went to him and said:

"Congratulations on this deal you just made! Since the Tsar allows you to conduct such a successful business in Russia, you should return his favor now and send one of your sons to the Russian army to serve in the Tsar's honor!"

Nathan wanted to curse when he heard these words, but he realized that it was a bad idea to swear at such a prominent Jewish community member. So he thought for a minute and said:

"I would love to please our Tsar and send one of my sons to help him to defend our motherland, but unfortunately, I need all of them here, to help with my business."

"But you have one hundred employees!" Meir exclaimed. "Surely some of them can help you."

"Not when it comes to counting my money. They could make a mistake," Nathan replied, "whereas my sons are very good at it." Meir laughed:

"That's the most ridiculous excuse I have ever heard! Stop talking nonsense and tell me which one you will choose to go and serve."

"It's not nonsense!" Nathan insisted. "Let me show you how they count money, and I'm sure you'll agree that they cannot be replaced."

Nathan quickly summoned one of his sons. Having performed such demonstrations before, the son eagerly said:

"Don't worry, Papa, I'll show Mr. Meir my counting skills."

Then he led Mr. Meir to a cash register in back of the office and showed him how he counted money. Soon after, Mr. Meir left, with a big smile on his face and a thick wad of cash in his pocket.

Next, Meir went to see another Jewish man, a moneylender named Isya, who had six sons, with a seventh child on the way.

"You must be tired of looking after so many children," he said. "Now it's six, but soon it will be seven. I can help by taking one child off your hands."

"Why don't you go away, Meir?" Isya said. "I'm not having any problems."

"You'll have a big problem, if you don't choose one son to be recruited into the Russian army."

"I realize the Russian army can't survive without one of my sons," retorted Isya, "but neither can I. Why don't you go somewhere else to find your recruits? I need all my sons to help me with my business."

"Ah!" laughed Meir. "They help you count your money?"

"What money?" asked the money lender. "It's true I'm called a money lender, but in fact, I myself never see any money: I only give it to people, and then it takes a long time before they return it to me. I've almost forgotten what rubles look like!"

"What do they count then?" asked Meir in surprise.

"My sons help me count debts," said Isya. "They write down who owes what, when they have to return it, and at what percentage. By the way, remember the large sum I lent you last summer, Meir, to buy a wedding dress for one of your daughters? When is the wedding?"

Meir shrugged his shoulders:

"She cancelled the wedding. Instead of marrying, she decided to continue living with us, until she finds the perfect mate. But she said her room was too small for her grand piano, so instead of buying the dress with the money, I had to build another, bigger, room onto my house. I can't repay you yet, but I will... In the meantime, tell me which son you'll send to the army."

"As I said," Isya insisted, "I need my sons to keep track of all the debts. If you doubt their abilities, you can see them in action. Motya, here, will show you the big ledger where we record all the debts, and how he can add and subtract them, and even make some of them disappear, just by erasing an amount in this accounting book, together with the name of the debtor..."

And Motya led Meir behind the counter, where he demonstrated his remarkable skills. Seconds later, Meir left the lender's shop in awe of how magically Motya had made his debt to him disappear completely.

Finally, Meir came to the poorest family in the vicinity – ours. My father changed jobs so often that if you picked one, there was a good chance he'd done it at least once in his life. He was a milkman and a cobbler and then he was a shoe maker and after that a tailor. He was equally bad at everything he did, except making music. Everybody told him he should just perfect his fiddle-playing and earn his living performing at weddings and funerals, but my father would always note:

"I enjoy music, so I can't charge money for my own enjoyment. As for making shoes or mending clothes, I really hate it, which is why I charge people for doing it!"

Unfortunately, people were more willing to pay him for playing the fiddle, than for fixing their shoes or bringing milk to their home, so our family was always hungry and cold.

"You can't feed your sons, Shmuel!" said Meir to my father. "You should be grateful to me for coming to recruit both of them for the Russian army, where they'll be looked after!"

"Please don't take them from me!" my father pleaded. "My children and my fiddle are the only good things I have."

"The last two fathers I visited told me they couldn't let their sons go to the Russian army, because they helped run their businesses. But from what I can see, Shmuel, the only business you have is fixing this old wreck you call home, so let me take down their names and get it over with."

My father was so overwhelmed by this proposal that he started crying, but this did not deter Meir. "Hurry up, Shmuel! The other fathers said their sons helped them count their money and debts. But you can't fool me like they did. The only things your sons can count here are the crumbs on the table, and your bitter tears."

I was only thirteen at the time, but seeing my father in such a desperate situation gave me courage. I approached Meir and said:

"Please don't send me and my brother to the army. We might be useless in business, but we can keep people's hearts and souls happy with our stories and music. Let us perform for you so you can relax after your long trip…"

And I asked Papa to play the fiddle. While he played, my brother danced, and I told a long story I'd made up. I can't remember what it was about, but I do remember that several minutes into our performance, Meir fell asleep for a couple of hours, right in his chair. Afraid that he'd wake up if we stopped performing, we kept playing, dancing and telling the story, even after he did wake up. When he awoke, he yawned and opened one eye, with which he observed my papa playing his fiddle. Then he yawned again and opened his other eye. Now he observed my brother and me with both eyes.

"You are still telling your story?" he exclaimed in surprise. "It couldn't have been very interesting, if I was able to fall asleep."

On hearing this, my father realized our efforts were in vain, and there was nothing left to do except send us to the Russian army. He started crying so bitterly that I stopped telling my story and rushed over to hug and console him.

Just then, Meir said:

"The other two fathers helped me put my finances in order. But you and your poor sons helped to heal my soul and restore my balance. Now I see that not everybody cares only about money. I see how much your son loves you, and I'm consoled and soothed by your music. And I'm in awe of your son's storytelling abilities, even though the story he told was so uneventful that I fell asleep. It's the end of the day, and it's too late to make any decisions about the army right now. I bid you good-bye for now and I'll see you tomorrow."

With these words Meir left, and we never saw him again.

50

– You were lucky! – Naftali said, once the old poet had concluded his story. – This fellow didn't even listen to your fable, he just liked that you felt sorry for your father...

– It's true, at the time I was not very skillful at storytelling, – said the old poet. – But some people can talk their way out of any situation, just by making things up. For example, I heard about a hardened criminal from an Argentinean prison, once, who would jump out onto the road and rob people at knifepoint. The travelers were so frightened by his huge frame and scarred face that they eagerly parted with their belongings.

– This is incredible, – interrupted Lyova. – This is already your third anecdote today!

– Only to encourage you to peel my potatoes! – smiled the old poet. – You see, you didn't notice that you are almost done!

He put the potatoes into boiling water on the stove and arranged the mushrooms in a skillet.

– By the time I finish my third story, our dinner will be ready. You see how easy household chores become, when one supplements them with storytelling? Let me continue about this bandit, only don't interrupt ... Naftali listened intently. He saw that the old poet had an incredible power – to keep everybody's attention. It seemed that the stories coming out of his mouth were endless, and that the boys' interest was undiminishing. Naftali got so carried away listening to Favel that he forgot about his misadventure with the key and the rhea. He also forgot that his parents were probably home by now, and growing worried about him. Completely impressed by the old poet's stories, Naftali thought that, like Favel, he too could make up different tales about his life in Russia and in Argentina.

For Favel, all the life events that had happened in Russia and in Argentina were simply a source of inspiration. Some of the events in the stories were not very happy, but still they aroused his listeners' curiosity and were entertaining. And Naftali thought that no matter how difficult his life and that of his parents was, he could always make it more colorful by retelling it and, with a little exaggeration, turning it into a real adventure…

Just then they heard knocking at the door that was quiet at first, but then got louder and more insistent. Eager to hear the story about the bandit, Naftali said to the old poet:

– Please, continue! Don't pay attention to that noise!

But that very second, the door to the old poet's room opened and Naftali heard his mother exclaim:

– I'll give him noise! We thought he had been abducted by Indians! There we were, checking every bush and dirty ravine in the cold pampas, and all this time he's been enjoying himself here, eating potatoes!

– I am sorry, – Naftali said, looking anxiously at his mother.

– Have you forgotten in which home you live? – she asked angrily. – Or is our home not good enough for you? We work so hard all day to make sure you are well fed and dressed, and instead of waiting patiently for us, you accept somebody else's invitations!

– I didn't know our son was so popular in the pampas that he's already being invited to important social events! – Naftali's father said, sarcastically. – But seeing as we've come uninvited, we should apologize to the owner of this house.

Favel Bavilsky nodded and answered casually:

– We are just telling stories, and there were indeed bandits and Indians in them. But let me assure you, none of them ever stepped into this room!

– I do apologize for interrupting your dinner, – said Naftali's mother, glancing at the boiling pot of potatoes. – But how is it he ended up here, without even leaving us a note?

– I didn't want you to blame Tulchinea, – answered Naftali, barely audibly.

– She didn't do anything, – exclaimed Naftali's father. – Unlike you, she's waiting for us at the door...

– She came back! – said Naftali happily. – Did she bring back the key?

– Now I understand, – said Naftali's mother. – The ugly creature couldn't steal food from the kitchen, so she swallowed the key! I've suspected her since my thimble and some of my precious jewelry disappeared...

– This lady loves to be elegant, if she borrows jewelry! – commented Favel Bavilsky. – But why would she swallow a key?

– She's not a lady! She's my pet rhea! – said Naftali.

– I must be getting deaf, – sighed Favel. – I thought you uttered "Dulcinea", so I assumed she was somehow related to venerable Don Quixote...

Naftali was dumbfounded by the very mention of Don Quixote so far away from the civilized world.

51

– We called her Tulchinea, not Dulcinea, – smiled Naftali's father in response to the old poet's question. – In honor of our town in Russia!

– So, Naftali knows about Don Quixote? I would gladly present him with the book, – volunteered the poet, – but I only have the first volume. I packed the second one in a different sack, which was stolen at one of the train stations. On finding it was full of books, instead of a pile of loot, the thief probably just threw them away.

– I can't believe it! – exclaimed Naftali. – I have only the second volume, so if you give me the first one, I'll have the complete *Don Quixote*!

– I'll try to find it, but you'll have to patient, since many things seem to have disappeared from my living quarters. I can't even find the belt I brought from Russia! – Favel said. – Very often people who devote their life to the arts are not in control of their material possessions... I only hope that I'm at least in control of my mind!

– A man whose only loss is a book or a belt wouldn't understand what it is to have a child disappear! – Naftali's mother announced, as though blaming her worries over Naftali on Favel. – My heart still aches from thinking my son had been abducted by bandits, Indians, or evil strangers who only mean harm!

– I agree that it's more worrisome to lose a son than a belt, – said the old poet, – but where bandits are concerned, they can have a good heart, too.

Lyova and Syoma, who had kept a low profile, trying not to anger Naftali's parents, started giggling and elbowing each other, now, and finally burst out laughing.

– I'm going to abduct you! – Syoma shouted to Lyova, and started pulling him into a dark corner by the neck.

– No, no, don't abduct me, – Lyova said, in a high voice – I need to feed my birdie! What can I give her? Let me feed her a key, it's so tasty! Yummy-yummy!

Naftali knew they were teasing him, but he paid no attention to them. He was very surprised that in the middle of the pampas, there was somebody besides him who knew and liked Don Quixote.

The old poet shushed the boys, looked encouragingly at Naftali and said:

– Don't be afraid of the bandits. They are human and have feelings, too. Maybe what they do is really awful, but deep down they know they are wrong, and afterwards they regret their actions. My hope is that by talking to them, one can help transform their murderous intent to understanding... Favel Bavilsky looked at the boys and Naftali's parents and, seeing that he still commanded their attention, continued:

– I just remembered an episode from *Don Quixote*... When Don Quixote and Sancho Panza were on their way to the city of Barcelona, they suddenly were surrounded by dozens of scary-looking men. But before jumping to conclusions about these people, they observed how they swarmed them and took all their belongings.

– I wouldn't just stand and observe! – shouted Lyova. – I would fight them off with my sword!

And to demonstrate, Lyova grabbed a ladle off the table and started fencing as though attacking invisible enemies. But Naftali only stared at Bavilsky, waiting for him to continue. Unlike Lyova and Syoma, the old poet's legends didn't inspire him to jump up and start fighting. On the contrary, after hearing a story, Naftali wanted to seclude himself in his room and make up his own tales.

Meanwhile, Favel Bavilsky continued:

– One of the bandits asked Sancho Panza and Don Quixote for all their belongings, and then divided them evenly among his colleagues. Even though what he did was bad, he still tried to be fair with his people, making sure they each got an equal share of the booty.

– What a gentleman! – said Naftali's mother sarcastically. – If you think this was a good bandit, your influence on my son is even worse than his teacher's! Listening to stories about "good bandits", Naftali might decide to become one as well. We should be going...

– Mama, wait, please! – begged Naftali. – I want to hear more of this story!

– When Don Quixote revealed his mild demeanor, – Favel continued, – the bandit, as though in exchange, bared his soul. He said he had a guilty conscience because of his misdeeds, but that his life was such that it made him engage in these despicable acts. On hearing of the man's remorse, Don Quixote said God would forgive him, because his desire to rob was a sign of sickness. The bandit had only to realize he was sick, and his salvation would follow.

Don Quixote suggested the man become a knight in shining armor and defend the poor and the weak! But the bandit declined... He only gave back to Don Quixote a portion of what had been stolen from him, and they parted ways. Still, Don Quixote believed the bandit was on his way to salvation!

– Was he? What happened next? – asked Naftali.

– I don't remember, – answered Favel. – Some bandits indeed become honest citizens right away, but for others, it takes time. For example, if your parents don't mind, I'll tell you the story of the Argentinean bandit I promised you earlier...

And, pouring out six cups of tea for his listeners, Favel told the following story.

52

– This bandit, named Hilario, was a bandit not because he was evil, but because he simply didn't know what to do with his life. With his huge muscles and endless energy, he first tried to be a gaucho, but couldn't bear the monotony of everyday work. He found it much more exciting to scare people who traveled on Argentinean roads than to harvest crops or fight nasty locusts. Yet, he was quite simple-minded and clumsy and always used the very same method of committing his crime. He would throw something onto the road – a large gold coin or a purse – and then wait for travelers to stop and check what it was. Then he would spring from the bushes with a long knife in his hand and threaten to kill anybody who would not surrender. He was so certain of his strength that he never once considered buying a gun.

Moreover, he thought that whoever carried a gun only did so to scare people and had no idea how to shoot. Luckily for him, he had never met anybody with a working rifle before, so he almost always succeeded in escaping the scene of the crime with his booty. His method of surprise attack had only failed once, when a former soldier wrestled the knife from his hands. But that time Hilario was able to run away.

Something very different happened during his very last attempt to rob travelers...

As usual, Hilario lay in the bushes and watched as a carriage approached the dusty spot on the road where he had placed a purse. In this carriage, there was an old farmer, and a doctor, who advised locals on how to treat their children's colds, how to help a cow give birth, or pull a rotten tooth. Every time the locals had a problem with animals or humans, they called him. And since there were no other doctors in the vicinity, this young man – his name was Alberto – had to travel great distances.

Even though he was almost too young to grow a decent mustache, he was very experienced. Once, on his way through the woods to help an injured hunter, he was attacked by a wild boar. Another time, lightning struck a tree under which he was sitting, but he survived without even a bruise. A third time a poisonous snake bit him, but he sucked out all the venom and just spat it out, saving his own life. Finally, after a pack of stray dogs followed him for a kilometer and one of them almost bit him, the doctor said "enough is enough" and started carrying a rifle with him.

But Hilario, who was hiding in the bushes, had no idea he was about to rob not a cowardly man, this time, but a weathered hero. He watched the carriage stop and the doctor jump off and walk toward the purse with the rifle slung from his shoulders. That very minute, Hilario emerged from the bushes with a knife. The young doctor was quick to grab his rifle, but Hilario was quicker. He grabbed hold of the rifle, too, and pulled it toward himself.

Here they were, two strong, young men fighting over the rifle, but one man's mission was to help and heal, while the other's was to take what did not belong to him.

"Do not pull the trigger, be careful!" cried out the doctor. He wanted to protect himself and the old farmer from the robber, but he didn't want bloodshed.

Unfortunately, Hilario misunderstood the young

doctor's intentions and grumbled: "You don't scare me with your rifle, scoundrel, just give it to me!"

And since he'd never handled a rifle before, he accidentally pulled the trigger and shot himself in the arm! Imagine his surprise when he suddenly found himself lying on the road in pain, with the rifle lying next to him! He tried to reach it with his other hand, but when he tried to move, a sharp pain shot right through his body.

"Let me help you, to stop the bleeding!" shouted the doctor and ran to the carriage for his satchel of medical supplies. But as the doctor knelt before him to examine his wounded left arm, Hilario pulled another knife from his riding boot and attempted to stab him.

"I'll kill you, I'll kill you!" Hilario repeated, growing weaker and weaker from the blood he'd lost.

"I'm only trying to help you," the doctor tried to explain, but Hilario did not believe him. Then, realizing that his condition was deteriorating, Hilario simply closed his eyes and said:

"You win. Do whatever you want with me now, even kill me, if that is your intention." "Why would I want to kill you?" the doctor asked, as he deftly cleaned and dressed Hilario's wound. He not only treated Hilario as he would a regular patient, but he even placed a pillow from his carriage under his head to make him comfortable.

Hilario quieted down for a minute and lay on the road, his head on the pillow, looking into the blue sky. Then the doctor said, guiltily:

"I shouldn't keep my patient the dirt. Let me help you into my carriage, so you can rest." Meanwhile, Hilario tried to get up and run back into the bushes, but he was so weak from the loss of blood that he collapsed.

"Where are you going? You are not healed yet!" the doctor said.

"I don't want to go to jail," Hilario said, "I thank you for your kindness, but please, let me go free..."

"My profession involves treating people and making them feel better, whereas I think jails are intended to make you feel worse!" the doctor replied. "You probably should go to jail for what you do. However, I'm not a policeman. But I can say that if you feel remorse over your life, you should go to a church, confess all your sins, and then turn yourself in. As for me, I need to attend to a sick girl in another town, so I have to speed up..."

"I can't believe that a man whom I almost killed for his possessions treated my wound," said Hilario. "Where are you headed? If you are going to Rosea, I would to ask you to take me along, to my elder brother's place. I would like to give you something in return for saving my arm."

And the doctor took the bandit to the town of Rosea where Hilario's brother lived and raised chickens. When they reached his home, Hilario asked the doctor to wait outside, while he entered the dwelling and soon emerged with something, wrapped in a bright red kerchief.

"This is for you!" Hilario said.

Intrigued by this unexpected gift, the doctor unwrapped the heavy object in Hilario's presence. Imagine his surprise at seeing a silver candelabra, commonly found in Jewish households!

"Are you of the Jewish faith?" the doctor asked, naively. "I am not a Jew, but my neighbor is, and he told me how much he cherished his candelabra."

When Hilario didn't reply, the doctor had a closer

look and noticed the letter "R" engraved on the bottom of the candelabra, which he knew stood for "Reuben". And he realized immediately that it belonged to his neighbor, whose son, Reuben, had engraved his initial on this prized possession, without his father's permission. The silver candelabra had been stolen from the neighbor's home one evening, while he was busy in the adjoining room, making Reuben recite passages from the Torah, in preparation for his bar-mitzvah.

The doctor hesitated before responding.

"Do you reject my gift to you that comes from the heart?" Hilario asked angrily, seeing his reluctance, and he reached for the knife on his belt, but only cried out in agony.

"If not for my pain," he said, "I would've attacked you again. I didn't mean to, it's just that whenever I feel that someone disrespects me, I lose control and want to lash out! The blood rushes to my head, I get angry, and then I start a vicious fight. It's how nature created me."

Afraid the bandit would change his mind and overpower him, the doctor said: "Thank you so much for your gift, dear Hilario."

But to himself, he thought:

"If I tell him I know it was stolen, he could get angry and kill me right here, so I'll keep silent and outwit him! I'll pretend I believe he is indeed very kind, in order to save my own life. At the same time, I'll prevent him from attacking other innocent people!"

The doctor was smart enough to hide the truth from Hilario, but he was still naïve to think he could convince the bandit to change his unlawful ways.

"It appears that our encounter has helped you, Hilario," he said. "Not only is your arm healing now, but so is your soul, since you thanked me with kindness."

"My dear friend, you are right," Hilario replied. And just as the doctor had, now it was Hilario's turn to lie. "I feel that our encounter woke me up and showed me the ugliness of crime. I'm ready to help other people, and if you would teach me to heal, and to raise the ill from their sick beds, I'm eager to listen!"

The doctor looked into Hilario's eyes and almost believed him.

"Why not?" he thought. "Maybe our meeting was fateful. It's not by chance that this bandit stole my neighbor's candelabra and gave it to me, so I could return it to Reuben's family… And it's not by chance that this bandit wants to assist others. I'll be the one who will help him find salvation!"

And the naïve doctor came up with a plan.

"Hilario!" he said solemnly. "Even though I'm a doctor proficient in treating flesh, I never forget about the soul. I indeed healed your arm – but along with your arm, your soul improved. Promise me you will turn yourself in and go to jail, and that you will tell other inmates about your healing and urge them to give up their bad actions and thoughts!"

"Sure, my dear friend," nodded Hilario. "As soon as we finish this conversation, I will run toward a jail as fast as I can, so that by the time you start treating that sick girl, I will already be sitting behind bars and preaching to the other inmates."

– And with these words, – concluded Favel Bavilsky, – the bandit and the doctor shook hands and parted ways.

53

Naftali looked at Favel Bavilsky questioningly.

– You don't like this story? – asked the old poet.

– I like it very much, – answered Naftali, – but wasn't it supposed to be a story about a bandit who was so eloquent with words that he was released from prison much earlier than expected?

– That's true, – confirmed the old poet. – I was so involved in the story, I forgot what my point in telling it was! Yes, Hilario was released from prison for being a great storyteller.

– Did he indeed turn himself in immediately after parting with Alberto the doctor? – asked Naftali's father, who was enjoying the company of the old poet and the three boys.

– No, no, – Favel raised his finger. – He laughed at the doctor's naiveté, and after the doctor rode away, Hilario started boasting to his elder brother about how smart and resourceful he was. He was so involved in himself that he didn't notice he'd upset his brother, who had been a bandit before, but was trying to be an honest man and earn money by raising chickens. Besides, the candelabra had been a gift to him from Hilario, and he didn't like that Hilario had grabbed it without asking.

Instead of turning himself in the next day, Hilario he robbed somebody right next to his brother's house, which didn't sit well with him at all.

"You put me in danger!" his brother said. "A local policeman knows about my past, and he'll think that I robbed this poor farmer, whose only mistake was choosing to travel on the wrong road."

But Hilario only laughed at his older brother, pointing at his dilapidated hut and thread-bare clothes.

"You've gained nothing with your honest ways, so after one look at your decrepit shack, any policeman who came would know you weren't a robber!"

"Say what you want," answered the older brother, "but I'm glad I'm not like you anymore, stealing from simple folk."

Hilario just smiled and left. He was very proud of himself and congratulated himself for fooling the doctor. Half an hour later, the policeman knocked on Hilario's brother's front door and asked whether he'd heard anything about the robbery which had happened nearby.

"I'm ashamed to say, but I do know who did it," confessed the older brother, and he told the policeman where Hilario was headed. The policeman jumped on his horse and chased after him. Within minutes, Hilario was apprehended and thrown in jail.

— And that's where he started composing stories? — asked Naftali.

— Oh yes, at first Hilario thought telling stories would earn him the respect of other inmates, so he started telling them stories about himself. They were almost all the same: how he sharpened his knife and hid in the bushes and then jumped out on the road and left with somebody else's belongings and jewelry. But after the third or fourth such story, the other inmates told Hilario they'd had enough and would like to hear something completely different... Afraid of losing their respect, Hilario thought and thought for several nights, even losing sleep! He would sit on his bunk for hours, thinking. Finally he broke his silence with a new story, not about his merciless robberies, but about a *bien-te-veo* bird – the bird all Argentineans love. And this story had no beginning, or end.

Each night the inmates would gather around Hilario, and he would share with them a new adventure from the bird's life. At one point, he started writing them down, and they became so popular, the inmates would memorize them and pass them around from cell to cell, so that even those at the other end of the prison could benefit from their rich texture.

One inmate really hated Hilario for his popularity and did whatever he could to get make his life difficult. He decided that presenting Hilario's written stories to the jail-keeper would be enough to get him in real trouble. Once he'd collected several of the sheets being circulated, he presented them to the jail-keeper and complained that as soon as Hilario had come to their jail, the inmates had stopped thinking about reforming themselves and praying to God to forgive their sins, and only looked forward to each new chapter of Hilario's "frivolous tales". The inmate also suggested that having learned to pass the stories from cell to cell, so the most literate prisoners would read them aloud while the others memorized them, they'd be passing escape plans next!

"Venerable sir!" the inmate addressed the jail-keeper politely. "Today Hilario is composing stories about a shrewd weasel and a careless bird; tomorrow his popularity will grow so much, he'll be able to stage an uprising and prepare a clever escape! He must be stopped."

However, as sometimes happens in life, this inmate's actions led to the completely opposite result. For quite a while already, the chief had been noticing that since Hilario's arrival, the inmates were fighting and quarreling less. Instead, they would gather in their cells every evening and engage in conversation. Even in their illiterate letters to family members back home they seemed milder and more considerate. Instead of only asking for food or clothes or even money, now they were describing how much fun they were having in the evening, when restless Hilario entertained them with one of his endless stories!

The jail-keeper took one of the sheets and started reading. The more he read, the kinder his face became. By the time he'd reached the end, he was roaring with laughter: apparently, the story he read was hilarious!

"He is so talented!" the jail chief said to himself. "Even though I like keeping him in my jail to make other inmates contented with their lives here, I would like to present his case to the citizens of this town, to show them what a positive influence a jail can have on its inmates! Who would recognize a former violent bandit in this wonderful storyteller? And if I showed the townsmen some of Hilario's stories, maybe they'd see me not as someone cruel, who feeds the inmates only bread and water and denies them any culture, but as a refined individual who appreciates the arts!"

So the jail-keeper published one of Hilario's stories in a local newspaper. After reading it, a certain major reviewed Hilario's case and promptly authorized his release.

– And so, – Favel Bavilsky concluded, – a talent for storytelling helped the bandit become free again! Nobody knows what happened to Hilario following his release. However, the locals were not afraid to travel alone after that, because the robberies in that area had stopped.

54

After school the next day, Naftali asked his father to help him find his key, which his rhea had stolen the night before.

– We can hoe the earth in the garden and see if she hid it there, or maybe dropped it when she was running away from you! Let me grab a mattock and begin…

– If I give that ugly creature a drink of castor oil, – Naftali's mother chimed in, – she'll return the key, along with everything else she's carried away from my kitchen pantry!

– How could drinking oil make her do that? – asked Naftali, not knowing what his mother meant.

– You'll see! – she replied.

– Just make sure the bird is outside when you do it, Raya! – Naftali's father said. – In fact, we'll be killing two birds with one stone: we'll not only get back the key, but we can also use her droppings to fertilize our garden.

– Don't throw stones at her! – Naftali exclaimed, unfamiliar with the expression. – It was my fault for leaving the key near her…

– Never mind, Naftali, – his father said, smiling reassuringly, – a little castor oil wouldn't hurt a bird that size. Besides, I'm sure your mother is only joking…

He began loosening the soil with a pickaxe, examining every clump of earth.

– Wait, I think I found something, – he suddenly said, and he dropped to his knees to inspect an object he saw in the grass. Naftali and his mother stood waiting impatiently, as his father yanked it out of the ground and cleaned it off, but it was only a rusty horseshoe.

Naftali's father had dug up most of the garden, before he finally said:

– I don't think your key's here... But just look at how fertile this soil is. When the earth is loose like this, seeds grow easily. In Russia, when I was a boy, my dad planted poppies with me. I still remember how we bought two pots, then made holes in the soil with sticks for the seeds and then checked them every day... Now I can grow poppies with you!

And Naftali's father took a handkerchief out of his pocket, carefully unfolded it and showed Naftali the poppy seeds that were in it.

– This is only the beginning! – Naftali's father exclaimed. – One of the government officials here told me we can build a wooden fence around our garden. That would be so much better than the ropes we have now. It would keep the stray horses and other animals from trampling or eating our crops... Won't that be great, Naftali?

– But how will we be able to repay the cost of these planks? – Naftali's mother asked.

– Don't worry, Raya, – her husband replied. – We'll earn enough to repay the cost of our voyage from Russia and the materials we've acquired here by selling what we grow!

– But your only experience is with horses! You've never grown anything besides those poppies you planted as a child!

– Raya, we'll learn, – Naftali's father reassured his wife, – everything will be fine! And soon the fence was built around the garden. Naftali's father was beaming:

– In Russia we had no land whatsoever, and now I

feel like a well-off landowner! I can't wait to start growing wheat and tomatoes!

Meanwhile, Naftali was less enthusiastic about his father's intentions. Secretly, he dreamed about moving to the city, closer to books and libraries, and becoming a learned man. Deep in his heart, he hoped his parents would change their minds and, instead of farming, that they'd leave the pampas and find jobs in the capital.

Little did he know then, that he would indeed be moving to the city soon. Nor could he have imagined the sudden, tragic, and shocking circumstances that would bring about the move, and affect him and his mother forever.

55

Naftali understood the benefits of having a wooden fence around their vegetable garden, but he had no use for it, personally. Besides, it was already provoking anger in others. On his way home from school one day, Naftali saw his old acquaintance, Estancio, walking shoeless and shabbily dressed. When Naftali waved at him, Estancio shouted:

– Here comes the rich boy, here comes the rich boy!

– I'm not rich! – Naftali shouted back.

– You hide your wealth behind the fence! – Estancio retorted, and he threw a stone at Naftali. When Naftali insisted his parents weren't wealthy, Estancio shouted: – Liar, liar, liar! – stuck out his tongue. On the verge of tears, Naftali ran home.

But when he got there, he saw that his father was in trouble as well.

Red-faced and confused, either from the hot sun or frustration, Naftali's father was in the garden, exchanging words with a gaucho on horseback, who was on the other side of their newly built fence. Naftali recognized him immediately: this short and stocky gaucho used to gallop around wildly on his pitch-black horse, scaring children and the elderly, who sometimes had to act fast to get out of his way. Once, Naftali saw him pummeling another man, who was taller and stronger. But even so, he was defenseless against the gaucho's vicious attack. Another time, Naftali saw him taking part in a horse race. When he only came in second, he started shouting fighting words and grew so enraged, he charged his horse at the winning horse, trying to make it throw its rider to the ground.

Afraid for his father, Naftali went to his side, ready to protect him, if needed. Naftali's father hugged him, as if to reassure him that everything was fine.

– No need to worry, Naftali, we are just discussing some issues...

The gaucho shouted something in Spanish that Naftali did not understand. Naftali's father said very politely:

– His name is Ermilio.

The gaucho jumped off the horse and approached the fence, shaking his fist. It was dark, polished, and smoothed by the sun – exactly like the gaucho's deep-toned, sun-burned face.

– Ermilio, – Naftali's father addressed him, – this is my son. *Es mi hijo*, Naftali. Do you have children?

The gaucho narrowed his dark eyes at Naftali, making the boy so uncomfortable, he couldn't even bring himself to smile or nod back. The gaucho then started gesturing excitedly and shouting in Spanish again. Naftali knew the language, but he couldn't understand a word of what Ermilio was saying, either because Ermilio was speaking too fast, or using unfamiliar words.

Naftali's father quietly said to Naftali:

– Ermilio wanted to let his horse graze here, but the fence prevented him, so he's not happy. I explained that we had erected the fence to protect our future crops and poppies. Then Ermilio told me that he possessed no land, himself.

While Naftali's father explained, Ermilio grabbed a flask from under his belt and started drinking. He was growing more agitated with every gulp. After drinking everything in the flask, Ermilio pointed to his own chest and started shouting:

– *Nada! Nada! Nada!*

Naftali's father was nervous but tried to remain calm. There was nobody who could help him diffuse this delicate situation. Ermilio lived in the area and they had to make peace somehow. Naftali's father continued:

– Ermilio complained that just a few months ago he could roam the pampas freely, but ever since the Jewish colonists arrived, he can only go here and there. He said he didn't feel free in his own country anymore!

Naftali looked at Ermilio, who kept repeating, *"Nada, nada!"* more loudly, followed by what sounded like Spanish swear words. His behavior was rude and aggressive. He kicked a plank in the fence a couple of times, then grimaced, glanced at Naftali and suddenly laughed.

– I'm joking! – he said in Spanish. He raised his foot as though to kick the fence again, but didn't. – It's well made! – he said instead, winking at Naftali. – My horse would love to have this wood for her corral. – Did you help your father build it?

– *Si,* – said Naftali.

– There, you see? – said Naftali's father proudly. – We understand each other! Before you came, Naftali, Ermilio here asked me why he, an Argentinean native, has nothing, whereas an immigrant like me can work on the land so soon after arriving. He kept repeating the same question over and over, without letting me reply. When he quieted down, I explained to him that in Russia, our situation was quite similar: Russians could own land and Jews couldn't! Russians could live off their land, harvesting the fruit and vegetables they had planted, whereas

Jews could only be peddlers, selling things door-to-door, working at menial jobs. And here, this destitute man with his hungry horse has no rights or possessions, like Jews in Russia. And, as in Russia, the government does nothing to help! I feel so sorry for him... After I told Ermilio this, we understood each other perfectly, because we have both experienced the same pain!

Not sure how to respond, Naftali just looked at his father, standing on one side of the fence, and then at Ermilio, on the other. Unexpectedly, Ermilio approached the fence once again and started shaking it as though testing its firmness.

– Please don't do that, – said Naftali's father politely. – I understand why you are not happy about us coming here and building fences, but please understand us as well... There is still plenty of grass for your horse beyond this fence.

But Ermilio wasn't looking at him. Instead, he took another little bottle out of his pocket, gulped down its contents and threw it over the fence so forcefully that it hit the front door of their house. Then he jumped into his saddle and galloped away without saying a word.

Naftali sighed with relief, and his father said: – He's not a bad man.

56

Naftali couldn't understand what this gaucho wanted from them. The life of the locals here remained a mystery to him, and despite his parents' urging, he still hadn't made any friends with the local boys.

He took down the basket of his beloved books from a shelf built by his father, opened a volume by Charles Darwin and found the pages where Darwin described his encounters with gauchos. Naftali had already read these pages in Russia, but at that time these gauchos were only dreams, only characters on a page.

Imagining that he and Darwin were sitting by a campfire together on a remote Argentine island, Naftali started reading the passages aloud, but pretending that Darwin himself was the one speaking. He was saying:

"Who else in the world is so independent? Free as the wind, gauchos have the sun as their guide, the meat of a mare as their food, and bare saddles as their beds. They use dung or dry bones to build a fire and spin tales of adventure while sipping mate. Not tied to any particular place, they travel light and at any second can gallop to the other side of the pampas, or even another part of the world."

In his imagination, Naftali supplemented Darwin's observations with qualities he himself wanted to see in these inhabitants of the Argentinean pampas.

Darwin described hovels made of robust thistle-stalks, where gauchos rested at night, after herding cattle from sunrise to sundown. Their roofs had gaps that exposed the sky and let the rain in. Naftali envisioned himself at the doorway of one of these, introducing himself in Spanish, so that the tough guy within, wearing a thick poncho, would let him in. Naftali would whistle, first, then talk in a friendly, relaxed way, so that the gaucho wouldn't mistake him for an enemy and attack. Warmed by the hot tea and enjoying the fragrance of the gaucho's lighted cigar, he would listen to the weathered man's account of the day's hunting adventure.

"I rode as fast as a lightning bolt!" the gaucho would say. "I spotted a rhea, threw my bolas and trapped it in a second. Then I leaned over on my horse, still going full speed, grabbed the rhea and placed it in a sack, hung from the saddle. What a wonderful trophy she was! Breathless, but not allowing myself even a second of rest, I spurred my horse on with my heels. She ran so fast I thought I might fall off. I spotted another large rhea and repeated my usual method of throwing the bolas and trapping its legs..."

Naftali paused to think. What else would this gaucho tell him? Would he ask if Naftali wanted to join his hunt for deer and armadillo, or maybe even wildcats, like a jaguar or puma?

Imagining this encounter, Naftali wondered how Ermilio would react, if he asked him to describe his days on the pampas? Judging only from Ermilio's rough, yet down-to-earth appearance, Naftali could not decide whether Ermilio would be kind to him...

Were the gauchos Darwin met nice to him? Naftali continued reading, and again he felt as though he were hearing Darwin's low and self-assured voice:

"Gauchos are proud and brave; they love to compete with each other in races. A long time ago they abandoned

the idea that horses should be free, deciding that a gaucho's primary goal in life was to gain complete mastery over these animals. Once, during my travels, I met a man who claimed that no matter how many times he threw his horse down, he never went down with it."

Naftali imagined Darwin frowning on such boasting, but not objecting to it, because arguing with a gaucho was dangerous. Gauchos didn't like to debate, preferring a physical fight. In the book, Naftali found a relevant excerpt:

"Gauchos carry with them long knives, and, if they have a different opinion on a certain subject, these knives can become a solid argument in a conversation."

Naftali was unsettled by these words, but continued reading:

"So many times during my travels I met gauchos with big scars on their faces... When I asked one of these strong and silent warriors about the origin of his scar, he did not say anything. He just rolled one of his little cigars, and, when a flame from his match lit his face, I saw that the scar was fresh and still had a couple days before it healed... Seeing this made me shiver: there was no way of finding out, who attacked this robust traveler and how often he engaged in these violent displays of temper."

From what Darwin had written about the constant quarreling and contests among Argentinean gauchos, Naftali supposed that contact with them could lead to trouble. At the same time, Darwin was impressed by their many good qualities:

"I had never met more welcoming and polite people. Not even once did gauchos show me any disrespect or unfounded rudeness. Without exaggeration, it would be ac-

curate to proclaim gauchos incredibly modest beings, who respect not only themselves and their guests, whom they treat well, but also their country, of which they are proud citizens."

Naftali put the book aside; it had not given him an answer. It painted two contrasting images of the very same gaucho: as a dignified and hospitable man, and as a brutish, unrestrained fighter, on the ready with his long, sharp knife.

Naftali wanted to discuss Ermilio with his father, and compare him to the gauchos in Darwin's book. In Naftali's opinion, Ermilio was both nice, by commenting favorably on the fence Naftali had painted, and rude, by kicking the very same fence. Still, as his father said, the free-spirited gaucho was ready to listen and understood many things.

– Papa, have you read Darwin? – Naftali shouted, rushing to his father's room. But his father wasn't there, so Naftali went to the kitchen. He saw a tea cup and an unfinished piece of bread on the table, but his father wasn't there, either. Nor was he in the corridor.

Suspecting his father might be in the garden, Naftali decided to check.

57

Suddenly Naftali heard a commotion outside their house: first, a loud bang, then men's voices, shouting. Then a horse neighed wildly, as though in pain. Naftali ran to the window and saw a horse in their garden, on its knees: apparently, it had tried to jump over the fence and fallen, and now it couldn't get up. Ermilio was standing beside it, still holding the reins. He walked around the animal, stroking its neck and inspecting its legs. He whispered something into its ear and wiped his hands on his pants.

Then, without warning, he threw himself at Naftali's father. Terrified, Naftali yelled for his mother, but she was out, either running errands or working in the garden.

Naftali was too afraid to look out the window. His father's voice had grown shrill, and the horse's neighing was much louder now. When he couldn't hear Ermilio's voice, Naftali was hoping he'd left, and that the danger had passed, so he peered out the window once again. Alas, Ermilio was still there, pinning Naftali's father against the fence, so that he couldn't move.

– Mom! Help! – Naftali shouted and immediately heard his mother yell out:

– Lazar! Lazar! Oh my God, Lazar! Get off him, get off him!

Naftali fell to the floor and put his arms over his head, afraid to listen. But when he heard Ermilio's grunting and his mother screaming, Naftali quickly looked out the window, just in time to see the knife in Ermilio's hand. It flashed as Ermilio raised his hand and brought it down again, hard – once, twice, three times. Naftali's mother screamed:

– He killed him, he killed him! Naftali ran toward the door.

– Mama! Mama! I'm coming! Wait, I'm coming! – he shouted. But when he tried to push open the door, he heard his mother say:

– Stay inside, Naftali!

She'd stopped screaming; her voice was firm and steady now.

– Mama, I'll help, what's going on, mama, please tell me! – Naftali was saying, over and over. There was an image in his head of the enraged Ermilio, and of his father's lifeless body, standing up against the fence, then sliding down to the ground.

The image of his father's limp body. The image of a raised hand, clutching a sharp knife. The image of his father carefully unwrapping a kerchief full of poppy seeds. The image of Ermilio's horse, which he had forced to jump over their fence. The image of his father with a pickaxe, softening the earth in search of the lost key.

Naftali pushed at the door, while his mother, pressed her full weight against it from the other side.

– Don't come out here! – she insisted, desperately.

Terrified, Naftali refused to think about why his mother would not let him out. With his ear to the door, he tried to listen, but the only sound was the horse, roaring in anguish. Then he heard Ermilio laughing. Naftali ran to the window, just as the drunken Ermilio staggered over to the window and peered inside. Their eyes met, but it was getting darker and more difficult to see; Ermilio looked at the boy, but didn't seem to notice him. Still, Naftali's heart was racing. He ran away from the window and crawled under the bed, mortally afraid that Ermilio, after killing his father, would now come after him. Listening for Ermilio's footsteps, Naftali held his breath and lay perfectly still under the bed.

Several minutes later, when Ermilio still hadn't entered the house, Naftali decided he must have left, so he tiptoed to the front door. What he heard made him run out the door and straight toward his father.

His mother was crying by his side:

– Lazar, Lazar, say something! Lazar, everything will be okay! Forgive me for laughing at your idea of planting poppies here... We'll do it! Lazar, open your eyes and say something!

Naftali's father was lying next to the fence. The horse was gone. The grass was green. Their neighbors were already running over to help, among them a village doctor. Naftali's father was moaned weakly, as though his wound was nothing significant. His moaning grew weaker and weaker. The green grass was soaked through and sticky with his blood. By the time the village doctor kneeled beside him, the moaning had stopped.

The doctor stood up and wanted to say something to Naftali's mother but stopped himself short. Then he saw Naftali and tried to hug him, but Naftali flinched. He was afraid to look at his father's pale face. He looked at his lifeless body and at the fresh earth, and then saw the handkerchief. It must have fallen out of his father's pants pocket. It was still folded and the seeds were surely still in it.

After the doctor, some of the locals and Naftali's mother had carried his father's body inside, Naftali picked up the folded handkerchief and, making sure that nobody saw, hid it behind the books on his shelf.

Then he wept, and he continued to weep for a very long time.

58

Two weeks later, Naftali opened his diary. Before his father's death, Naftali could discuss with him whatever questions he had, whereas now he found himself alone, facing only a blank page that could receive his words, but never respond to them. His mother had become melancholy and withdrawn since her husband's murder. Every morning she woke up early and went to the grave, until noon, then returned to look after the household and cook. Then she'd sit in the corner for hours, crying, and talking to his clothes as she sorted through them. Soon there were piles of clothing all over the floor, and when Naftali asked why, his mother wouldn't answer the question. Naftali was afraid she was losing her mind.

She didn't want Naftali going to school, either.

– What if Ermilio's relatives ambush the school in revenge? – she said. – I heard they've thrown that killer in jail, but he has brothers. People are saying it was your father who attacked Ermilio, because his horse accidentally jumped over the fence...

– But it's not true! – protested Naftali. – When Ermilio got upset over our fence, Father explained that we had plans to grow vegetables and needed to protect our future crops...

– Plans! Plans! – Naftali's mother retorted bitterly. – Our only plan now is to leave here! And the sooner everybody forgets about what happened here, the better!

– Where would we go? – Naftali asked, but again, his mother gave no answer and only kept to herself, sorting clothes and household goods, and dividing them evenly between sacks and suitcases.

Naftali wrote down his thoughts:

"Things have gotten much worse now that my father is gone. My mother cries all the time, but I try to stay calm. I still cannot believe what has happened. He was always so wise. He knew how to address guests who visited our home in Russia. Even when they argued among themselves, my father would say a few words, and they would quiet down. These words were not enough here in Argentina. He was misunderstood. I do not know what to do without him. Now his place at the table is empty. Even the tales that Favel Bavilsky tells don't interest me anymore. He told us about conscientious bandits – bad people who commit crimes but feel remorse and try to better themselves. Does Ermilio understand what he did? I'm not sure what his viewpoint is, but whatever he feels, it won't change the situation. My father is gone."

Naftali paused briefly and continued writing:

"I'm not the same after his death. I used to converse with him before, but now I just stare at his place at the table. I enjoyed reading books before – now I see no fun even in perusing them. Tulchinea, who brought joy to me, has disappeared. I'm afraid that Estancio snatched her when she was outside. I don't even want to think about what he could have done to her. Perhaps, she ended up in a soup! I'm very upset. My mother is desolate. She has changed, too. She has prohibited me from going to school, at least for the time being. She is afraid something might happen to me on my way there, that I might be accosted by bandits or Ermilio's relatives. After he attacked and killed my father, he was apprehended by our neighbors. Now, from time to time, they bring us some food. They just leave it on our porch, anonymously. They feel sorry for us. One of them commented that, before, a bright future awaited me, but that now, I'm done for, that without 'a man in the family', I won't be able to make it. He said that unless my mother remarries, we'll never have money. Hearing him talk like that made me angry. My mother loved my father so much, she cannot even think about anybody else.

Yet, she's becoming unpredictable. She doesn't let me leave home even to play with Syoma and Lyova. When she saw me sitting in a tree, she shouted at me, as though I had just committed a sin. She told me to immediately climb down. She was afraid I would fall to the ground like a ripe apple. Now I can't go anywhere without her being worried sick. She says she's already lost my father and does not want to lose me, too."

And, finally, Naftali wrote: "Not sure how to occupy myself, I woke up one day and pulled all the weeds out of our would-be garden. As for the handkerchief that fell out of my father's pocket, I want to keep it forever. I carry it in my pocket all the time, with the poppy seeds inside. It is a memory of him that is always with me."

Naftali hid the diary in the basket, under the *Don Quixote* volumes.

* * *

Later in the day his mother said:

– I'm ready! I don't think you have many belongings to pack, so it will only take you fifteen minutes.

– Why should I pack? – Naftali inquired. He had no idea what his mother was talking about.

– Naftali, we are leaving. I thought you knew. There is no way we can stay here after what happened to him.

Naftali hid his face so as not to show that he was ready to burst into tears.

– Besides, – added his mother, – we cannot repay our debt to the people who sponsored our trip to Argentina. With your father alive it was still possible, but it's hopeless, now, with only you and me. We have to disappear, without telling anybody a word!

– What if they start looking for us? – Naftali asked, worried about his mother's idea to run away.

– We'll be far away by then! – she said. – We have a little money that your father and I had saved for our life here and for your future, but if we stay, our sponsors will take it. Pack your things, and at sunset there will be a carriage here waiting for us. We need to leave when it's dark!

Naftali did not expect this turn of events. He'd lost his father, and now he was losing his familiar surroundings. Ahead of them was the unknown. He had no idea how they would be able to support themselves somewhere, but he didn't dare contradict his mother's decision.

– I can't stay in a place that was so cruel to us, – she said. – Besides, the sooner they forget about us here, the safer our money will be. To be honest, I had hoped our sponsors would forgive our debt, but they didn't. Just before Ermilio came, your father had spoken with one of the officials making their rounds here, reminding the settlers about repaying. Maybe he was so nervous, he said the wrong thing to that gaucho...

– My father didn't say anything inappropriate to Ermilio! – protested Naftali. – He was extremely polite and even explained to him that Jews in Russia were treated poorly, too, like the gauchos here...

— Naftali, Ermilio does not care about faraway Russia, — his mother said. — Neither he nor his father nor his grandfather ever left this area in search of better future. He knows nothing except the pampas and horses, because they are his livelihood. And he doesn't want to know about anybody else! But let's forget about this evil man. Today a carriage will take us away...

And so their lonely journey began.

After riding for several hours in the carriage Naftali's mother had hired, they spent a night at an inn. When the proprietor asked where they were headed the next morning, Naftali's mother pretended not to hear the question. She was afraid he would disclose their destination, should anyone come looking for them.

– I hope you are not going far! – he warned. – The weather is unpredictable during spring. Anything can happen, so I advise you not to travel without a guide.

Naftali's mother was so afraid the owner would ask about their destination again, she didn't ask about the possible dangers, if they traveled alone.

They soon found out that this was a mistake.

The next morning they had a light breakfast, left some luggage with the innkeeper that they would fetch, once they had settled in their new place, and continued their journey. They had rucksacks on their backs, filled with enough snacks to last till their next stop, plus they were carrying suitcases, so Naftali became tired quite soon.

– I told you to leave your books at the inn! – his mother said angrily. – We could have picked them up later, once we found a new place, and some work, to earn some money.

Naftali answered:

– They're not heavy, – Naftali replied, – I only brought my two volumes of *Don Quixote* and the Tolstoy stories Papa bought me...

Upon hearing the word "Papa", Naftali's mother's

expression changed. Afraid she might cry, Naftali stroked her forearm, but she pushed him away.

– It was your father who brought us here! – she said, bitterly. – *He* was the one who chose Argentina and convinced the others to move. Our neighbors blamed him for their misfortunes. They even told me to my face!

– Would we have been safer in Russia? – asked Naftali.

– No! I was always afraid for you and your father, worried about ignorant boys slandering you, or when the next pogrom could be... Naftali sighed. Apparently, neither Russia, nor Argentina were without their shortcomings.

– Mama! – he said. – Let's stop talking about what was, or could have been, and do something now! The wind has gotten so strong, I can hardly walk! Look, look at the trees! They're practically bending over. This one has already broken in two! What if it's a hurricane?

Naftali's mother dropped her suitcase on the ground.

– I'm tired too, Naftali. Let's have a snack, and then continue. We are still a long way from where we're going.

And that very minute, Naftali felt a raindrop. The sky was suddenly dark, the temperature dropped and a strong gust of wind blew Naftali's hat off his head and carried it away, along with everything else it had picked up.

– Mama, maybe we should return to the inn, – said Naftali. – Remember what the owner said about the bad weather?

– We'll be fine, – she answered, and before Naftali could insist, she stood up, put her rucksack back on, grabbed the suitcases and started walking. All Naftali could do was follow her.

– We need to walk quickly, – she said. – What if our sponsors have realized we've left and are already looking for us? I don't want them to bother us about our debt. I'm doing this for you, son, so we'll have some money left for your education. I never wanted to go against your father's will, but I don't see you as a farmer. I see you as a teacher, living in the city. Besides, I couldn't bear to keep living where my husband met his tragic end!

And Naftali and his mother continued walking. It was raining more heavily, everything was swirling in the wind, the birds were flying and chattering wildly over their heads. Stopping to remove a grain of sand from his eye, Naftali reached into his pocket for his father's handkerchief with the poppy seeds, but it wasn't there. Desperately, he checked both pockets and then the rucksack, but it was gone. Naftali grew very upset, listing aloud every place he'd been, where he could have lost it – his home, his school, to say bye to Lyova and Syoma, without his mother knowing, his father's grave, Favel Bavilsky's place, to hear one last fairy tale.

– What did you say? – asked Naftali's mother.

Naftali shuddered. He didn't realize she was walking so close to him. But she hadn't heard him mention the school, because she said:

– Did you say "fairy tale"? Let's tell each other fairy tales! The time will pass more quickly that way. Look at this tree, for example! It is so imposing and comforting at the same time; one probably could even take a nap in its trunk... Have you ever read a tale about a tree? Tell me one and then I'll try to make up another!

– That's too easy! – Naftali said, drying his wet face

on his sleeve. The rain drops were now falling more frequently. – I remember one by heart, from Tolstoy's book. It is short and simple, and I can finish it before it starts pouring. Then I hope we'll find cover!

– If we walk more quickly, – his mother said, – we'll reach where we are going in just one hour. Meanwhile, tell me this Tolstoy tale.

Naftali started:

– Two young boys were strolling through the forest, when they chanced upon a huge bear. The boy who spotted the bear first, climbed the nearest tree as fast as he could. The second boy did not have time to escape, so he lay down on the road and covered his head with his arms, fearing the worst.

The bear approached.

The boy in the tree held his breath, watching. The boy who lay on the road did not move either: he was terrified. The bear touched him with his paw, then lowered his head and sniffed him. When the boy on the road still did not move, the bear decided he was dead and lost all interest in him.

As soon as the bear left, the first boy quickly scampered down the tree and laughed at the second boy. He asked him if the conversation with the bear had been pleasant: "He lowered his head, and his nose almost touched your ear. Did he tell you something interesting?"

The second boy looked at the first one, seriously, and said: "Yes, he certainly did." Still laughing, the first boy asked, "What did he tell you?" And the second boy replied: "The bear told me it's not nice to leave your friend alone, in danger."

And the first boy said nothing in response, because

he was ashamed.

– What a wonderful story! – commented Naftali's mother. – The first boy learned a great lesson. But I would like to remind you, Naftali, not to climb trees like that boy.

– It's only a story! Tolstoy probably made it up! It never happened! – objected Naftali.

– I know it's just literature, but I'm the only one responsible for you now, so I don't want you to do stupid things. Trees are quite dangerous, so never climb on them like you did in Russia.

Naftali got upset. Instead of praising him for how well he remembered Tolstoy's story, his mother was scolding him for climbing ridiculous trees! How unfair that was!

Noticing his sudden change of mood, his mother asked:

– Don't you want to hear my story about a tree?

– I don't want to hear anything about trees anymore!

– Naftali, – his mother hugged him, – don't you understand that I care about you? Now I have to act as both parents, so I have to be doubly vigilant and keep an eye on you. But now it's my turn to tell a story involving a tree.

Naftali stopped in his tracks.

– Yes, tell me, but let's rest.

When they stopped, the sky was darker than before, even though it was midday. The rain had stopped, although the wind was even stronger. All the birds had disappeared and there wasn't a soul in sight. Oblivious to these changes in the weather, Naftali's mother started her story.

60

– Some time ago there was a little girl who had to stay home alone, while her father was working. Despite his warnings, she wanted to go outside. She was playful and loved nature, so she disobeyed him. At first, she just walked around gathering flowers, but then she made a garland and wanted to float it in the water. Her father was always afraid that she would fall into the river and, even though he taught her how to swim, he forbade her to approach it. Yet, since her father didn't come home from work till night-time, the girl knew he would never know if she went to the river. She took her garland and hurried to the river bank. But when she got there, she spotted a puma! Her first impulse was to run away or climb a tree. But, unlike in your story, Naftali, there was no suitable tree on the shore – just sand and some bushes. The girl stood staring at the large and dangerous animal. And the animal was looking her straight in the eyes!

In a split second, the girl realized that the puma did not intend to attack her, and was only concerned about her cubs. Suddenly, two of her litter fell into the water. Acting quickly, the girl jumped into the river and pulled out the cubs. As they were hardly breathing and wet, the girl removed her cardigan and wrapped it around them, warming them up. She kept them close to her breast, to make sure they were reviving, and even sang them a lullaby as she often did with her dolls. The puma was grateful!

– Fascinating, – commented Naftali, – but didn't you say there were no suitable trees on the shore? Then your story can't count as a story about a tree.

— I haven't finished! — answered Naftali's mother. — The girl came home, dried her clothes and cooked dinner as if nothing had happened. When her father returned, he asked her what she had been doing that day, but instead of telling him she had gone to the river, she listed her other activities: "I swept the floor, arranged a tea party for my dolls and made my own copybook out of paper sheets, using a thread." Satisfied with this answer, her father repeated his usual warning: "Please don't go outside, especially to the river bank. I don't want you to drown." The girl promised, again, that she wouldn't leave the house during his absence.

The next day, after her father left for work, the girl went to pick flowers again and made another garland, which was even more intricately woven than the first one. And again, she wanted to go to the river to float this garland on the water, because flowers on water looked very beautiful. But this time she never made it to the river because a group of Indians captured her. They surrounded the little girl, demanded her valuables and became enraged when she told them that she had nothing on her. Then they asked her to tell them where she lived so they could take everything in her house. But the girl was more afraid of her father's anger than of the Indians, so she kept silent. And the Indians got so upset with her, they tied her to a tree. "Just stay here, you stupid girl," they said, "and we'll be back in the evening to check on your bones."

— Bones? — exclaimed Naftali.

— Yes, bones, — answered Naftali's mother. — The Indians thought that wild animals would devour the girl, but when they came to the tree at the end of the day, they saw her alive. Moreover, next to her sat the puma: she was so grateful to the girl for saving her cubs, she decided to protect her from other wild animals!

– This is really a great story, – said Naftali, – but now we really need to hurry, because I see water coming toward us.

– I know there's flooding in this area, – admitted Naftali's mother, – but I hope we'll have reached our destination before the water rises...

– Otherwise, we'll end up like those helpless puma cubs in your story, – Naftali completed her sentence, – swimming in water and not being able to get back to dry land.

But Naftali's mother ignored his joke.

– This does not look good, – she said, – my feet are already wet, and so is the bottom of my suitcase, and it's heavier than before.

Naftali and his mother stopped talking and walked faster. They managed it for about an hour, but then, frightened by a massive body of water coming their way and rising quickly, they looked around in search of higher ground. There was no hill, no living being, or house – only water, high enough now to make Naftali roll up his pants. His mother tried lifting her long skirt, but she couldn't hold it up and carry the suitcases at the same time.

– If we really try, we can reach our destination before the water rises up to our necks, – she said, but her tone wasn't very convincing.

Naftali figured they'd probably be alright, since their heads would be above water and they would be able to breathe. But they wouldn't be able to walk. The water was rushing in loudly, now, and had risen up to his calf.

Naftali could see that his mother was growing more and more anxious. He didn't ask her what was on her mind. He just kept walking, carrying his suitcase and rucksack, though he was exhausted, and they were becoming increasingly heavier.

His mother stopped for a minute and looked around. She was getting confused.

– It's only a half kilometer further, straight ahead, – she mumbled. – Or maybe to the right? It's hard to tell in the rain...

Naftali was sure that the straight road would lead them to a city, where he could become a teacher or a writer, but now his mother wondered if they should turn left.

Finally they stopped, dead, in their tracks. Naftali had never seen his mother so unsure of herself and he felt sorry for her.

– I said I'd take good care of you, and look where I've gotten us, – she groaned.

– It's not your fault, Mom, it's because of the flood! – Naftali reassured her, shivering, now up to his knees in water.

They were standing near a group of tall trees.

– Naftali, can you climb up and hang our suitcases on the branches? – his mother asked. – Otherwise, all our belongings will get soaked.

Naftali couldn't believe his ears: what she'd forbidden him to do just an hour ago, was now a necessity.

– And after that, Naftali, – she added, sheepishly, – please help me climb up, too. We have no choice, but to sit tight and wait till the water recedes.

And so they found themselves sitting in two different trees, facing each other, watching the water rise, and their hopes of a quick rescue evaporate.

Like the young boy in the Tolstoy story, Naftali and his mother had climbed the tree to escape danger – not in the form a wild animal, however, but of a flood.

61

Naftali sat in his tree shivering from the cold, and uncertainty, while his mother hung on for dear life in hers, trying her best to keep her balance: she had to keep grabbing at her shoes to keep them from slipping into the water, where her hat was already bobbing around.

Naftali remembered a former classmate in Russia, who told him that, before death, a person sees in his mind's eye everything that ever happened to him, as though in a dream.

Naftali feared that the dreadful moment had come.

He attempted to conjure up his infancy, but he couldn't recall anything, except for what his parents had told him about the time he fell out of his crib. Then he remembered the first time his parents sat him in the water of a nearby stream, when he was three, and his father pulling him out, when he got water up his nose and cried for help.

And now his father was dead! And this was not a quiet a Russian stream, but an untamed Argentine an flood!

Forcing himself not to look at the floodwaters, Naftali continued to evoke his past, before he perished. He remembered braving the Russian winters, and traversing the huge drifts of snow in his felt boots, on the way to school; he remembered the pastures, where he and his friend Syoma took Syoma's sheep every summer; the farmer's markets, where besides household goods, you could buy wooden *matreshkas*. And the drunken man who burst into their house, but whom his father fended off, the fire set by the Cossacks that destroyed all the Torahs... And the kind Russian man with a beard, who took Naftali by the hand when he had gotten lost in the forest and led him to a familiar road... The good and the bad...

Once he'd recalled everything that had ever happened to him, his life would come to an end. Naftali had listened attentively when his classmate told him this, but he didn't like the idea now! Did he really come to Argentina to end up in a tree? Was this the future his father had envisioned for him, and the reason his parents had saved their money?

How sad his father would be, to see his son, helpless, in this wet tree!

Naftali saw his father's face before him, as he had every day, since his passing. He usually pictured him on the last day of life, during the fateful altercation with Ermilio, and he felt guilty about hiding behind the door, instead of running at the angry gaucho assaulting his father!

But this time was different; his father was smiling, and his face – calm. Just then, Naftali thought he felt somebody's hand touch his hair. He looked up to see if his father was on the limb above him, and he decided his dad would want him to act, instead of uselessly recalling the past. But how?

Naftali closed his eyes and imagined himself floating, lifeless, in the murky waters – how awful this would be! Then he closed his eyes again and saw himself in the future. Imagine his surprise at seeing himself as an old man, leaning on a cane, but still full of energy, standing next to the very tree on which he was now sitting, except the ground was dry and the sun was shining. He was surrounded by children on a school trip, listening to him speak. Suddenly the old man looked up at the tree.

"And then Don Quixote appeared..." he said.

At this point, one of the boys in back of the group shoved the boy in front of him. "What did he say?" he asked.

"That somebody came to rescue him and his mom from the trees they were stuck in, during the flood," the second boy replied.

"But didn't he say it was Don Quixote, on the Argentinean prairie? Was it a mirage?" "What's a mirage?" another child asked.

"It's when you see things that aren't actually there," a girl in pigtails explained, "like in a dream, except you're awake!"

"So he was saved by a dream about Don Quixote?" inquired yet another boy. Meanwhile, the old man continued:

"...Don Quixote appeared, put us on his horse, and the horse carried the three of us to dry land..."

– How could we have been saved by Don Quixote?! – Naftali thought, back in the present. – What would Don Quixote be doing here, anyway, when he and Clara are in Paris, oblivious to our sufferings?

Naftali knew he'd 'seen' his future, but it didn't seem right, there was nobody here, never mind Don Quixote...

He looked around. It was getting dark, but the wind had not quieted down. Pieces of wood, branches, and even dead birds rushed past them in the flood waters below. The water was rising slowly, but steadily, and soon it would reach Naftali's feet. How distant he was, now, perched on this limb in his tattered clothing, from the old man in the neatly-pressed suit he'd glimpsed in the future! Nothing, besides his vision, indicated that he and his mother would be saved...

Suddenly, it occurred to Naftali, that if he'd mentioned Don Quixote in his future, he had to find a way to summon him here, now! All he could think to do was to cry for help, and he did.

– *Socorro! Socorro!* – he shouted in Spanish, so loudly that his head hurt.

And the very second he pronounced these words, Don Quixote and his horse appeared! He was wearing a poncho over his leather bombachas. Nothing about his appearance, neither his beaten up boots, nor his wide-brimmed hat, reminded Naftali of the refined gentleman he had met in Russia, or seen in the pictures in his Don Quixote book. Yet, this man had a dignified air about him, despite the rising waters and roaring wind. He approached slowly at first, as though unable to see them yet.

– *Socorro! Socorro!* – Naftali shouted again, hoping to attract Don Quixote's attention. When he heard his mother begging God to save them, in Russian, he started shouting even louder and waving his arms in the air. Suddenly his mother said:

– Keep quiet, Naftali! This person must be a bandit! Don't attract his attention! Instead of being excited about being rescued, his mother was afraid.

But it was dark by now, and Naftali knew this was likely their only chance of being rescued, so he ignored his mother and kept shouting.

Slowly, the man and his horse waded through the rushing waters toward them, and by the time they had reached the tree, Naftali's mother was terrified.

– Be careful, Naftali! This man is a gaucho! – she said, loudly enough for the man to hear.

Both the man and his horse were breathing heavily, and his voice was gruff, but very calm.

– Don't worry, come on down, I will take you to safety! – he said, in heavily accented Russian, much to the astonishment, and relief, of Naftali and his mother.

Under the weight of three passengers, the horse was barely able to walk, but the gaucho kept repeating, "It's nothing at all" – in Russian – as though he were trying to cheer them up. Naftali stared down at the water, the whole time, amazed by the power of nature.

As soon as they reached dry land, the gaucho said, matter-of-factly:

– And now it's time for us to part ways... I am happy that I was able to help you. Some time ago, a Russian doctor treated me when this horse broke my ribs, but I was too poor to thank him properly... Now, by saving two Russians, I've finally repaid my debt to him!

With these words, the gaucho galloped away at full speed on the horse that, just seconds ago, could barely walk. Naftali's mother watched as the gaucho rode into the distance.

– I'm so relieved that bandit finally left, – she said.

Naftali didn't say anything, though the speedy departure of the man who saved them was very mysterious, indeed.

He and his mother finally reached a little tavern. They went in to rest and ask for directions. On realizing that they had been fighting for their lives in the flood, the owner exclaimed:

– You're lucky to be alive! – he exclaimed. – A couple

of people from our village, who were trapped in the ravine, are still missing.

— If not for a man who plucked us out of the tree, we would have had to spend the night there, in the water! – said Naftali. – He came out of nowhere, as though from a dream, responding to our pleas for help...

Naftali paused to take a breath, then continued, even waving his arms for emphasis.

— But listen! – he exclaimed. – He spoke Russian, like us, even though his bombachas and wide-brimmed hat were unmistakably Argentinian. He had a silver dagger on his belt, too, but it looked ancient and so unlike the ones ordinary gauchos wear...

— Judging from your description, – said the proprietor, – I see you've met "Cuchilla"!

— I knew he was a bandit! – Naftali's mother whispered, so only Naftali heard. – Even with my limited Spanish, I know that nobody honest and straightforward can be named "Blade"!

— It could only be him, – the man continued, – because on his rare visits here, he always used the strangest words in conversation. Some were Russian, which he claimed he'd learned from a Russian doctor, while under his care, and some sounded Spanish, but different. I know he was speaking Spanish, because it seemed familiar, but apparently it was an old form of Spanish, because sometimes I couldn't understand a thing! He always seemed so mysterious...

— But why do you call him Cuchilla? – Naftali's mother asked. – Does he like to get into knife fights?

— Mama, he saved us! – reminded her Naftali.

— I don't know why they call him Cuchilla, – answered the proprietor, – he never told us his real name. And we don't know where he lives, either. But when we ask him where he's from, he always says "I'm from Cuchilla de Montiel", which is an area in the province of 'Entre Rios', not far from here. Have you ever been there?

– Many Russians live in Entre Rios, – Naftali's mother replied, – and we come from there too, but we have never been to Cuchilla de Montiel. We've never even heard of it.

– I have! – Naftali blurted out, then stopped short. He knew exactly what had happened, now, but didn't want to share his secret. He wanted this conversation to be over.

But Naftali's mother wanted the opposite, hoping the proprietor of the tavern would now offer them hot tea and some food.

– What were you going to say, Naftali? – she asked.

– Oh, nothing... I was mistaken, – he replied, and, hoping to change the subject he groaned: – Mama, I'm so hungry!

– My apologies! – exclaimed the tavern owner. – Here I am talking, instead of offering you some hot maize and eggs. Be my guests! – and with these words he led them to a table.

Naftali was glad they'd forgotten about "Cuchilla". He knew nobody would believe him if he said they had been saved by Don Quixote; he didn't want to be laughed at. But when he heard "Cuchilla de Montiel", he immediately remembered reading in the first pages of his book about Don Quixote that Montiel was where he had begun his adventures. Before Cervantes made it famous in his writings, nobody had even heard of it. And now, "Montiel" was a code word, confirming what Naftali already suspected: that he and his mother were rescued by nothing short of magic.

When Naftali grew up, he wrote a book about *Don Quixote* and its author, Cervantes. Naftali's book became so famous, he was often invited to speak to school children about his life and his subjects. He liked to take the pupils to the very place in the pampas, where he and his mother had sat in the trees during the terrible flood. And there, now a grown man with children of his own, and many years after the dramatic events, Naftali described how, having almost lost all hope of surviving the rising floodwaters, he cried out for help. And out of nowhere, a mysterious man on a horse appeared, and carried him and his mother to safety.

ISBN : 978-1-911424-87-1
SKU/ID: 9781911424871

ORIGINAL COVER:
Title: THE LITTLE GAUCHO
Artist: Fabio Perla
Technique: monochrome pencils on card board mounted on wood
Year: 2016

Editor: Monica Turoni
Book design by: Wolf

Publishing Company:
Black Wolf Edition & Publishing Ltd.
2 Glebe Place, Burntisland KY3 0ES, Scotland
www.blackwolfedition.com